The Vampire Hunter's Price
By Victoria S. Pritchard

Preface

Jamie McKinsey is a bounty hunter, but she doesn't hunt run-of-the-mill bail jumpers. She hunts illegal supernatural creatures in a world where an infection can create the undead, vampires and lycanthropes stalk the night, and magic is illegal. When a local businessman waltzes in and offers her a small fortune to find his kidnapped fallen angel wife, Jamie finds herself in a world of intrigue, danger, and the inevitable double cross. Can she survive long enough to find Adora and keep herself from becoming infected with vampirism? Will she end up in the crosshairs of one of her fellow hunters and pay the vampire hunter's price, her life?

ISBN: 978-0-9850876-2-3
First draft January, 2012.

Acknowledgments

I would like to thank my editors, my mom, Lois, and sister, Elizabeth. They have put so much effort into this book and without them it would never have been finished. I'd also like to thank my brother Steve for reading it, helping with the cover, and encouraging me to write more. Thank you, dad, for encouraging me and never telling me I couldn't do it. Thank you Robyn and Jacob for putting up with me while I wrote every evening, allowing me the time to finish this book, and encouraging me. There wouldn't be a cover without Jordan, thank you for helping me design and shoot it in your spare time. Finally, I'd like to thank Josh, Jordan, and Lindsey for allowing me to bounce ideas off of them. Without all of you, this book would have never been finished.

Chapter Index

Preface	2
Acknowledgments	4
Chapter 1: Harold	7
Chapter 2: GRM	13
Chapter 3: Hook, Line, and Sinker	22
Chapter 4: Mr. Bateman	32
Chapter 5: Demon	45
Chapter 6: Barry	60
Chapter 7: Ghoul	74
Chapter 8: Coleman	87
Chapter 9: Purity	91
Chapter 10: Missing	101
Chapter 11: Total Purity	113
Chapter 12: Kendra	126
Chapter 13: Escape	142
Chapter 14: Streets	156
Chapter 15: Chautauqua	171
Chapter 16: Vampire	181
Chapter 17: Intruder	189
Chapter 18: Svetlana	198
Chapter 19: Recon	213
Chapter 20: SER	219
Chapter 21: Hospital	227
Chapter 22: Allie	241
Chapter 23: Dead Cows	250
Chapter 24: Revelation	265
Chapter 25: Treatment	274
Chapter 26: Miracle?	285
Chapter 27: Strings Attached	303
Chapter 28: Kris	317
Chapter 29: Svetlana Once More	325
Chapter 30: Erick	332
Chapter 31: Confrontation	338
Chapter 32: Adora Unleashed	348

Chapter 33: Escape   353
Chapter 34: Cleanup   362
Chapter 35: New Roommate   369
Chapter 36: Werewolf   377
About the Author   381

Chapter 1: Harold

"What can I do for you Mr...?" I asked politely as I sat down behind my desk in the offices of McKinsey and St. James, LLC. My office, if you could call it that, was a ten foot by ten foot box with pale yellow walls, a large peeling oak veneer desk, hollow steel door painted baby blue, and no personal affects whatsoever. Classy, I know, but considering how much time I spent there, it made more financial sense than a large glassy office in some fancy downtown high-rise. It was a cold, hoar-frosted Saturday, but in my business, I met with the clients on their time, not mine.

"Johanson," the little man on the other side of the desk replied, fidgeting with his tie and twisting the ring on his left pinkie. Silver, as was his cross shaped tie pin and his cufflinks, so he obviously wasn't doing too badly for himself. Which begged the question, why was he in my office, the office of a supernatural bounty hunter?

I waited, calmly sipping my tea and clicking my red lacquered nails against the handle. Mint, with sugar, none of that artificial sweetener crap, it gave me a headache. My long, pale fingers clasped the mug loosely as I blew across it, trying to look nonchalant and interested at the same time. My bronze and copper bracelets tinkled softly whenever I shifted my arms, a merry counterpoint to the humming of the heating vent. Silver and gold were too expensive for the likes of me, mainly because silver worked marvelously on the supernatural baddies of the world and was in high demand and gold was, well, gold.

Next to the door was a large mirror, helpful for identifying those whom the establishment had labeled as Illegals. Vampires, lycanthropes, angels, demons, faeries, extraterrestrials, even humans, all of us reflected an aura in a silver backed mirror. Trained psychic sensitives, like me, could see this aura and make a fair guess as to what flavor of entity they were dealing with. I surreptitiously peeked around my fingers to see his reflection, relaxing a little as his aura showed swirling gray with streaks of white and black, totally non-sensitive human.

I caught my own reflection in the mirror and a little smile tugged the corner of my red lips. My own aura swirled around my head, pinpoint colors flashing blue and green amidst the gray-backed white and black streaks. My shoulder length blonde hair curled softly around my oval face as my ocean blue eyes stared back at me with piercing intensity. I had taken the time to put on makeup today; I looked pretty good in my fitted pink dress shirt with the three top buttons undone along with a floor length black skirt, slit up to the middle of my thigh with sheer black stockings. Its slits provided ease of movement as well as allowing easy access to either the 45 at the small of my back or the 9mm strapped to my right thigh, plus I thought it was sexy. The slits gave flashes of my knee-high, four-inch heeled black boots and I thought I looked pretty intimidating, all 6'6" of me counting the heels. Not that it seemed to be having any effect on the little man on the other side of my desk.

He was short, perhaps 5'4" maybe 5'5", and slender, no more than 130 pounds. His hair was receding, salt and peppered, with a neat goatee also peppered with gray. All of this was background; his eyes were the first thing you noticed, clear and icy blue as a winter's day with laughing wrinkles around the outside and neatly trimmed gray eyebrows hooding them. His nose was masculine, not much more to say about it, and he had a strong chin with a confident lilt to it. He said jump and expected you to jump.

His suit was charcoal gray, elven silk, well tailored, and probably cost more than I made in a month. His light blue silk shirt and green tie set off his coloring and eyes perfectly, something he knew quite well from his posture. Still, he was fidgeting, and clearly nervous about something, I just had to out wait him and find out what it was.

Truth be told, I was nervous too. After that last fiasco in Dallas, I really needed a job and someone this well off would not have come to someone like me without a really good reason. Our office assistant, Kristen Stephanos, hadn't given me very much information before I met Mr. Johanson, just told me I should meet him and think very seriously about taking his job.

"Perhaps this was a mistake," Johanson said, twisting in his chair to reach for his coat, making a move to stand.

"What was a mistake?" I asked quickly, seeing my job about to walk out the door. I set my coffee mug down and leaned forward, trying to catch his gaze and convince him he wanted to stay. "What can I help you with, Mr. Johanson? I'm sure you came to me for a reason." I smiled my most winning smile, all teeth, red lips, and complete insincerity.

"Well..." he said, settling back into the chair and resuming the spinning of the ring on his finger. "It's just..."

"Just what, Mr. Johanson?" I asked brightly, flashing my pearly whites and hoping he wouldn't leave.

"It's just, I've talked with other hunters, and all of them told me I was better off without her and they wouldn't even think of taking my case, that I should go to the police. I can't go to the police and no private investigator will touch my case because she's an Illegal. I'm desperate! I don't know who else to turn to!" He slumped in the chair, cradling his face in his hands. I noticed the balding spot on the back of his head, and he suddenly looked small and frail. I half rose from my chair, desperately trying to think of some comforting words to say, but my mind stayed infuriatingly blank. I stood there, half standing, half crouching, while he gathered himself.

"No," he finally said, giving himself a visible shake and throwing off his strong emotions with an effort, "no, I came here to ask you for help because you are the only hunter in Denver who asks questions before she shoots and shows any sympathy to my cause and my company. Please, Ms. McKinsey, please help me find my wife, Adora."

"Adora Johanson..." I mouthed as I sat back slowly into my chair. "You're *that* Harold Johanson?" I asked, nonplussed.

"Yes, Ms. McKinsey, didn't your secretary tell you?" he asked, confusion furrowing his brow and narrowing his eyes.

"It must have slipped her mind," I said faintly as I sat back in my chair.

Harold Johanson was sitting in my office and needed my help to find his wife. His fallen angel wife. I didn't know what to say.

Chapter 2: GRM

Harold Johanson was the head of Global Rights Media, Inc. and one of the main antagonists of the establishment. His company regularly featured newspaper and blog stories about Illegal activity and openly advocated more and better rights for many of them.

Sufferers of HBV (also called lycanthropes) and Stoker-Dracul syndrome (also known as vampires) were marginalized, the lepers of the 21st century, and many counties allowed them to be executed by a licensed hunter if they proved themselves a danger to society. That's right, people suffering from a medical illness could be hunted down if you had the right paperwork. Grays and faeries didn't have as many rights as humans and they too could be hunted if they were involved in criminal activities. Magic was illegal and something a lot of people were afraid of, so practitioners of the Forbidden Arts could be hunted just like any criminal.

Harold led the vanguard of people who'd a problem with the current paradigm and advocated better rights and treatment for all Illegals. His reasons were his own, partially due to his wife, Adora Johanson, being a fallen angel and partially because he liked poking sleeping bears with pointy objects.

By fallen angel, I mean true, honest to God, angel from Heaven who rejected the rule of God and had fallen to Earth in disgrace. Or so she told people. I was a skeptic, being a Deist, and I was not convinced she was not simply another alien race come down to make our lives difficult. As if we needed more trouble from extraterrestrials, the Grays were enough of a handful in and of themselves. Still, she looked very angelic, ethereal and beautiful, tall and pale with large dark eyes. *No wings or halo though*, I thought sarcastically.

"Mr. Johanson... Uh, what happened to Adora?" Brilliant. Wow him with your wit there, blondie, that's a surefire way to lose this bounty.

"Your secretary didn't tell you anything?" he asked, arching his right eyebrow and pursing his lips. He leaned forward, steepling his fingers and trying to pin me with his gaze.

"I've been a little out of touch and rushed for time," I grumbled, flashing back to losing my sorcerer bounty in Dallas. I'd almost had him. He'd been cornered in a warehouse at gun point when his summoned demon had burst in on us and nearly torn me limb from limb. I had apparently outrun my backup, they were nowhere to be found, so I had emptied my magazine into the demon and run like a scared rabbit as the demon's Hellfire laid waste to crates and boxes all around me. Demons aren't usually nine feet tall and super aggressive so when this one came in guns blazing, I knew something was very, very wrong. So I ran.

Of course, the police pinned the whole thing on me, saying if I hadn't cornered the sorcerer and I hadn't outrun my backup, he wouldn't have summoned the demon and wouldn't have destroyed that city block. These were the same police who'd hired me to capture him in the first place, a fact conveniently forgotten when things went topsy-turvy.

Supernatural Emergency Response (SER, basically supernatural SWAT) had finally arrived and had shot the sorcerer nineteen times. Too much? This was a man who sold his soul. Nineteen times was actually a commendation to their shooting skills. One sorcerer in Orlando was so powerful and psychotic, they had to call in the National Guard and run him down with a tank. Even then, his demon flung the tank off him like it was a toy to get to the man and collect his soul. I'd been lucky they hadn't tagged me with a clean up bill and had at least paid for my airfare back to Denver.

"Adora has been taken for ransom," Johanson said softly. "They want twenty million dollars, and I would gladly pay that, but they also want me to stop advocating for 'aberrations'. I won't, I can't, it would betray everything I believe in and alienate Adora. How could I get her back by alienating her? I'm stuck, I have nowhere to turn, and I need your help, Ms. McKinsey. Please help me find my wife." He leaned forward, hands on his knees, knuckles white with his gaze locked firmly on mine, willing me to understand and take his case.

I squirmed under his gaze, unable to meet his eyes. I was a bounty hunter, dammit! Not a nurse maid! I didn't do missing persons cases, I did cases where I found an Illegal causing problems, and shot it. Well, sometimes.

I was a licensed hunter and hunters were usually a psychic sensitive (or just sensitive for short) who took bounties on the less savory members of the supernatural community. There were some vanilla human hunters, but they either had to be a complete badass or really, really lucky to make it long in my business. Vampires, lycanthropes, zombies, witches and warlocks, extraterrestrials, rogue angels, demons, and faeries, anything not run-of-the-mill human who decides they want to cause problems for human society could be the target of a hunt.

In most cases, once-human creatures were more likely to trust or tolerate a sensitive because our magical and psychic abilities tended to attract them, making it easier for us to get close to them. Frequently, if a person was attacked or came up missing and the perpetrator of the crime was supernatural, it was likely the victim was a sensitive. Many people lived their whole lives not knowing they were sensitive, and no one really knew how many of us there were, but anyone who ever had hunches that came true was likely a sensitive. Sensitives were also the only people who could be turned into a vampire or lycanthrope.

If a vampire, lycanthrope, or zombie caused problems, the state or federal government would hire someone like me to go take them out, usually with a bullet from a distance. Lycanthropes were easy, catch them on a full moon and shoot them with a silver bullet. Zombies, too, weren't terribly challenging, although they usually required consulting the fire department and then using a flamethrower on them. Sometimes, at least in the city, most people called SER and had them come out with their oven on wheels to incinerate the victim. I liked flamethrowers personally.

Vampires were my least favorite of the once human variety because they were the hardest. Instead of being unthinking or animalistic things, vampires were cunning, vicious predators. A bullet from a sniper rifle was my favorite way of dealing with them, but a Master vampire might not be killed by a single bullet. A hunter might need to brave their nest and kill the rest of the vampire family first, although any hunter stupid enough to go alone was in for a very short career. In all three once human cases, the body had to be burned because the pathogens that created them could still be transmitted from a dead body.

Faeries, witches, and extraterrestrials were a different can of worms. They were more difficult because they had some rights under the American constitution and a hunter could be brought up on charges if he or she violated those rights. Faeries and extraterrestrials, mainly Grays purportedly from the Zeta Reticuli star system who crashed millennia ago after some intergalactic battle, were recognized as thinking, living creatures and a hunter couldn't just shoot them unless his or her life was in danger. Fortunately for the hunter, it was pretty easy to claim self defense because 'hey, I didn't know what that dull metal rod in his hand was so I assumed it was a weapon and shot him!' worked just fine in court. Faeries, too, couldn't just be killed but they were usually more of the trickster variety and fairly easy to capture and transport to their home territories. People didn't like the term reservation but that was essentially what they were.

Witches and warlocks, sometimes called practitioners, were sensitives, like myself, who chose to use their psychic and magic powers for nefarious purposes and frequently learned the Forbidden Arts to commit crimes or simply for personal power. They, too, had to be captured and remanded to the authorities where they were tried and, if found guilty, forced to undergo radical brain surgery to remove the part of their brain that made them sensitive, a process called severing. They usually didn't live long after that. More often than not, witches and warlocks would force the hunters to defend themselves and would fight to the death.

Finally, demons and angels were my least favorite of all of the various kinds of hunts but, thankfully, they were rare. Demons were inter-dimensional beings (in my opinion they were inter-dimensional beings, some people really thought they were demons like in the Bible or Torah) summoned by a sorcerer who sold his or her life force, or soul if you want, to these beings for magical power.

Demons themselves, as far as anyone could tell, were immortal and couldn't be hurt. That's fun, emptying a magazine into a charging demon, hitting them repeatedly, and it having *no effect*. Crosses and other holy objects sometimes kept them at bay, but if there was any doubt in your heart, you were dead meat. I personally liked to find the sorcerer and shoot him or her (usually him), prompting the demon to harvest their soul and leave through a smoking hole in the ground. It was a really, really good, even life-saving idea to have some serious backup when hunting a sorcerer and his or her demon. I'm talking National Guard with tanks backup, something I learned the hard way.

Angels came in two flavors: divine and fallen. Divine angels were easier to deal with than fallen ones because they weren't evil. At least, no one had encountered an evil one, and they were usually just messengers. Hunters rarely were called on divine angels; we usually got the fallen variety. Fallen angels were angels who'd supposedly renounced God and decided to live on Earth. Having lost their divinity, they were flawed, just like people, and sometimes they ran afoul of the law. If that running afoul activity involving using their innate magical abilities, a hunter was called in to capture them and remand them to governmental custody. They were often too much for the police to deal with. I hated trying to capture an entity who was effectively immortal, magically more powerful than any sensitive, and really, really hard to kill. Gold bullets would do it, but they were very expensive. I kept a couple magazines of them just in case, but I'd only needed to use them once before.

Chapter 3: Hook, Line, and Sinker

"Mr. Johanson," I started, trying to come up with a tactful way to tell him I wasn't a detective.

"I'll make it worth your while," he continued like I hadn't spoken. "I'm a man of means, as I'm sure you're aware, and I'll pay you five hundred thousand dollars."

I choked, my face turning bright red as my mind rebelled at the figure he had named. *Five. Hundred. Thousand. Dollars?* I thought. There was no way I could turn down that kind of money, not after the disaster in Dallas.

He sat back, a small smirk on his face as he crossed his legs and settled his hands on his knee, one on top of the other. He knew he had me and was just waiting for me to say okay.

"Okay," I choked out, "but I need some more information first before I absolutely agree to take your case." Always be cagey, see if you can get more out of them; that was what my daddy always taught me. Oh, who was I kidding? I was going to take the case and we both knew it.

"Anything I can help you with is yours, Ms. McKinsey," he said smoothly, one hand idly spinning the silver ring on his pinkie. He had relaxed a lot; obviously he had much more faith in my abilities than I did.

I thought furiously, trying to come up with pertinent information I would need to track Mrs. Johanson down. I took a deep breath and sat back in my chair, the springs creaking under my weight and threatening to dump me. My notebook was in the second drawer on the right of the desk and I thought there was a pencil in there too, but I rummaged through the rest of the desk first to give me some time. Finally, I pulled out my battered black-covered sketch book and a chewed up yellow pencil with no eraser.

"When was the last time you saw her?" I finally asked, peering over the edge of my notebook to see his reaction. A slight frown creased his face and his eyes darkened in thought. He chewed his lip and sat back in his chair, gazing up at the ceiling like he couldn't remember the last time he saw his wife. *Close relationship there,* I thought, which was odd considering his earlier desperation and apprehension.

"The last time I saw her was on her birthday. Really the day she descended, but we called that her birthday just for simplicity's sake. December the 10th I believe," he said.

"So you last saw your wife a *month* ago?" I demanded, incredulous. To his credit, he didn't flinch, instead returning my glare with a calm, level gaze, his husky-blue eyes piercing through me and daring me to judge him for the life he led.

"Yes," he replied calmly, "we went out for her birthday and ate at Pike's Steakhouse. She seemed distracted, but Adora is easily distracted and I didn't pay it any heed. She's always involved in charities, Salvation Army, CFIC, that sort of thing. Anything to keep her busy, she bores so easily."

"CFIC?" I asked, scribbling furiously.

"Charity for Illegal Causes," he clarified with a cross expression. "The charity my company started to advance the cause of Illegal rights. Perhaps you've heard of it?" he asked, arching an eyebrow and staring at me.

"Ah," I replied, feeling dumb. "And when did you get the ransom request?"

"This morning, my assistant found the note taped to the steering wheel of my car. She was running errands and found it when she returned from the drycleaner. I have it if you want to look at it," he said as he reached into the pocket of his suit coat. He presented me with a plain piece of white paper, folded twice, held between his index and middle fingers of his right hand. I took it gingerly, inspecting it like I was going to find fingerprints with my naked eyes. When I opened it up, there was a ransom note out of any bad mystery novel, letters cut from a magazine or newspaper to spell out the threat and the promise.

Johanson,
We have your aberrant wife and if you don't do exactly as we say, we'll kill her. Bring 20 million dollars in unmarked c-notes to the corner of E. 26th Ave and Colorado Blvd. Close CFIC and stop trying to get those aberrations rights they don't deserve. If you aren't there at 6:00 am on Friday the 14th, we'll kill her. No cops or we kill her. We expect to hear about CFIC closing before the 14th or else we kill her.

That was all, fairly straight forward I supposed. Unimaginative, brutal, but straight forward, although it was very challenging to kill a fallen angel.

"No fingerprints? Nothing in the car that the messenger may have accidently dropped? No one saw anyone getting into your car? Where was it parked when the message was delivered?" I asked, turning that paper over to see if there was anything else written on the other side. There wasn't. I held it up to the mirror to see if there was a supernatural aura that would tell me what kind of creature did the kidnapping, but again there was nothing. Either it had been too long, which wasn't very likely, or they were so powerful they could conceal their aura and keep it from bleeding onto the paper. I didn't think the latter was likely based on the wording of the letter, there were very few powerful supernatural critters who thought of themselves as aberrations, but it was always possible.

"No fingerprints," he confirmed, "and no other forensic clues. No hairs, no auras, nothing of value we could find. The car was parked off Thornton parkway near the drycleaners there. We asked for the security tapes of the businesses in the area but they were all pointed away from the car when the note was delivered and no one saw anything they can remember."

"So you don't know when exactly or from where she would have been taken?"

"No, although our maid says she saw her on Wednesday during the day so it would have had to be Wednesday night or Thursday sometime, maybe Friday morning."

I pursed my lips and chewed on the end of my pencil, looking down in irritation when the pencil end turned red from my lipstick. "So there's been no contact other than this letter, no phone calls, nothing of that sort?"

"Nothing."

"Odd. Usually kidnappers want to make other threats, make sure their threats are being recognized and the cops aren't being involved. It smacks of lack of planning or inexperience to me.

"Human supremacist groups would be the logical first place to look," I continued, "I don't know who else would have such a problem with your charity work. I'll get in touch with a contact of mine and see if I can get an appointment with Purity."

Purity was a humans-first organization, taking a hard-line stance against elves, faeries, vampires, lycanthropes, even sensitive humans. If you weren't vanilla, non-sensitive human, they had a problem with you. Lycanthropes, vampires, and zombies they believed should be quarantined until the infections burned themselves out, which of course is silly because the pathogens that caused the conditions occurred in nature. Not all cases of *Reanimagus mobilius*, the bacterium responsible for zombieism, or Human Bestialism virus (HBV), the virus responsible for lycanthropy, were from bites of infected people and good luck quarantining all the vampires in the country.

More radical members of Purity believed vampirism, lycanthrope, and zombieism were all punishment for sinful behavior and all sufferers should be killed on sight. Most Purity members believed we should exterminate the Grays and the Faeries or round them up and send them to Anareola, the elven nation to the west of the US, and then close the borders to elven traffic. Human sensitives, too, they believed were unnatural and needed to be exiled or severed from their powers. Thankfully, such thinking was the minority in the general population. No one knew for sure what made a person sensitive, although it did seem to run in families but it skipped generations, sometimes several.

"I don't think they'd tell me if they did the kidnapping but maybe they'll slip up. They're the most virulent anti-Illegal group and I have a friend who knows someone who's a member. Let me start there and I'll get back to you as soon as I learn anything." I rose to escort him out.

"Splendid," he replied, also rising and extending his hand. His relief was palpable. I felt really bad for him because I had no idea what kind of success I would have. I had never looked for a missing person before, but then it probably wasn't that different from locating a bounty who didn't want to be found. I shook his hand, his palm dry and coarser than I was expecting, and led him to the door.

I led him back out into the main area of the office, a pale blue three sided room with a twin walnut colored doors on the long side and offices on the two short sides. Our secretary, I mean office assistant, Kristen Stephanos, was sitting at the desk between my office and the office of my partner in crime, Jackson St. James. She was staring intently at her computer screen, but knowing Kristen, she wasn't reading Quantum Physics Letters, more likely Facebook. She turned to us as we walked away from my office and flashed Mr. Johanson a bright smile. She was young, only twenty one, with olive skin and waist length dark brown hair, a pretty oval face and exotic almond shaped dark eyes. She also had a fiery temper and an excellent attitude for an office assistant, e.g. she didn't take crap from anyone.

"Everything all right, Ms. McKinsey?" she asked brightly.

"Yep, everything's fine, just showing Mr. Johanson out. Is Jackson in his office?"

"Yeah, he's talking to a client but he'll be done in a sec," she replied. "You have another appointment at eleven. He's here already; I'll send him in when you're ready."

"Okay, thanks."

"I'll be in touch when I find something out, Mr. Johanson," I said, turning back to face him and opening the right door to see him out. "I know time is of the essence so

29

I'll begin working on this as soon as I have talked to Jackson about any help he can offer. Sometimes he has contacts and/or information I don't have access to." I smiled my most confident grin at him, hoping he didn't see the severe doubts I had brewing under the surface, and offered my hand one more time.

"Thank you, Ms. McKinsey, I-"

"Jamie," I interrupted, "please, I'm not formal in my business practices."

"All right, Jamie. I know you'll find her," he replied as he shook my hand, a small smile on his face. I noticed he didn't tell me to call him Harold. He was already dialing his cell phone, I assume for his limo to come pick him up or something, as he walked out the door.

As he walked from Ms. McKinsey's office heading for his car, Harold Johanson dialed his cell phone, calling his office assistant. She picked up right away, probably expecting his call.

"Hi, Mr. J, how'd it go?"

"As expected, the offer was more than she could refuse. She's got the most chance of finding Adora, I think, she's a more powerful sensitive than she realizes and she has powerful friends, even if she doesn't know it yet. Just to be sure, make sure the other hunters keep away from her and if they find anything relevant, make sure she stumbles across the evidence. Contact Jennifer, have her leave some evidence for Ms. McKinsey to find, maybe one of her minions, but tell her not to be too obvious about it and not to get her Master involved. We need to nudge Ms. McKinsey in the proper direction."

"Yes, sir, I'll be certain she's discrete."

"Excellent. Also contact Dr. Schmitz, tell her to have her treatment ready. Someone might need it before the curtain falls on this play. Good bye."

Harold pocketed the cell phone, pulling his keys from his pocket, unlocking his Bentley, and starting the engine. He pulled away from the curb with a screech of tires, heading west toward his home. Hopefully, the seeds had been planted for his plan to succeed.

Chapter 4: Mr. Bateman

I shut the door behind me, leaned against it, and sighed. How in the heck was I going to get the nutcases at Purity to listen to me? What was I thinking? I was a hunter, not a private investigator! I needed to talk to Jackson and then see if I could get I touch with my best friend Barry.

"Jamie?" I'd forgotten about Kristen. "Are you all right?"

"Fine," I said, "just thinking about how to help Mr. Johanson."

"I hope you can, his wife is so hot, I wish I looked like her! Would you like to talk to Jackson? I think he's free or I can send your next appointment, Mr. Bateman, in to see you."

"Mr. Bateman...?" I muttered. "Oh! The farmer with the lycanthrope problem, may be a lead to the Denver County Sheriff posting on the werewolf who killed the little boy. Yeah, send him in, please; I can talk to Jackson in a little bit."

"Sure thing, Jamie. I mean, Ms. McKinsey," she turned with a saucy wink. I smiled, slightly exasperated, and headed for my office.

Sitting in my chair, I reached for my coffee mug and took a sip. Bleh, cold tea when I was hoping there was some warmth still in it. Sighing, I stood up and headed for the door, chugging the cold tea as I went. I pulled open the door and nearly ran face first into a solidly built older man. He grabbed my arms to keep me from falling and held me straight out in front of him.

"Oh gosh, sorry, miss, but your sweet little helper said you were ready for me. Guess I shoulda knocked first," he said with an abashed grin.

"No worries," I said, stepping back to invite him in. I guess my fresh cup of tea had to wait. I gestured toward the seat and he sat himself down with a thump and the smell of sweat and Old Spice. He was taller than I was, solidly built from a life of manual labor and I estimated him to be in his late forties. His sun browned skin was heavily creased around his eyes and mouth, but they were laugh lines more than frown lines. His big hazel eyes were a little sad and his short-cut hair was silver white, what little I could see under his John Deere cap. He wore a button up blue shirt and his jeans were clean, his boots obviously freshly scrubbed.

"Can I get you anything?" I asked, hoping he'd ask for some coffee or something and I could get a fresh cup of tea.

"No, no, thank you miss, your pretty helper already offered me some coffee and if I have any more I'll float away," he replied with a good natured grin.

"How can I help you, Mr. Bateman?' I asked flashing him a toothy grin.

"Mike," he said, "call me Mike, everyone does."

"Call me Jamie then," I replied.

"Sure thing, Miss Jamie. See I have a cattle ranch, a few thousand acres, out by Brighton. I run it with my wife and my two sons, been in the family for a hundred and fifty years. Well, anyway, about three weeks ago, maybe a little more, I found one of my cows killed out in the furthest pasture from my home. See, she'd been killed by, uh, something tearing her throat out. Whatever it was didn't eat a whole lot, just some of the organs, but it was brutal, tore her up real bad. Not much out that way of natural predators that would take on a cow, mountain lion maybe, but this was way more brutal than a puma attack. Puma usually will bite from above, break the neck you know."

"Of course," I replied faintly.

"Then I thought maybe wolves, but usually a pack of wolves don't just leave a kill in the field like that, plus they'd eat more than just a few organs. Don't know that there's been a bear sighting in the area in a long time, and black bear don't usually take on a full grown cow, too many other easier things. I'm thinking it may be one of them shapeshifters, a werewolf or something. I saw the bill the governor posted for that werewolf who killed that kid and I wondered if maybe it was him."

He settled back into the chair and looked at me expectantly, crossing his hands over his stomach and crossing his legs at the ankle in front of him.

"Mr. Ba... Mike, did you see any tracks around the corpse?"

"Nope, nothing, but the area 'round the kill was tore up pretty bad, I probably wouldn't've noticed anything. There was a trail through the grass, though, and it definitely came from the woods on the edge of the field. Looked like a pretty good size animal made the trail but I'm thinking just one, not a pack or nothing'."

"Hmm, I'll certainly look into it for you; the next full moon is in four days so I'll be out there then, if that's okay with you. Make sure none of your family or employees are out there after dark, I don't want to shoot them by accident. Is it okay if I come scope out the area if I have time in the next couple days? I'm working on another case but if I get time, I'd like to look and see if I can feel any supernatural traces."

"Sure thing, Miss Jamie, just give me a ring on this number," he passed me a plain white business card with his name and a phone number on it, "and me or someone else would be happy to take you out there. Need an ATV or an MUV, can't get there with a car so just give me a ring. It's my cell so I should have it on me most of the time."

"Thanks, Mike; I'll see what I can do. If it's the werewolf the bounty is posted for, I'll give you fifty percent of the bounty for giving me the lead on it." I rose and gestured for the door as he rose and held out his hand. We shook and Kristen showed him out.

Time for another cup of tea, I decided and wandered over to the microwave in the corner of the main office area to brew it.

"Jamie?"

"Yeah, Kristen, what's up?' I asked as I leaned back against the counter in the corner waiting for my tea to steep.

"Jackson's available; he knows what you want to talk to him about so he's just doing some paperwork 'til you come in. He said he has some ideas too. Also, I wanted to ask you, my mom's birthday is on Friday, can I take the day off so I can take her out for a day of shopping and out to lunch? Jackson said it was okay and neither of you has any appointments." She looked at me imploringly. "Please?"

"Sure. Say hi to mom for me and have a great time."

"Thanks, Jamie!"

"Jamie, are you done with your client?" It was Jackson standing in the door of his office, leaning on the door jamb. He was always striking, and hard to miss in a crowd, standing six foot six and painfully thin, no more than a buck forty. He was also very pale, skin so white it was almost translucent but with a blush of color on his long cheeks. His hair was white blond, curling around his ears, but his eyes were dark, dark brown. They looked huge in his slender face, almost like the characters in a Japanese anime film. Today he was wearing a green tunic-style short-sleeved shirt with loose khaki slacks and brown loafers. He was not much into the whole dressing up thing. With my heels on, I looked him in the eye but usually I looked him in the chin.

"Yeah," I replied, "you have a second for me?"

"Sure, come on in, sister." He always called me that, sister or sweetie, something like that, mildly condescending, but he didn't mean it that way, he was just old school. He looked like he was his thirties, but I knew for a fact he was over a hundred years old.

He turned and headed for his desk as I followed him in. He moved with an ethereal grace, a slender, flowing lope I had always envied. I walked into his office, blowing across my tea, and heading for one of the tan leather chairs around his little oak table. His office was much larger than mine, maybe three times the size, with a mint green paint job. *Still a box though,* I thought as I sat in the chair furthest from the door.

He sat behind his desk, another oak-veneered particle board piece of crap, but his wasn't peeling as bad as mine. He, too, had a silver mirror on his wall and I watched his aura swirl about his head as he sat down. Jackson had a fairly unique aura; I had never seen one exactly like it. Gray, with streaks of white and black, ribbons of silver and gold, and flashes of green and blue just like mine. The only other place I had seen a similar one was around Adora Johanson but hers didn't have the flashes of blue and green.

Jackson was a sensitive, a practitioner, also called a warlock, in secret, and his skills in the Forbidden Arts came from his fallen angel father. He usually handled the cases of witches and warlocks that came through our doors because his angel ancestry made him very resistant to their powers. He was a demi-human, someone with blood from both a human ancestor and a non-human ancestor. Some scientists thought all sensitives were demi-humans way back when, but there was little proof for that theory. I personally thought we were just another variation in the kaleidoscope of humanity.

Jackson's desk was cluttered with knick knacks, crystals and amulets he had found or made, and pictures of his wife and kids. His wife was lovely, originally from Japan and pretty much the polar opposite of Jackson. Akane was petite and by petite, I meant less than five feet tall and probably ninety pounds soaking wet, with large very dark eyes and thick blue-black hair. She was very sweet most of the time, but everyone who knew Jackson and his family knew who ran that household, and it wasn't Jackson. Their daughter, Hideko, was the spitting image of her mom with her dad's height, a lovely sixteen year old just learning to drive, while their son took after dad. Takashi was a precocious ten years old, with the ethereal grace and slender build of his dad but the almond eyes and blue-black hair of his Japanese heritage. I wasn't usually much for kids, I didn't really have the patience to deal with them, but Jackson's were always sweet and polite so I didn't mind having them around.

"Have you decided to take the Johanson case?" Jackson asked as he settled back into his brown leather desk chair. *His chair wasn't busted,* I thought mildly piqued, and then I shoved that thought from my mind. It wasn't worth getting jealous over.

"Yeah," I said, taking a sip of my tea. Mmm, minty. "He offered me more than I could turn down although I'm at a loss how to start. I thought maybe I'd talk to Barry, see if he can get me a meeting with Purity, maybe from there move on to one of the other human supremacy groups, if Purity is clean. Something about that ransom note is bothering me; it's too... too Hollywood, too similar to movie ransom notes. It's almost like a teenager made it. Can you take a look at it; see if you can discern anything with your Arts?" I asked, checking to be sure the door was closed.

Jackson being half human, half fallen angel was like a very powerful sensitive, but magic was illegal regardless of your heritage. If he was caught, he'd be forced to be severed from his abilities and few sensitives lived long after that. They described it as going blind and deaf all at once and many of them just wasted away after severing. Jackson never did anything nefarious, he was a good man, but the hysteria against magic was rampant.

Consequently, he was very careful to hide his abilities and knowledge from anyone but me and his wife.

"I can try," he replied, "I assume you have already looked for an aura?"

"Yep, nothing. Maybe it's been too long, maybe they deliberately concealed it, maybe I'm losing my touch, I don't know."

I handed him the letter, sitting back to drink my tea as he examined it, reading it through several times and holding it up to his mirror. He pursed his lips and furrowed his brow, frowning at the offending letter. He stood, walking over to the mirror, and holding the letter within a couple inches of the surface. He hummed a short melody, the pitch gently rising and falling, and a faint shimmer formed around the image of the letter in the mirror. It looked like heat-waves emanating from the edges of the paper, but nothing really definite. He frowned, the shimmer obviously meaning more to him than it did to me.

He quit humming, turning to walk over to a safe set in the wall behind the door and spinning the lock to open it. Inside were papers, some gold and silver amulets, and a silver bowl, tarnished with age and countless hands. It was quite large, perhaps twelve inches across, two deep, and half an inch thick with a flat bottom.

The inside was shined to a mirror polish and free from tarnish. It probably had more silver in it than any piece I had ever seen, and would have cost me six month's income on a good year.

Jackson walked past the door, locking it as he went by, and set the bowl down on the table in front of me. He retrieved five silver candlesticks, plain and simple in design with five pure white beeswax candles in them, from the safe. He laid them out on the table in a pentagon pattern around the silver bowl and lit them all with a flick of his hand. I always wondered how he did that and knew I could learn, but was afraid to start down that path.

He started chanting, nonsensical words I knew, just a repetitive pattern to get himself into a trance, and placed the ransom note into the silver bowl. He held his hands out in front of him, shoulder width and parallel to the ground, as his chanting rhythm picked up in tempo. The silver candlesticks and silver bowl began to glow with a pure white light, getting brighter and brighter, until I had to look away.

Jackson continued to stare at the paper, now hovering six inches over the silver bowl. His chanting undulated, going higher and lower in succession, slowly building tempo, faster and faster. Finally, the mirror finish in the bottom of the bowl began to show the outline of a face, a woman, very lovely, ethereally pale and slender. *Adora*, I thought. Her face was twisted in concentration as a pair of masculine hands with a simple gold band on the right ring finger reached in from outside the view and did something to the paper.

Suddenly, there came a knock at the door, sharp and sudden. Jackson's chanting broke off mid-syllable, as he gestured to snuff the candles. Adora's ransom note fell to the table top with a soft thump as the vision of Adora disappeared. He hurriedly grabbed the silver objects and shoved them into the safe, locking it with a spin of the dial.

"Yes?" He called out, out of breath, a half annoyed, half worried expression on his face

"Jackson, your wife is on the phone. She tried to call your cell but you didn't pick up. Hideko is sick and she needs you to go pick her up from school," replied Kristen.

"Thanks, Kristen; just transfer it to my office."

"Did you get anything?" I asked, anxious.

"Not very much, just some flashes of a fallen angel I think was Adora and something else, something very powerful. Demon, I think, but I'm not entirely sure, could have been a vampire. No human presence though, that's odd, but maybe it was overpowered by Adora and whatever that other presence was. Sorry I couldn't help more, but I suspect your meeting with Purity is going to be a waste of time. Still worth looking into though," he looked at me expectantly and then handed me a silver amulet on a slender chain.

"What's this?" I asked, turning it over in my hands. It was solid silver, in the shape of a triangular Celtic knot work, hanging from a slim silver chain. I probably would've spent a month's salary on it if I had bought it myself.

"Protection," he replied, closing my fingers around it and pushing my closed hand closer to me. "You can give it back when you come back if you don't want it." He turned back toward his desk, about to answer the phone, when I pulled him back around and gave him a brief hug. Disengaging, I shot him a grin and slipped out the door as he answered his phone and I headed for my office. I clasped the chain around my neck, layering it with the copper chain I was already wearing, and turned toward my office.

Chapter 5: Demon

Jackson St. James closed the door softly behind Jamie, head down in thought. He'd sensed more than he had let on, more than one fire-laced presence in addition to the demon or Master vampire and Adora. There was a very good chance there was more to this whole thing than was apparent on the surface, but he needed to see how Jamie handled it. She showed startling moments of ability and clarity, but still made foolish decisions sometimes.

Sighing, he reached for the phone, not wanting to keep Akane waiting.

"Hi honey, whatcha need?" he said, reclining into his desk chair and fiddling with a silver amulet on his desk. It was the twin of the one he had given Jamie and would let him track her anywhere in the world. In and of itself, it offered no protection, but the twin in his hand would heat up if Jamie was in danger from a mystical source and grow icy cold if she were to be injured.

"Hi sweetie," replied a mocking female voice. Jackson sat up straight, nearly dumping himself from the chair, and swore softly.

"Director, I didn't expect your call, how can I help you?" Usually one of the telepaths on the team would give him the head's up for an assignment, but not this time it would seem.

"You've got an assignment, it's there in Denver. We've tracked a sorcerer to an office off Colfax, you're to perform aetheric recon and see if his demon is anywhere near by. If so, you're to retreat and regroup, our contacts in SER will take it from there. If not, you're to confront and capture the sorcerer, sever his aetheric link to the demon. If you can capture him, great, if not, then his death will be a great loss to our society," the Director's voice dripped sarcasm with that last bit. She loathed sorcerers but then no one else much liked them much. "I'll have Gunther download the instructions and mission parameters to you when he gets in, make sure your mind is open enough to receive them." She clicked off abruptly, not even saying goodbye, but he'd grown used to her lack of tact.

Jackson had no idea what her real name was, everyone just called her the Director. He'd met her for the first time after a high profile case in Dusseldorf, Germany, involving a powerful Russian fallen angel. Part of a team hired to confront the angel and bring him to justice, Jackson had been instrumental in curbing his powers and allowing the more experienced heavy hitters, McClellan and

Burns, to get in close and neutralize him permanently. The Director had pulled him aside at the German polizei congratulatory dinner, posing as a German diplomat, to offer him a position in Division 99. He found out later both Burns and McClellan were also in Division 99 and had been watching him as he worked.

The Director had been much younger looking than one would think the director of a government agency should be, but she hadn't aged in the nearly thirty years since he had first met her. That night she'd been dressed in a poured-on white dress baring one shoulder with her blonde hair plaited in a complicated braid atop her head. Her face was oval with full red lips, high cheekbones, and a slightly downturned nose. Her eyes gave her away, though, the gray-green color of an angry ocean and cold as deep space.

He found out later the face she wore was just one of many. She was a changeling, a kind of faerie able to alter their physical appearance at will. Her natural form, he knew, was more akin to that of a Gray alien, no nose, a slit mouth, and large black eyes. Most changelings were brightly colored in their natural form, some mottled several colors, but her natural form was a ghostly bluish white.

He waited a few minutes before feeling the gentle touch on his mind of another psychic. Gunther was always very polite in his mind-to-mind contact, so Jackson acknowledged him and allowed the psychic data transfer to occur. Suddenly his mind was full of information, maps and memories that weren't his crammed into his receptive memory. Within a couple moments, his brain had sorted the information and catalogued it, filing things away as if they were his own memories and he knew where he had to go.

Jackson sighed, dialing out to Kristin and asking her not to disturb him for the next two hours and to hold all his calls. He rose to lock the door and reopen the safe containing all his foci. Air magic was his specialty, like many with angel blood, but his human blood gave him a measure of power in fire and water as well. Today, though, he would need his skills in air if he was to travel to the aether, so he pulled his silver candlesticks from the safe once more and aligned then in a pentagon on the floor.

He lit them with a flick of his wrist and a focused thought, accelerating the atoms in the wick until they caught fire. Sitting cross-legged on the mat in front of his desk, hands loose on his knees, eyes closed to clear his mind, he began a low chant. Using fire magic was most similar to an adrenaline rush while air magic was more like meditation and water magic was like swimming through a deep lake. Earth magic was more visceral, focused on the practitioner instead of the outside world, and his natural arrogance made it difficult to change himself. As a consequence, earth magic was very challenging for him. He knew this, and tried his best to temper his arrogance with realism, but his angel blood sang to him constantly, swelling his ego and creating an elevated sense of self-worth.

Gazing into his silver mirror, he concentrated, focusing on his own dark eyes, and imagining his body lighter than air, drifting toward the ceiling. As his chanting reached a fever pitch, his head felt like a helium balloon rising to the stratosphere, and he looked down to see his body sitting in the circle of candles, his chest still rising and falling in rhythm. He soared free, passing through the ceiling with a dizzying moment of blackness as he passed through the solid matter.

Jackson's essence flew free through the pale blue winter sky, gazing at the rimed streets below with something approaching contempt. *Foolish mortals*, he thought into the aether, *scurrying about their little lives.* He knew these thoughts were uncharitable, but here in the aether his angel side took over and he couldn't help but see them as insects. His powers dwarfed theirs; he could set himself up as the next God if he wanted to. Perhaps he should, provide them with a purpose, a new deity to worship. Soaring over the 105th longitudinal ley line, its searing silver energy reaching high into the atmosphere, he felt its power boiling through him.

Shaking the thoughts from his head, he moved on, quelling the egomaniacal rumblings of his angel blood to the deepest regions of his psyche and soaring over downtown toward the building on Colfax where his assignment waited. A white building loomed, one he recognized with a jolt as he passed through the walls of the Purity building, searching for a fire darkened essence he had never encountered yet knew as well as that of his own children.

His search ended in a little room deep underground, with no windows and no artificial lights to break the viscous darkness. The sorcerer was sleeping, lying in a simple military cot with no other accoutrements deep in the offices of Purity. Jamie was coming here later; she'd probably already gotten through to her friend to setup the meeting, which left Jackson in a quandary. He'd found his quarry, but he knew if he called SER here they would likely prevent Jamie from learning anything about her case, leaving her high and dry. The Director had told him to try and sever the aetheric contact between the sorcerer and his demon so he decided to try before he called in SER.

Gliding close to the sleeping man, Jackson looked closely to try and see the ephemeral strand connecting the man and his demon, on the lookout for any sign of the demon. Contrary to popular belief, demons could be hurt, and on the aetheric was one of the few places they weren't massively superior to mortals. If it came down to a fight, Jackson had a good chance of besting a demon here on the aetheric, but the fight would cause spiritual turbulence for most of the Denver area for several weeks to come and he didn't want to deal with that just yet.

There, he thought, his attention causing the gossamer thread to pulse softly. Leading from the man's navel was a glowing string, a twisted red and black line disappearing over the edge of the bed and down into the ground. Following a pact line was dangerous when it led into the ground, the demon on the other end would have a huge advantage if Jackson didn't have access to the power of the air.

"Intruder," hissed a voice, a sound like scree running down a steep hillside. Jackson's head snapped up, focusing on the source of the voice in the corner of the room. The demon sat cross-legged on the floor, the twisted black and red thread coming up from the ground to end at its navel. It wasn't large, maybe three feet high, but the shifting outline of its form made it hard to say for sure. The features of its face shifted constantly, now the wizened, lined face of a grandmother, next the cherub cheeked grin of an infant, sometimes showing horns, sometimes not. No one really knew the true face of a demon, because it was said that those who found out never lived to tell.

Instead of confronting the demon, Jackson retreated, rocketing through the ceiling and out the top of the building. Most likely the demon wouldn't follow, they didn't like sunlight, but if the thing felt he was a threat, it might. Fortune smiled upon Jackson as he hovered above the building, because the demon didn't follow. He'd need to contact SER, have them raid the building and deal with the sorcerer.

As Jackson waited to see if the demon pursued him, a black car pulled up to the curb and let a woman out. She was too far for Jackson to see clearly, but he thought it might be Jamie; she was certainly tall enough and blonde. He hovered closer to see if it was her, keeping his distance so as not to alert her to his presence. She had a determined look on her face, an almost angry expression, but she couldn't know what situation she was walking into.

Jackson debated contacting her, but decided against it. *This could be a good chance to see how she handles herself first hand,* he thought as he hovered over her, watching her stride confidently into the Purity offices. He didn't have time to contact SER before she went in, but maybe she'd have more luck than he thought.

As he watched her go, Jackson decided to save his strength, thinking it might be necessary to venture out again later. A powerful demon could give him a run for his money, it was probably out of her league entirely.

Relaxing, Jackson allowed the natural pull of his corporeal form to reel him back in toward his office. He closed his eyes, such as they were, and relaxed, trying to expend as little energy as possible as he drifted back to his body. A psychic flicker caught his attention, something in the aetheric moving to his right, and he snapped his focus around as he arrested his motion back to his body.

He didn't see anything, but that didn't mean very much, there were a lot of buildings a presence could hide behind and mask its signature. Thinking fast, he altered his course, floating off ninety degrees from his previous destination and appearing to relax. After a moment, the presence flickered again, this time from his left, so he bolted after it, moving as fast as possible to try and get a fix on it. He thought it was the demon, trying to follow him back to his body, but it had no idea who it was dealing with.

The presence flickered ahead of him, moving off at high speed, but he was faster, gaining ground second by second as he rushed after it. It tried everything it could to evade him, plunging through buildings or swerving around them, flying high into the atmosphere and plummeting to skim the ground.

A flicker to his left caught Jackson's attention again, a minute filament flashing in the sunlight, stretching from the fleeing presence like a rubber string. For now, he ignored it, focusing on catching the other presence, which had dived again and was skimming along the streets, weaving in and out of the crowd. He worried about it taking a hostage, possessing someone on the street, so he abruptly changed tactics, swerving to intersect the filament.

Flashing red in the sunlight, it looked very similar to a thread from a sorcerer to a demon, leading credence to his theory about the presence. Hovering close to the strand of essence, Jackson examined it, probing it with his air powers, finding a concentrated fire and earth essence. Definitely demon or vampire.

Water power would weaken the strand, maybe sever it entirely, but it might bring the demon roaring back. It'd be at a disadvantage in the sunlight, but would probably fight all the harder if it thought it would lose the soul it had been promised. Pursing his lips, Jackson considered, weighing possibilities. Jamie was walking into the Purity building with a sorcerer she knew nothing about, a dangerous business whoever it might be, and if he could sever the link between the demon and the sorcerer she'd be a lot safer.

This demon was much smarter than average. It knew enough to try to follow him to his body and it would try to destroy it before he reentered, killing him. Jamie didn't have enough mental control to stop an average demon, but her faith was strong so she might be able to hold it at bay long enough to escape. Still, he felt guilty about leaving her to its tender mercy, so confronting it was his only option. Quickly but deftly, he wove a bubble from air and water, pulling water from the plumbing lines in the building next to him and air from all around him to form a force globe enveloping him. No elements could penetrate his shield as long as his will held out, but he knew the demon's will might be a match for his.

Jackson focused his considerable ability, drawing more water power from the moisture in the air and from the pipes in the nearby building and forcing it between the strands of the filament. As the area between his hands began to unravel, smaller strands bulging and then snapping as the water power countered and doused the fire, he kept an eye out for the demon. The last thing he needed was to be taken by surprise and ambushed by the thing.

As he expected, the thing came roaring from the ground beneath him, now ten feet tall and grossly muscled with red skin and a gaping needle filled maw. Its eyes were balls of flame in its canine-like face and its massive paws were now tipped with glistening black talons. It's physical form didn't really matter here on the aetheric, but it was trying to intimidate him and doing a damn good job of it.

Reaching for him and roaring, the demon struck his water and air shield with a cascade of sparks, howling in rage and clawing with all its considerable power at the ephemeral bubble between it and Jackson. Whether or not it could get to him before he severed the contact with the sorcerer depending largely on the willpower of the sorcerer and his own willpower. If he was stronger than the sorcerer, he'd be able to complete his work before the demon tore through his shield.

Sweat broke out on Jackson's ethereal brow as he struggled to maintain both his shield and the disruptive powers focused on the strand of fire. He was almost halfway through the strand, but the demon was tearing long scratches in the substance of his shield with its power, the bubble bowing inward from the force of the attack.

The strand snapped, aetheric force expanding out in an explosive backlash, sending Jackson and the demon tumbling through the aether like twigs in a hurricane. When Jackson was able to right himself, the demon was nowhere to be found. He spun, reaching out with his air senses to try and locate the demon, but felt nothing. He'd not been injured, luckily, but keeping his essence intact had drained a lot of his energy.

Tracking back to the explosion site, he approached slowly, worried about aetheric turbulence from the explosion, when the demon came howling from the ground, completely berserk. It had reverted to the form he had first seen it in, three to four feet tall with a shifting face, but every face was twisted in rage. He recognized faces from the crowd the demon had flown over, faces from history, even his own for a brief instant, all screaming for his blood.

They grappled in the air, water and air stabbing at the demon while fire seared around Jackson, singeing his ethereal clothing and hair. Forming a loop of water held together with air, Jackson finally managed to lasso the demon around the head and left arm, pulling tight to spin it around and loop another strand around its knees and finally its right wrist. Once it was trussed up like a hog for slaughter, he threw a gossamer net of water around it, pulling it tight to immobilize the thing.

"*Wait*," it hissed, voice like nails down a chalkboard, "*wait, I'll make you a deal, wait!*"

"*No deal,*" Jackson replied, wrapping another strand of water around the trussed up demon and pulling it toward a fountain in a square below. The fountain wasn't flowing, but the reservoir beneath it would give him enough water power combined with the air around him to banish the thing permanently.

The demon continued to plead and beg, alternately threatening, and pushing with all its strength against the water binding it and raising great stringers of steam, but to no avail, Jackson's bonds held. Jackson began a chant to help focus his mind, pulling strength from the reservoir below the street, and focusing the power into tight strands around the demon. Layer after layer of gossamer water net formed over the demon, covering it while it keened a grating, almost ultrasonic cry of pain.

Its cry cut off abruptly as the water covering grew complete, a shifting bubble of iridescent liquid the deep turquoise of the Caribbean Sea one moment, green-gray of the angry North Sea the next. As his chanting reached a fever pitch, the bubble began to contract, bulging strangely as the demon inside struggled in vain. The bubble collapsed inward, falling to the size of a drop of rain and then falling to the pavement below to shatter with a small *plop*, empty.

Jackson breathed a sigh of relief, singed and exhausted but relatively unhurt, as he closed his eyes and allowed himself to be drawn back to his corporeal form, safe after defeating the demon.

Chapter 6: Barry

As I exited Jackson's office and walked back into the entrance area of our offices, Kristen was on the phone, gossiping about one of her many friends, gesturing wildly. I sighed, wondering if I was ever that young, even though I was only about five years older than she was, but I had seen more than I hoped she ever saw. She came from a fairly wealthy family, mostly worked for us to keep busy, and hadn't ever really had to deal with the really real world. My parents were poor, working class people, and growing up we didn't have a lot. I'd been working since I was sixteen and hunting since I was twenty two, as soon as I got out of school. I sighed again, shaking my head with a small smile on my lips, and headed for my office to look for my cell phone.

I hated cell phones, they were the bane of my existence, but they were also what kept me in business. Without the darned thing, I'd have a rough time tracking my quarry when I was hunting and Kristen wouldn't have any way to get a hold of me most of the time. Mine was in my purse, somewhere, and I had to dig for it. I needed to call one of my best friends, Barry.

Barry McAllen was an engineer, quite successful, and just about the complete opposite of me. He was vanilla human, no sensitivity, nothing interesting aside from his astounding ability to make friends. Everyone loved Barry, he was just so open and friendly and we'd been friends since childhood, probably the only reason he still talked to me, because he leaned toward the conservative.

He had connections with a couple of the humans first groups although he was not an active member. I was hoping he would be my in with Purity, but if what Jackson had found was true, it might be a dead end. Still, worth a try, mainly because I had no idea where else to go with it and maybe they were in with a sorcerer or something. That thought stopped me in my tracks for a moment, ludicrous but strangely plausible. Nah, that wasn't likely, but it was the only thing I could think of.

I pulled out my battered flip phone and thumbed through the address book for his number, noticing the cracked screen was worse than earlier and I was going to need to give up the ghost and buy a new one soon. He answered on the third ring, trying to be funny.

"Hello? You want Chinese? Egg roll?" I smiled in spite of myself; he was certifiably insane I think.

"No egg roll," I replied, "not hungry, need a favor."

"No, no favors here, just Chinese food."

"Come on Barry, I need some help, quit clowning around!"

"Sorry," he replied, "couldn't resist, you're so easy to get going. What's up, my little psycho friend?"

I was usually his psycho friend or something similar. He called all sensitives psychos even though very few of us were truly psychic. He just liked trying to get me going and succeeded embarrassingly frequently.

"Working on a new case," I said, "and I need to talk to someone in Purity a.s.a.p. Something you can help with or should I brave the lion's den alone?"

"Phew, Purity, going for the jugular right away I see. Couldn't have started with, hey, how are you my brilliant, handsome friend, no, not Jamie McKinsey. Sigh. Why Purity?"

"Cut it out, Barry, I'm serious."

"I'm super, thanks for asking. Woke up after a nice night's sleep, had a nice breakfast, it's been a good day so far."

"Barry, you're killing me, come on I need your help. Seriously."

"Crabby crabby, Jamie, what's got your panties in a knot? You know Purity doesn't like you, not after you exposed their little plot last year. Why do you need to see them anyway? Couldn't you just go into a bear's den covered in honey? Probably be safer for you."

"No further, okay? This is confidential."

"Right, no talkie talkie."

"Adora Johanson has been taken for ransom and her husband has hired me to find her. I have no idea where to start but the ransom note referred to her as an aberration so I thought maybe one of the humans first groups would be a good start. Purity immediately leapt to mind, and I thought maybe your friend could get me an interview with one of their higher ups."

"Adora Johanson has been taken for ransom? Shit, Jamie, you are in way over your head with anyone who can take a fallen angel against her will. Purity is just vanilla humans, how in Heaven's name would they have taken her?" I could tell he was worried; he rarely cussed unless he was very upset. Something about his wording niggled at the back of my mind, but I couldn't put my finger on it. I pushed it aside, not able to concentrate on it right now.

"Jackson found traces of something else, something powerful, vampire or demon maybe angel, around the ransom note. Purity has been known to use unorthodox means to accomplish their ends; maybe they hired a sorcerer or something to help them out. In their ransom letter, they referred to her as an aberration. Most vampires and angels don't refer to themselves as aberrations so I thought maybe Purity could've hired someone with power. They've done it before."

He sighed, a burst of static over the speaker that made me flinch.

"Okay, Jamie, I love you so I'll tell you this only once. Drop it. Drop the case; this is too big for you if they are holding an angel against her will."

Again the niggling feeling in the back of my head. What felt wrong about what he just said? "I can't," I replied, "Johanson offered me too much money; I need to at least try."

"How much is your life worth? This is really, really dangerous, hun."

"I know, but I need to try. Can you get me the meeting with Purity or should I just walk in and hope they don't lynch me?"

"I knew it, I knew I shouldn't pick up the phone, I looked down at the screen and thought to myself, 'self, it's that weirdo Jamie calling, she's nothing but trouble, don't answer it.' But, nooo, I had to answer it and now I'm honor bound to help you. Yeah, I can get you a meeting, be down by Colfax by one and they'll let you in. I gotta make some calls first, if they throw me a curve ball I'll call you so keep your phone handy. It'll be with George McBarrister so ask for him by name. You owe me, if you survive this case, so make sure you have reservations at the Pike's Steakhouse for two."

"Right, two reservations for Denny's, coming right up. And Barry? Thanks. I owe you one."

"Just don't get yourself lynched, I gotta make some calls," he grumbled as he hung up.

I had almost two hours to get to the Purity office on Colfax and it was only about fifteen minutes away so I decided to get some lunch. Jackson had probably brought his lunch, vegetarian because practitioners got bad vibes from animal protein, and Kristen was, uh, interesting to have lunch with, so I decided to call my friend Allison.

Allison Schmitz, MD, PhD was a doctor at the University of Colorado Health Sciences studying vampirism and prions. She and I had known each other as long as Barry and I had, but we had a different sort of relationship. We had met at our Taekwondo school when I was in middle school and she was in college. I trained because I enjoyed it; she trained because she wanted to be able to defend herself. We were both still training there, I was a fourth degree black belt, she was a third degree, and we pretty well ran the school. Allison was very quiet, intense, and a workaholic. She wasn't married, had no kids and no interest in either, and had a virulent hatred of vampires, which made it interesting when she found a subject to research, usually one I brought back for her.

Her family had been killed by a rogue Master some twenty years ago and she was Hell-bent on finding a cure for the prion (called Stoker-Dracul syndrome) responsible for vampirism. Vampirism, like zombieism and lycanthropy, was caused by an infectious agent but Stoker-Dracul syndrome had a metaphysical connection too. Someone bitten by a vampire, servant or Master, might contract Stoker-Dracul syndrome but if the biting vampire didn't complete the ritual, the victim would develop an illness very similar to bovine spongiform encephalopathy and would die fairly quickly. After death, they would arise again as a ghoul. Ghouls were nasty characters, similar to zombies in that they were dead and rotting, but ghouls were far more intelligent, cunning, aggressive, and agile. If a Master was powerful enough, he or she could control the ghouls they created, sending them to terrorize or to kidnap victims for their sustenance.

Flamethrowers were your best friend when dealing with a ghoul.

If the biting vampire was a Master, he or she completed the metaphysical rituals, and the victim was a sensitive, they would create a servant vampire. Servants were the lowest of the low in the vampiric hierarchy, not any stronger than humans and without any other great supernatural powers. They even lost whatever powers they might have had as a sensitive. They were beholden to their Master for everything from food and shelter to protection from other Master vampires and weren't too challenging to deal with. Silver worked quite well but wasn't totally necessary because normal copper jacketed rounds worked almost as well. They healed only a little faster than a vanilla human so running them over with a truck was very effective as was sunlight. Many servants would cower from a holy symbol of any variety and thus a cross, Star of David, or something similar was standard hunter apparel. I preferred a cross, having been raised as a Christian.

Periodically, a Master would run afoul of a vampire hunter or another Master vampire and there would be an open territory for a new Master to take over. Sometimes rampant population growth would force the creation of a new territory, kind of like when they added all those new area codes. Master vampires were created by other Masters by the same rituals used to create servants, performed again on a worthy servant. Masters were much more challenging to deal with than servants and many of the vampires in fiction were based on actual Masters.

A run-of-the-mill Master was much stronger than a human, able to lift a car with little trouble, and extremely fast, some able to dodge bullets if he or she was aware of the shooter. They could grab your mind in theirs and force most people to do whatever they wished, up to and including complete mental domination.

Sensitives like me were resistant to this mental control, but not immune, part of the reason we made better hunters than vanilla humans. Most Masters could summon wolves and bats to do their bidding but couldn't turn into either, contrary to popular belief. Masters could be killed with silver or even massive damage, but they healed very quickly from non-silver damage. I'd seen a Master heal from a shot from a rocket propelled grenade once, but others have been killed from a single sniper shot with a silver bullet. Masters can't tolerate sunlight, but they will laugh if confronted with a holy symbol.

Most Masters had a family of servants, maybe another Master or two, but rarely more than ten other vampires living with them. Too many others attracted attention and Masters hid themselves from the law with all their considerable ability. If found, hunters and police alike were authorized to eradicate a family down to its last member and would usually receive a nice finder's fee for their trouble.

When a Master was created, he or she was freed from the control of the creating Master but the creator would gain power as well. Eventually, if a Master created enough Masters, they would become a King or Queen and their power would increase exponentially. There were approximately ten to twelve Kings or Queens in the entire world at any given time and ousting them frequently required action on the part of a branch of the military due to the large number of lesser vampires in their families.

Thankfully, most vampires who reached this level were fairly mentally stable and less likely to cause trouble or attract the attention of the establishment. One of the North American Masters on his way to becoming the King of North America was named Erick McBean and the government thought he was somewhere west of the Mississippi. Erick was one of the more benevolent Masters, or so I had heard, but that was like saying something was a benevolent lion or grizzly bear.

Stoker-Dracul syndrome damaged the centers of the brain involved in morality and compassion, so most vampires were textbook psychopaths, predators in human form. Depending on how long they had been infected with Dracul-Stoker syndrome before the metaphysical rights, some vampires were more cold blooded than others.

As far as anyone knew, all varieties of vampire were immortal, they never aged and only severe damage could kill them. Jejong, the Queen of China, was thought to be more than ten thousand years old and it would likely require a nuclear strike against her if she ever went off the deep end. China maintained they would be happy to do so, regardless of other casualties, if anyone could find her and give them her location. So far, no one had come forward with that information.

I thumbed through my phonebook again, looking for Allison's number. It was only 11:20 so she was likely in the lab. I hated going to her lab, it smelled horribly and I was terrified of catching Stoker-Dracul syndrome, but sometimes I had to go and pry her away from her work. I hoped today wasn't one of those times.

I settled back in my chair, crossing my legs at the knee, and waiting while her phone rang and rang. I sipped my tea as the phone clicked over to her voicemail and I swore softly under my breath. I hung up and redialed the number, not interested in leaving a message. It rang through again to her voicemail and I left her a message to call me if she got the message before 11:30. She wouldn't, but it was worth a shot. I guess it was lunch alone, because I didn't feel like going over and ousting her. Again. Sigh.

Standing, I grabbed my ankle length leather trench coat and my black leather purse from the back of the door and slid my arms into the silk lined holes. I tied the front closed and swung the long strap of my purse across my body. I wasn't worried about being mugged, I could take them if they weren't armed and I had a 38 special in my purse, easy to get to, if they were armed.

"I'm headed for Mickey D's if you need me and I have my phone," I tossed over my shoulder to Kristen as I walked out. She waved without turning her head, intent on whatever she was looking at on her computer. I snorted, and headed out the office door to the ice-coated streets of Denver.

It was cold today, a blustery twenty degrees and the sun was shining bright white and frigid. It'd snowed a couple days ago and all the north facing rooftops were still glaringly white with unmelted layers of winter precipitation. Our streets were clear, the government usually did fairly well clearing them, but there was a thick gray slush band between the sidewalks and the asphalt, not something to step in. Bundled people hurried about their business, covered heads down against the gusting wind, hands shoved deep into winter coat pockets.

Down the street from our offices was a McDonald's, somewhere I frequented a bit too often. Contrary to popular belief, if one avoided the Big Macs and fries, it wasn't hard to eat fairly well at most fast food places and I liked their salads and orange drink. I settled my large-lens black sunglasses with multicolored crystals at the temples over my eyes and headed for the McDonald's with a cocky stride. People were staring, but at six foot two barefooted, I was used to being stared at, so I just smiled politely and moved on.

I ordered my usual, added an order of chicken nuggets, and took a seat in the corner, next to a window so I could bask in the sunlight. Mmm, rabbit food with artificially colored and flavored water and mechanically separated chicken, yummy. I pulled my ebook reader from my purse, immersing myself in some trashy romance novel as I ate. I glanced down at my watch when I was finished and 11:30 had come and gone with no sign from Allison, so I headed out into the icy streets again.

Chapter 7: Ghoul

It was now after noon so I needed to call a cab or catch the bus to get to the Purity offices. I didn't drive much, no need in downtown Denver, so I walked, relied on cabs, or took the bus to get everywhere. My old, beat up Honda Accord got me where I needed to go whenever I needed to go outside the confines of the bus system but it was just too much trouble for a short jaunt across town. It was too cold to walk (I hate winter!) so I pulled my wallet out to see if I could afford a cab. I could, but the bus was cheaper so I headed for the bus stop nearest the McDonald's.

The slush in the street was ankle deep, gray with dirt and road grime, and it had splashed all over the bus shelter. There was a homeless man hunched over a shopping cart on the right side of the bus shelter, looking like a grimy bear, so I headed for the other side, stopping behind the structure to avoid being splashed by traffic rushing by. I stood behind and to the right of the shelter, resting my weight on my left leg with my right leg crossed over the top of it and pretended to examine my phone. I wasn't afraid of the homeless man, but there was a good chance he would try to hit me up for money if I paid him any attention and I didn't have enough to give him any right now. Most charities said not to give handouts to panhandlers, to donate to the shelters instead, and I tried to do my best, but every once in a while I encountered a person I knew for a fact was homeless and I felt better giving them a little bit. Small salve to my conscience I guess, but it helped me sleep at night.

Out of the corner of my eye, I noticed the homeless man shift his position and sniff the air, turning his head toward me as if he was trying to get a fix on me. He groaned, a low bestial sound, and I stiffened. I slid my phone into my front pocket and unzipped the back pocket of my purse, reaching in to wrap my palm around the Smith and Wesson nestled in there. It was a 38 special, only six shots, but enough to deter most people just by sight. The homeless man shifted his head, bringing his head around to face me, and I swore. His eyes were clouded, dull, and his skin was pasty gray with weeping sores on his nose and cheeks. He had greasy black hair and a week of beard growth, but was otherwise fairly nondescript. His coat was hanging open, revealing a sullied red flannel shirt and unbuttoned khaki twill pants with ragged black shoes, but he wasn't shivering. He was sniffing the air like a dog and I realized he was dead, fairly recently dead from the look of him, but dead nonetheless. I guess I was lucky he had chosen to come after me instead of some hapless passerby.

I backed away slowly, retrieving my phone and dialing 911. Encounters with plague victims weren't unheard of, the vaccine wasn't always effective and it needed to be updated every five years, but neither was an encounter an everyday experience. My gun wouldn't be of any use against him, it would shoot right through him and he'd never hesitate. I needed a flamethrower but I didn't have mine, so the police were the closest people to have one. He grunted as I hit send on my phone and shuffled a step toward me, reaching out with his hands, grasping his fingers, and grunting again as if he could already taste my flesh.

"Hi, I'm at the intersection of East 8th Avenue and Colorado Boulevard at the bus stop on the corner and there's a homeless man infected with *Reanimagus* here looking me over like a snack. Can I please have SER here a.s.a.p? I'll try to keep him busy but I would really appreciate some help."

"Thank you, ma'am," the operator replied, "we'll have a unit out there as soon as possible. Are you armed?"

"Yeah, I'm a hunter so I can handle myself, just please get the roaster out here as soon as you can. Thanks." Click.

He jerked at the sound of my voice, grunted again, and let out a low moan as he shuffled faster toward me. He had apparently bitten his tongue or his lip because red black goo was dribbling from the left corner of his mouth. I dodged around the bus shelter to my right and he came after me, suddenly breaking into a run. He moved much faster than I thought he would, almost grabbing the trailing hem of my coat, and I realized I wouldn't be able to escape him running around the shelter. I wasn't sure if he was actually a plague victim, he might have been a ghoul, but because of his poor condition, he wasn't as fast as ghouls usually were.

I spun, lashing out with a side kick to his mid section, and then whirling into a spinning hook kick to his head. My heel caught him just below the eye, crushing his cheek bone and snapping his head back, while he flailed for my leg. He went down in a heap with a scream, startling me. He was a ghoul, just a really broken down one and he struggled to his feet much faster than I hoped. His face was bleeding but not as much as it should, thick, black, coagulated blood leaking slowly from the long gash my heel had left under his eye. Yep, very recently dead, maybe this morning even. I hoped I was his first intended victim because I could handle him. Most people couldn't.

I looked in his eyes, dreading the flash of intelligence, but I knew I was being optimistic. He was a ghoul, not just a plague victim, which meant there was an active vampire family in the area. Not good, not good at all.

I lashed out again, side kicking him in the chest, the face, and again in the chest. He stumbled back, clawing at his face where I had punctured his left eye, and I spun to kick him one last time in the chest with a roundhouse kick that knocked him into traffic just as a semi zoomed by. The truck clipped him with the front of the cab, spinning him to the ground and crushing the left side of his body. He lay still for a moment, almost as if trying to catch his breath, and then, grotesquely, he tried to get up. His left arm and left leg were broken, flopping uselessly, and his face was a smashed ruin on the left side. He pushed himself forward with his right leg and pulled with his right arm, still hungrily trying to get to me and his meal.

My savior tractor trailer had screeched to a stop, snarling traffic, and the driver leapt out to see who he had just apparently killed. He came running toward the ghoul, but stopped dead when he saw the pulped figure still trying to stand. He doubled over, puking into the slush, turning it a foul smelling pink, as he leaned on a stopped cab for support.

The owner of the cab got out, shouting in heavily accented English at the trucker, but a good Samaritan arrived in time to keep the two apart. My trucker friend was in no shape to do anything but lean on the cab so the good Samaritan handed him a bag to breathe into to help him calm down and sat him down on the curb. A crowd had gathered at this point, far too close to the struggling ghoul, but he was focused on me and ignored everyone else.

"Back! Get back!" I shouted, visualizing a child or little old lady becoming lunch for this smashed thing. "He's undead, get back!" Wrong thing to say, I realized, as the mood turned from horrified fascination to terror. People starting running, any direction as long as it was away from me and the smashed horror still trying to make his way to me, including into traffic. Traffic had stopped behind the semi, thank God, so no one was injured and I could hear the eerie wailing of the SER siren. The ghoul wasn't going anywhere, but neither was I so I settled back to wait.

Twice, I had to kick his arm out from under him, and he would fall back to the pavement with a grunt and a splat. Morbidly fascinated people had started to gather again and there was a very large crowd by the time SER got there. Their maroon police vans pulled onto the sidewalk with a wail from their siren, a pair of tactical vans just like SWAT used.

"MOVE!" a very large man in heavy body armor bellowed as he exited the driver side door of the first van. The crowd split like the Red Sea before Moses and he strode up to me, ignoring the pulped mess at the my feet.

"McKinsey, I figgered it was you when I saw a giant blonde standin' in front of the zombie." It was Lieutenant Mark Coleman, in charge of SER for this area of Denver. We'd had our run-ins, but he usually was a good guy, although I would have appreciated him not always trying to get into my pants. Totally not my type. He was huge, as tall as me in my heels but close to three hundred pounds of muscle. He was a serious weightlifter and had to be to go toe to toe with some of the supernatural nasties around, although a Master vampire would still tear him to little pieces.

Coleman was dressed in the maroon jumpsuit and heavy body armor of SER with his tactical shotgun slung over his shoulder and his rifle held loosely in his left hand. The visor of his riot helmet obscured his face but I knew his broad, dark face was probably leering at me with his white teeth and dark eyes. His hair was mostly black, shot through with gray, cut very short to his head and he had a scar down the left side of his face where a lycanthrope had torn into him. Luck was on his side that day; he hadn't come down with HBV. Coleman was African-American at least partly and somewhat attractive, if you liked over confident braggarts, but he was a great guy to have at your back. I usually called him when I needed serious backup.

"Coleman," I said coolly, "took you long enough to get here. You just letting *Reanimagus* victims wander about nowadays? I thought the city agreed to fund that whole no person left unvaccinated thing."

Coleman pulled up his visor and scowled at me, the motion tugging and puckering the left side of his face as the scarred tissue tried and failed to move the way he wanted it to.

"Watch your mouth, McKinsey; ya know them vaccines ain't a hundred percent. Plus, ya know how hard it is ta keep track of all them homeless people out here? We do our best, but sometimes our best ain't good enough."

"I know, Coleman," I said soothingly, sorry I had pricked his pride. "I didn't mean it as an attack on you; I'm just still a little hyped up on almost getting eaten. He's actually not a zombie, he's a ghoul."

He snorted, sneering at me. "You're as likely to get eaten by a zom as I'm likely to win Ms. Teen USA. What'd ya do to him, anyway? He's been pulped."

"Knocked him into that semi," I replied, pointing to the tractor trailer stopped a couple hundred yards down the road. The driver was still sitting on the curb, still breathing into a paper bag, but the cab driver was back in his car trying to get back into traffic.

"Nice. Kickin' him into the tractor trailer, I'll have ta remember that one, works better than blastin' them I bet. Call it the McKinsey maneuver or something," he said with a wink.

"Shit," he said, comprehension dawning in his dark eyes. "Did you say he wasn't a zom, he's a fuckin' ghoul? Damn, I gotta call that in, you just stay here like a good girl," he said, winking again and striding away toward his van. He returned a second later, a scowl on his face. "I told the higher ups about the ghoul, they ain't happy. You sure he's a ghoul?" he asked.

I rolled my eyes and stepped away from him. "Whatever, I know a ghoul when I see one. Take a good look at him, I'll bet he's got a nasty bite. Probably not just one, either, they probably drained him." I said, looking down at the struggling ghoul and pointing at the black splotch under his chin where he'd bled out onto the concrete. "You want some help getting him into the roaster or cleaning up his mess?" I asked, trying to be nice and hoping he'd turn me down.

"Nah," he said, much to my relief, "the boys'll get him roasted and toasted and the sidewalk cleaned. You need something to get that crap off your boots?"

"Yeah," I replied as I realized I had blood and other goo all over my right boot, especially the heel. "Must've kicked him harder than I realized, gross." He laughed, a thunderous baritone, and led me to the dark red SER truck where his coworkers were securing the ghoul and heating up the oven, called the roaster, to incinerate him.

Zombies, vampires, ghouls, and lycanthropes had to be incinerated because they were still contagious after death and it was the only way to get rid of the zombies and ghouls. If they weren't incinerated, they kept trying to come after you. SER always had two trucks, one like the standard police tactical van with the same heavy equipment but with silver plated ammo, and another that was a mobile oven on wheels to deal with the end result of a SER call. Coleman handed me a bottle of bleach wipes and I started cleaning up my boots. Thankfully, nothing was on my clothes, otherwise I'd need to burn them. Leather could be wiped clean, part of the reason I favored it.

"Where were you headed?" Coleman asked when I had finished putting the wet wipes in the biohazard bag to be burned.

"Oh shit," I swore as I realized it was 12:35 and I wasn't even close to my appointment at Purity. "I was headed down to the Purity office off Colfax. There's no way I'm going to make it by 1:00. Crap, crap, crap."

"Purity? You thinking about joining that group of knuckleheads? They'd kick yo' butt out in a hot minute when they realized who ya was. Ya need a lift?" he asked with a wink.

"Sure," I said, batting my eyes and smiling at him. Hey, if you got it, use it, he knew I wasn't serious. I hoped.

"Hey! Gibson! Get over here!" Coleman bellowed suddenly, making me flinch. A short man in the same jumpsuit but without the armor or weaponry broke off from the group preparing the roaster for our undead friend. He trotted over and saluted Coleman.

"Whatcha need Lieutenant?" he asked, casually standing there with his hands on his hips. Terry Gibson was second in command of the SER for this area of Denver and he was much more my speed, although a little short for my tastes at five foot four. He was young, only about twenty three to twenty four, with straight black hair and startling blue eyes. He had an open, heart-shaped, honest face with plump lips, a small straight nose and the thickest black eyelashes I had ever seen on a man or a woman. Most women would kill for his eyelashes and he seemed completely oblivious to the effects they had on women around him. He was also ripped, as in Hollywood actor kind of ripped and he moved with the grace of a stalking cat. My mind went somewhat blank when he was close, and I said brilliant things like...

"Uh, hiya, Gibson, what's up?" Ugh, brilliant.

"Hey McKinsey, thanks for bagging that zom for us. Wish I coulda been there when you kicked him into the semi, I'll bet that was wicked cool." He said, flashing a white smile at me and then turning back to Coleman. My heart skipped a beat and I blushed or at least I hoped I was blushing, otherwise the heat on my face meant I was standing too close to the roaster.

Coleman glanced at me suspiciously and turned back to Gibson. "McKinsey has an appointment she's gonna miss 'cause she was doing our job, you want to give her a ride to the Purity office off Colfax?"

"Sure, be happy to, keeps me from clean up duty," Gibson replied with another wink in my direction. Nope, I was definitely standing too close to the roaster; my face felt like it was on fire. "Come on, McKinsey, let's get a move on," he said, walking toward a black Crown Vic. I followed, smacking Coleman on the back as I walked by and giving him a saucy look. He grunted and turned back toward the struggling ghoul, shouting orders and getting his men organized to clean up my mess.

Chapter 8: Coleman

Mark Coleman watched the squad car with Gibson and McKinsey disappear down the street with a shake of his head. He wondered when she'd figure out Gibson just wasn't into chicks and stop making goo goo eyes at him. She was a sweet girl and great to have at his back in a fight, he almost thought of her as a sister, but she was really clueless sometimes. He snorted, heading back to the ghoul and the messy cleanup job she'd left for SER.

As he approached the ghoul, one of the other officers in a Tyvek suit zip tied its arms and legs together, immobilizing it and keeping it from continuing to try to pursue a meal. It's constant grunting was getting on his nerves, but there wasn't much he could do about it. His superiors wanted verification about it being a ghoul, but he really didn't want to touch the damn thing. With a glance to the sky as if to say 'why me', he headed for the back of the SER van to find a pair of gloves.

Standard issue for SER units consisted of two dozen pairs of autoclavable synthetic leather gloves that were tear and puncture resistant among other things. He found a pair and bent to inspect the ghoul, pulling its head back by the hair to get a good look at its neck. It snapped and snarled at him, twisting hard enough in his grasp to tear a chunk of hair along with the attached scalp off its head, so he let go of the thing with an oath. There'd been a strange mark on the neck, maybe vampire bite, but nothing bloody so he wasn't sure.

"Smith, get over here and hold this damn thing down, I need a closer look at that bite there," he shouted, gesturing at one of the maroon clad officers loitering by the second van. Officer Smith was new, the low man on the totem pole, so he got the shit jobs. Smith wandered over with a scowl, looking between Coleman and the ghoul with an expression of disdain. His narrow olive skinned face, dark eyes, and downturned mouth were particularly suited to looks of disdain and irritation, it was one of the things Coleman didn't especially like about him. Smith was also a member of Purity, some of the reason he'd kept him away from McKinsey.

Gesturing for Smith to lean on the ghoul's head and pin it to the ground, Coleman squatted to get a closer look for a bite. Smith grimaced in disgust, carefully lowering himself to the pavement until he could put his entire weight on the thing's temple. It struggled, bucking and twisting, but was unable to free itself from Smith's weight.

Upon closer inspection, the mark on the ghoul's neck was a bite, but it looked bizarre, almost unreal, but very brutal. Whoever had done this had either been in a big hurry or else the poor man had fought them. Looking at the state of the ghoul, Coleman doubted the man had had enough strength to fight anyone, much less a hungry vampire. There was no blood in the puncture wounds, nothing in or around the wound, just torn nearly bloodless flesh that looked like hamburger. The ghoul hadn't been completely drained, there was blood on the sidewalk and the front of the cab from its encounter with McKinsey. Not a lot, but enough that the neck wound should have bled if he'd been alive when it was done.

Coleman pursed his lips, thinking hard, but he couldn't think of any reason someone would bite a ghoul after it was dead. *Unless it was another ghoul who bit it*, he thought, wrinkling his face in thought. Another ghoul would explain the violence of the wound, but undead didn't usually attack other undead. He shrugged, convinced it was in fact a ghoul, and that was enough for his superiors.

Pushing up from the ground, Coleman signaled the rest of the squad to throw the thing into the roaster, standing back as it struggled to reach someone, anyone, it could bite. Three white Tyvek-suited men grabbed the corpse while a fourth wrenched open the roaster, releasing a blast of heat strong enough to make Coleman turn away. The fourth officer opened the door just far enough for the three men to throw the ghoul into the searing hot chamber before slamming it shut again and giving the thumbs up for the driver to crank up the temperature. The ghoul screamed, a high keening sound, not because it was in pain, but because it was locked away from its meal. After a few moments, it fell silent as the scent of roasting flesh filled the air. Coleman hated that smell, so he walked away to get the equipment they would need to clean up the sidewalk and the semi driver's truck.

Chapter 9: Purity

I followed Gibson to the Crown Vic and slid into the front seat as he cranked it up. He flipped on the lights and we eased into traffic, headed for Colfax. He hummed tunelessly to himself, tapping his fingers on the steering wheel and not looking at me. Zombie had my tongue; I was pulling a complete blank on small talk.

"So, uh, what kind of music do you like?" I asked inanely.

"Just about everything," he replied. "Not too fond of that hip hop stuff but, you know, it's not terrible if there's nothin' else on." He went back to humming and tapping his fingers.

"Um, do you ever go to the clubs? The Church or anything?" I asked, groping for anything to talk about.

"Nope, mostly just work, hit the gym, you know," he replied, humming. I gave up, sitting back into my chair and pouting a little. Guess I was losing my touch, that creepy old cougar at the ripe age of twenty six. *Maybe he's gay.* I thought, hopefully. That thought cheered me up a little and I sat up in my chair to watch the town go by. I loved Denver, but it sure was cold in the winter time. We passed gray building after gray building, rimed in frost even in the early afternoon, with a crowd of heavily bundled people bustling through the streets.

We eased into a parallel parking spot outside the Purity office building, a gleaming white office cube with shining windows and manicured bushes heavy with white snow from the last blizzard. Purity was obviously not doing too badly, not with the money it would take to keep their office that shiny and new, so maybe, just maybe, they were doing well enough to hire a sorcerer to kidnap Adora Johanson. I sure hoped I was right with my sorcerer theory, because if I wasn't, I had no idea where to go next.

"Here ya go, McKinsey, Purity HQ. Watch your head in there; they ain't playing with a full deck if you catch my drift. By the way, here's my number, feel free to call me next time you have a problem you need help with." He handed me a white business card with his name and phone number in maroon ink. My heart skipped a beat again, thinking maybe I had made an impression on him, when I realized it was his professional business card. My heart sank into my toes and I mumbled an ungrateful thanks as I got out of the car. He pulled away slowly, giving me a cheery wave and a smile as he merged back into traffic, headed back to the ghoul scene I guessed.

I gave myself a shake and pulled my head up, throwing off the disgruntlement. I needed to be on my A game, Purity didn't like me and I was going to need to trick them into giving up their information if they had any. I walked into the main foyer of their building, headed toward the administrative assistant's desk. Their entry way was tiled in brown marble veined with gold with pure white walls hung with portraits of great humans. Non-sensitives only, no freaks in their corporate office if they had anything to say about it.

Seated at the massive pale gold wood desk (real wood, too, not veneered like my monstrosity) was a sweet looking older woman. She looked to be in her sixties, white hair tied into a bun at the back of her head, with neat makeup and a pleasant motherly expression. Her button up blouse was a pale purple and about two sizes too big. Pearl earrings and necklace loose around her throat looked real, shiny and iridescent, glowing against her pink skin.

"Hi!" I said brightly, hoping to start the meeting off on the right foot.

"Hello, dear," she replied, "can I help you?"

"Yeah, I'm Jamie McKinsey and I have an appointment with George McBarrister at one. Is he ready for me?" I asked, smiling winningly.

"Oh, you," she replied with a scowl. "No, he doesn't have time for the likes of you, please wait in there," she pointed to my right to a little door off the main entry way. She pointedly turned away from me, giving me the cold shoulder and maximizing the window for the solitaire game on her computer. My smile faltered and I headed off to the little door without another word. Truth be told, this was going about as I expected it to go. I opened the door and entered a little rat hole with a rickety chair and little else. It was dirty; perhaps eight feet square, with a scummy sink in one corner and an old mop and bucket in the other. I took one look at the chair and decided I'd rather stand.

Thirty minutes later, Ms. Attitude at the front desk beckoned to me to follow her as she walked through the large double doors to the left behind her desk. They were tall, maybe eight feet high with golden wood shined to a high polish. She ignored me, making no more moves to acknowledge my existence than she would a cockroach. Frankly, she probably would have paid more attention to a cockroach, probably screamed and smashed it.

We walked down a glass lined hallway, large, expansive offices with constipated looked underlings on both sides. Finally, we reached another large set of golden wood doors at the end of the hall. She knocked, and without waiting for an answer, entered through the right hand door. I followed, half expecting her to slam the door in my face, but she didn't.

The office we entered was expansive, maybe twenty feet on a side, with lush gold carpet, a massive golden wood desk directly ahead, and a white upholstered sectional sofa to the left. A gold wood coffee table sat next to the sectional while to the right there was another gold wood table with a half dozen white leather chairs around it.

Seated behind the desk was a hugely fat man, no more than five foot five, but easily three hundred pounds. He had greasy black curls and a pencil thin black mustache set in a doughy, fat face. His eyes looked almost black and were wide set in his uncooked biscuit dough face. He was one of the most singularly unattractive people I had ever met. His white sausage fingers had large gold or silver rings on every one, many too small and appearing to cut off the circulation, while his suit was well tailored white elven silk. No amount of tailoring could hide his bulk, though. It made him look like a giant marshmallow someone had left too long in the fire, blackened at the end. He looked up with unconcealed irritation creasing his porcine face, an expression that only intensified as he caught sight of me. He flicked his hand at his assistant and she left without a word.

"Mr. McBarrister I take it?" I hazarded, extending my right hand and advancing toward him. He froze me with a glare, looking at my extended hand in disdain, and remained seated.

"Ms. McKinsey, my associate Mr. McAllen suggested I meet with you against my better judgment and you have thirty seconds to convince me he was correct. Begin," he said. His voice was high and nasal, someone who was beat up in high school who loved lording his success over those he saw as his tormentors.

"Mr. McBarrister, thank you for agreeing to see me, I had some questions I wanted to ask you about a recent disappearance. Do you mind if I ask them?"

"Twenty seconds," he replied. Okay, he wanted to play hardball, I could play hardball. Maybe I could bluff him out.

"Look, Georgie, I know about the sorcerer you have on hire, and I know what you have been using him for. That blunt enough for you?"

A look of panic swept over his bulbous face, quickly quelled but there. Victory sang through me, triumph making me cocky. He surreptitiously moved his left hand to brush a statue on his desk. A small red button began to flash at the base of the statue and my triumph shifted suddenly to a queasy uneasy feeling. I had a really bad feeling about this whole business.

He remained silent and I waited, seeing what his next move would be, as I loosened the zipper on the rear compartment of my purse and surreptitiously slipped my hand around my revolver. A white door I hadn't noticed opened to his left and a small African American woman walked into the room. She was petite, maybe five foot two and a hundred pounds, with very short cut hair and skin the color of coffee with cream. She was wearing a well-tailored gray suit with a white dress shirt and sensible black heels, expensive. She moved with a predatory grace and the look she gave me was pure liquid poison. This had gone from uncomfortable to bad much faster than I had thought possible.

"Yes, George?" she purred, glaring at me like I had shot her mother.

"Kendra, this... person, has said some things I believe you should hear. Perhaps you would like to continue, Ms.

McKinsey?" I swallowed hard, uncertain why this little woman unnerved me so. She must be Kendra Phelps, his second in command and, if rumor was true, a real psychopath.

"You were saying about our supposed sorcerer?" he supplied with a sneer.

"Right, your sorcerer. I know you hired him and I can prove it so we need to talk about who you have, well, illegally confined." A look of relief flashed across his face and I knew I had pushed it too far. From his reactions, I was pretty sure they did have a sorcerer on payroll, but if they had kidnapped Adora, either he didn't know about it or he was a much better actor than I gave him credit for. Sorcery was very illegal, as was consorting with a sorcerer, but I didn't have any proof. Yet.

"I think I've heard enough," Phelps snapped, "and I think your fictional tales need to end. You have no evidence of anything, you know it and we know it, so I think you need to leave. Now, Ms. McKinsey. Follow me please," without waiting for a response she strode toward the white door she had entered through and disappeared down the hall.

"Mr. McBarrister, I wasn't finished," I tried one last time, "I'm ready to go to the police if..."

"You'll do nothing of the sort Ms. McKinsey," he interrupted. "You have nothing or the officer you arrived with would have arrested all of us. Now, please leave, and tell Mr. McAllen I see no reason to continue any interaction with the likes of you." He flicked his hand toward the side door and lowered his head to concentrate on his papers. I gave up, walking back to the double doors I had entered through and attempted to pull them open. They didn't budge, locked tight.

"You can't get out that way, Ms. McKinsey. Ms. Phelps will show you out. We can't have you wandering our offices unattended and I'm far too busy to deal with you right now." McBarrister said sharply, not looking up from his papers. I conceded with ill grace, shooting a glare at the top of McBarrister's head, and headed for the side door, thinking furiously about what I was going to do next.

As I walked through the door, it slammed shut behind me with a loud bang and I nearly jumped out of my skin. I was in a white hallway, perhaps ten feet long and as wide as my outstretched arms, with another door at the other end and a double bulb fluorescent light overhead. It cast a buzzing blue-white light over the hallway, but there was no other sound, only my breath loud in my ears.

There was no sign of Phelps, I assumed she had gone through the opposite door, and so I followed suit, nervously fingering the revolver in my purse. As I opened the door, I realized there was no light in the next room and alarm bells went to ringing in my head. I backed up until I hit the original door I entered through and my left hand found the knob. Locked. Shit. I turned to pound on the door with my fist, demanding they open the door, but nothing happened. I partially pulled my revolver, gripping it tightly, and tiptoed to the dark outline of the far door, hoping my eyes would adjust.

"Now, Ms. McKinsey," Phelps' voice came from the darkness and I edged forward through the doorway. I turned as the door slammed shut bringing the gun to bear just as a massive weight struck the back of my head. The door swirled into grayness as consciousness faded. The last thing I saw was Phelps' sneering face.

"Thou shalt not suffer a witch to live," she hissed as I faded to black.

Chapter 10: Missing

Jackson St. James was sitting at his desk, reading emails, when his phone rang, a two tone pulse meaning a call from outside the office. He'd returned from his aetheric jaunt exhausted, but a quick meal high in protein and a nap had restored much of his energy.

"McKinsey and St. James, Jackson speaking, can I help you?" he answered.

"Hey, Jackson, it's Mark Coleman, how are ya?" replied the voice on the other end of the line.

"Mark, I'm well, busy, but the lines are strong today." The ley lines running through Denver were some of the strongest in the country and powerful sensitives were very sensitive to their ebb and flow. "How can I help you?"

"It's about McKinsey," Coleman replied, "you know she went over to the Purity offices right?"

"Sure, she gave me the head's up when she left, told me to storm the gates if she didn't come out. Why? Didn't she come out?" Worry had begun to creep into Jackson's voice. His assignment had been to watch McKinsey, find out if she was suitable for membership in Division 99, but he had grown quite fond of her, seeing her almost as another daughter. He hoped she hadn't bitten off more than she could chew going in to deal with McBarrister and his cronies, but they were a law abiding organization, if intolerant. They wouldn't dare try anything, would they? Without the demon, he'd been confident she could handle herself, but this latest news worried him.

"Nope, not yet she ain't, I got Gibson sitting on their front door step and he says he ain't seen a wisp of blonde hair coming out from their little shithole. He's gettin' worried and so I am, it's been almost three hours."

"Is it time to storm the gates then, Mark?" Jackson asked, concerned.

"Don't think so, I'm gonna send Gibson in there, see if he can get a scent of her. If he can find her, maybe we won't need to storm the gates. They're okay with SER, they ain't gonna like you being anywhere near their place."

"True, I'll leave it in your capable hands, then Mark. If worse comes to worse, please tell me and I'll see what I can do about finding her."

"Sounds like a plan, Jackson, keep your cell on and I'll buzz you when I know more. Talk to ya later."

Jackson hung up the phone, leaning back in his chair and lacing his fingers behind his head, thinking. His arts could track her, he certainly knew her aura well enough to pick it out of a crowd, but he hesitated to use them without a really good reason. The amulet he had given her would make pinpointing her location quite a bit faster, but he didn't want to undermine her abilities. If she was to join his organization, she needed to be able to work independently and not be completely dependent on others.

Jackson checked his phone, fully charged, and reached for his coat. He had a premonition he would be up late tonight, so he was going home early to spend some time with the kids and Akane. Pulling his brown pea coat on over his tunic, he grabbed his worn, brown leather satchel and locked his computer before heading for the door. Kristen had gone home already, leaving the office in semi-darkness, so he turned off the remainder of the lights, locked the main door to the offices, and headed out into the twilight of winter evening Denver.

Gibson waited in his patrol car, heat on full, outside the Purity offices for any sign of McKinsey. Coleman had asked him to make sure she was okay, so he'd wait out here until she showed her little blonde head. He knew she liked him, and he supposed she was cute, but she had the wrong equipment for his interest. Still, she kicked some pretty serious ass and he was worried about her walking into that den of idiocy.

It'd been three hours, a super long time as far as he was concerned, but he really didn't want to go in there if he didn't have to. Coleman had left it up to his discretion, so he figured maybe a couple more minutes, then he'd broach their domain.

It was getting dark, he realized, the sun setting behind the Rockies with startling speed as he sat idle. Sighing, he pulled his maroon parka on over his maroon jumpsuit and killed the car, sliding out the driver door and meandering up the icy sidewalk toward the Purity building.

A gaudy entryway met his eyes as he walked in, poorly laid brown marble tiles veined with gold and portraits of stuck up looking old people on the walls. Behind an ostentatious oak desk sat the secretary, an old lady with a sour expression on her face. She arranged a sickly sweet expression as he approached, but he had seen the bitterness below and wasn't fooled. Still, sometimes he could charm these old cougars into letting him have what he wanted, maybe it would work on this old broad.

He grinned his most winning smile, perfect white teeth and sparkling eyes with an easy swagger to his step as he approached the desk. The secretary fiddled with the pearls around her neck, smiling back, but it wasn't a real smile, just the façade she had thrown on when he entered.

"Hey, there..." he checked the name plate circumspectly, "Edith, how're you doin'?" he asked, sauntering up to her desk and resting a casual palm on the corner, flashing her his best grin.

"I'm having a blessed day, young man, how can I help you?" she replied, the façade not wavering as she met his gaze. His grin faltered, losing a shade of brightness, so he switched tactics. Pulling the unzipped side of his parka away revealed the SER emblem, to which her eyes flicked briefly before returning to his face.

"I'm Sergeant Gibson of Denver SER, I'm here looking for a friend of mine who had an appointment here and then never met me afterward like we planned. You haven't seen her, have you? Really tall, blonde hair, blue eyes, pretty? I'm just worried about her is all," he said, winking and grinning. Edith's expression never changed, she lied straight to Gibson's face.

"Sorry, my dear, I haven't seen anyone fitting that description. We've only had members come in today, are you sure she made her appointment? Maybe you should check the local bars around here, maybe something will turn up. Or the gutters. Have a blessed day," she finished, dismissing him and turning back to her game of solitaire. Gibson stared open-mouthed, dumbfounded at her rudeness, but unwilling to accuse her of lying to her face.

"Well, perhaps I will, and while I'm there, I'll be sure to look for your manners, bitch." She ignored him, intent on her game, so he spun on his heel and stomped out, slamming the door as he left.

"See if SER comes to help you next time, you old bat," he muttered under his breath as he walked out. Once in his car, he radioed Coleman.

"Coleman, talk."

"Hey, lieutenant, it's Gibson. I just checked on McKinsey and the bitch secretary lied to my face, told me she hasn't seen anyone meeting her description like I didn't watch her walk in that rat hole. We got trouble, I think. You think we can get a warrant and search the place?"

Silence greeted him from the radio for a long moment, long enough that he was about to ask if Coleman was still there when he came back.

"Shit, no, Gibson, she'd be dead or moved before we got in there. Take at least twenty four hours to convince a judge and McKinsey be long gone by the time we got in there. Nah, I'll make a few calls and see what I can do with some other people I know, you go ahead and go home. You got the nightshift, right? Go get some sleep."

"Right o, lieutenant, roger that. Give me a buzz if you find her, she don't deserve to be done in by them Purity dicks." Cranking his car up, he eased into traffic, heading for home and a date with a warm bed, hopefully not an empty one.

Coleman sat in his office, a tiny moisture-stained cube in the bowels of the Denver County Police Department with yellow walls and a faded dark wood door. His desk was cluttered with half finished paperwork and there were a pair of certifications on the wall behind his desk. He debated with himself about calling Jackson again, and then made a sudden decision. He dialed the number on his cell, punching the numbers hard and swearing to himself. Jackson picked up on the fourth ring, sounding wary.

"Hello?"

"Hey Jackson, Coleman again, we got a situation and I ain't sure how best to handle it. I sent Gibson in after McKinsey but them Purity turds denied her ever being in the building. I don't know what they done with her, but I ain't gonna be able to get a warrant for at least twenty four hours to bust the place down. If you got any way to help her out, now'd be the time to do it."

"Thanks for the head's up Coleman, I'll handle it as best I can, be on the lookout for a call from her or me. I'd work on that warrant just in case though, maybe it'll be useful. Call me if you hear from her and I'll do the same. I gotta make some arrangements, bye."

Sitting back in his abused leather chair, Coleman dialed another number into his phone, the number of a local magistrate, and started the ball rolling to get a warrant.

Jackson sighed, flipping his phone closed as he moved to stand from the dinner table. Hideko was going on and on about her day at school, every little thing a crisis, while Takashi shoveled food into his mouth like someone was going to steal it from his plate. Akane sat across from him, next to Hideko, making the appropriate noises while only half paying attention to her daughter's ramblings. She noticed Jackson stand and held up a hand for

Hideko to be quiet, spearing her husband with a questioning glance.

"Jamie's in trouble, I need to see if I can help," he said, standing and pocketing his phone.

"Of course, dear, do what you need to do," Akane said, turning back to allow Hideko to resume her diatribe about some school rival and resuming her dinner. Softly, Jackson blew another sigh, this one relief that Akane wasn't going to give him trouble about interrupting dinner. He headed toward the stairs, trying not to make too much noise, but knowing he could have walked through the house with a bass drum and not interrupted his daughter's musings. His caution was due to Takashi, who was taking a little too much interest in all things mystical. He didn't want his son walking in on him when he was on the aetheric so it was better if Takashi didn't see him leave the dinner table.

He'd had a premonition he'd need to reenter the aetheric tonight, hence why he'd come home early, but he wished it had waited until after dinner. His stomach growled as he mounted the stairs, heading for his sanctuary.

Outside, the night was cold and clear, not a cloud in the sky, and it wasn't a good time to be entering the aetheric. The ley lines were running high tonight, this close to the full moon, and higher still from the proximity to dusk. Any actions taken on the aetheric tonight would resound for many hours to come.

Reaching into his pocket, he retrieved the twin triangular knot pendant, cold to the touch but not freezing. He frowned down at it, wondering why he hadn't felt the chill through his pocket, his concern growing. Jamie was injured, of that he was sure, but not severely or else he would have felt the cold more intensely. Still, it bore looking into to make sure she wasn't in over her head.

Jackson walked into his study, closing the door behind him and locking it to prevent his kids from entering. This was the seventh bedroom in his house, his sanctuary and a place of refuge and meditation when he needed time away from the hustle and bustle of his life. There was a recliner, old and threadbare, in the center of the room with metal circles in the white oak floor around it in a pentagon shape. His candlesticks snapped into the metal circles, allowing him to remove them when he wasn't in the room and keep his kids from finding out what he really did in here, alone.

Jackson padded to the other side of the room, spinning the dial on another wall safe and pulling five silver candlesticks from it. This set was the original set he had inherited from his father, heavy with age and power, an alloy of silver he'd never been able to duplicate. They made entering the aetheric easy, staying there easier, and coming back much harder. They boosted his power immensely, had he been using this set when he fought the demon the battle would have been no contest.

Snapping each candlestick into the receptive port required a simple twist of his wrist, lighting them no harder, just a simple flick of his mind. He settled into the recliner, leaning it back and putting the foot rest up so he could stretch out and relax. He didn't need a mirror focus with this set of candlesticks, just silence and a moment to relax. He let his eyelids fall, focusing on his heartbeat and feeling himself release from his corporeal form with a sudden lifting. Floating, serene, he allowed himself to drift, gathering his energy for the jaunt ahead.

Focusing on the amulet in his ethereal hand, really a facsimile of the amulet created by his mind, he channeled air through it to create a virtual image of the city in his mind. Warmth grew on the left side of his face and he turned to soar into the heat, following the warmth like a childhood game of hot and cold. His search led him to a building several blocks off Colfax, down into the basement and through several walls before he found her.

Jamie was lying in the dark in a little cell at the end of a hallway, bound but not gagged or blindfolded. He thought she was unconscious, so he called out softly to be sure. She didn't stir and he had no physical hands to shake her with, so his options were limited. He risked a brief contact with her mind, but she was out cold, nothing but her subconscious greeted his probe. Left in a quandary, he paused to consider. He could wait for her to wake, risking his strength, or he could find someone or something to come in a help.

Making a decision, he rocketed through the wall, brief flashes of darkness as he passed through the solid matter momentarily disorienting him, as he recalled the barely sensed presence in the trees outside a nearby building. Once outside, he cast his air senses out and called to the minute presence he had perceived. It answered, floating up to him in curiosity as he explained what he needed.

After he was finished, he headed back toward Jamie's cell, sliding through the walls once more to find her struggling awake.

Chapter 11: Total Purity

I struggled awake, clawing my way back from darkness to pain. Pain and the inability to move my arms. I thought they were bound but it was hard to tell through the red haze. There was something rough on my left cheek, something that moved like a thin layer of gravel, so I thought I might be on asphalt or concrete. Cracking my left eye led to no new information, it was completely dark, but I didn't think I was blind, just in the dark.

I waited and the pain slowly faded to a dull ache and the red haze retreated to the edges of my vision. My head felt like a two hundred pound weight and it throbbed with every beat of my heart. I probably had a concussion, I decided. Hollywood would have people believe they would leap back to life with a cocky grin after being knocked unconscious, but the reality was any hit hard enough to knock you out was serious and would likely have nasty consequences when you woke up. If you woke up.

There was definitely something binding my hands, it felt like a handkerchief or some other piece of cloth, definitely not handcuffs or anything metal, and my feet were free. I still had my boots on, but my trench coat was gone. Dammit, that was expensive. It's really hard to find clothes long enough for a girl my height and when I did find them, they were costly. My purse was gone, too, and with it my revolver.

As I rolled onto my back, I could feel my 45 was gone, but when I rolled over completely to my right side, I felt my 9mm dig into my thigh. At least I was armed if I could get my hands free. I squeezed my thighs together as hard as I could and felt the solid weight of my stiletto clipped to my garter belt. Awesome, if I could get it out, I could cut my hands free, but that left me with a decision. Try now and take the risk of someone walking in on me, or wait and see who'd kidnapped me and then escape after I knew.

It was a fairly safe guess that my kidnappers had something to do with Purity, but I hadn't thought they were stupid enough to pull something like this, although I still had no idea why they had kidnapped me. There were people who knew I was coming here, including cops, who wouldn't take kindly to my kidnapping.

The decision was taken from me as I lay there in the darkness. The outline of a door appeared, written in light on the far wall. I realized I was in a closed room, maybe twelve feet by eight feet, with a filthy linoleum floor and plain sheetrock walls. I was lying on the floor in the right corner furthest from the door. There was a single light socket in the ceiling overhead, a fixture without a bulb. The new light from the hallway behind whoever had walked in shot pain through my head again and I groaned, trying to roll away from the offending light.

"So you're awake, freak. Get up! Get up now!" It was Phelps, standing in the doorway silhouetted by the light from behind her.

I lay there thinking about what a bitch she was but I didn't move. She screamed at me a couple more times but I was in too much pain to pay her any mind. Maybe she'd just go away. Instead, I heard rapid heeled footsteps and felt a sharp pain in my ribs. I groaned trying to curl around my injured ribs when she hauled back to kick me again. This time, she caught my left arm as I raised it to defend my head, leaving a gash from the toe of her shoe and a nice bruise. I grunted, trying to beg her to stop, but she kicked me again, this time glancing off the fingers of my right hand. Shit, I was right handed.

"Stop, please," I croaked, the words sending waves of pain through my battered head and now injured ribs. She hesitated, mid-kick and then went through with it anyway. I grunted again as she made contact with my stomach and I vomited all over her shoes and lower legs.

"You bitch!" She shrieked, slipping to one knee in my vomit and making for the door. "You fucking freak bitch! I'll kill you! I'll shoot you like the dog you are!" I heard the distinct *click, click* of a shotgun being loaded when another voice, a male voice, interrupted, talking urgently. She argued with him for a moment, screeching at him, but he argued low and firm. I caught the words demon and gone but little else. I couldn't understand anything more before the door slammed shut and I was left alone again.

I cradled my injuries, trying my best to keep from vomiting again, the smell of my previous indiscretion sharp and sweet in my nostrils. *McDonald's doesn't smell nearly as good after it comes up again,* I thought sardonically. I started laughing, a hysterical, panicked cackle that scared me. I forced myself to take slow, measured breaths through my mouth, trying my best not to breathe through my nose. *Relax, girl,* I thought, *you've been in worse situations before. Think.*

Breathing deep and relaxing helped numb some of the pain, or maybe it was just shock, I didn't know, but I didn't really care. I decided to risk getting my stiletto out. My hands were tied behind me, so I needed to arch my back and see if I could get my hand to my garter belt. My skirt had shifted, the slits in the front and back instead of on the sides, and I managed to get me hand around the folded blade. I nearly passed out from the pain in my ribs, but I managed. I pulled it free with a snap of my garter belt, popping myself in the thigh with the elastic, and I yelped. *Shit,* I thought, *please, please don't come and check on me, please.* I held my breath, praying, but no one came.

I maneuvered the thumb stud under my fingernail and pushed, allowing the spring mechanism to thrust the four inch blade out. Now I just had to flip the blade so I could cut my bonds. Delicately, a little at a time, I spun the blade in my fingers, and then my injured hand spasmed, and I dropped it. It hit the floor with a soft thud and I swore. Thankfully, it hadn't rolled, just fallen straight down, and I managed to pick it up again without cutting myself. I carefully sawed the cloth and it split with a soft sigh and then a sharp prick as the point of the blade dug into my arm. I swallowed a gasp and flexed my fingers, wincing as blood began flowing back into my fingers with a burning, tingling sensation.

I sat up, leaning my back against the wall, and felt my right thigh. My 9mm was definitely still in my concealment holster because apparently it was okay to kidnap a girl, but not to search her intimate areas. I slipped it out, thumbing the stud to release the magazine, and felt for the bullets. Seven shots, six measly little silver plated hollow points plus the one in the chamber, to get me out of wherever they had me stashed. If all else failed, I still had my stiletto and it was a mean knife, but bringing a knife to a gun fight was always a losing proposition.

My head jerked up at the sound of keys in the lock. I hurriedly slid the 9mm back in its holster, a challenging endeavor in the dark, and slid the stiletto back into its holster, also not easy. Grabbing the cloth, I wrapped it loosely around my hands again and pulled them behind my back just as Phelps opened the door again. The light was blindingly painful again, but I doggedly stared into it this time, blinking away tears until my eyes adjusted. She was dressed in fatigues, black cargo pants and a black tank top with combat boots. Obviously, I had ruined her spiffy heels, point for me.

"Awake again, freak?" she asked, a sneer on her lips. Her dark eyes snapped with fury, I was willing to bet it had something to do with vomit-soaked shoes, and she looked angry enough to chew nails.

"No thanks to you, bitch," I replied.

"You're lucky you're breathing at all, whore. If I'd had my way, you'd be sucking air through a giant hole in your chest right now. But don't worry; you'll be dead within a few hours. We're going to use you as an example of what happens to freaks who stick their nose in where it doesn't below. Total Purity has had enough of you abominations and we're going to start cleansing the world of them, starting with you!" Her voice had risen to a strained pitch by the time she was done. She stood in the doorway panting when she was done with her monologue.

"Total Purity?" I asked, confused.

Her eyes narrowed further, becoming mere slits in her dark face. "You've never heard of us?" She asked, her voice low and growling.

"Nope," I replied, trying to incite her.

"We are the next iteration of Purity, we are the future! We will rid the world of filth and reclaim it in the name of our Lord God!" Great, I hated zealots, they were completely unreasonable.

"Think your pet sorcerer and his demon can take us all on, do you, Phelps?" I hazarded a guess, a sneer on my face.

Her eyes narrowed and she brought a crooked finger to her lips, thoughtful.

"Yesss…" she hissed, "how did you find out about Carl? We were sure no one outside the organization had a clue about him and in you waltz, all arrogant and proud, and try to threaten us with him. He believes in our cause, he wants the world rid of people like him, and with his help we will succeed!" Her eyes were crazed, darting wildly around the room as if she expected an army of freaks to charge her from the darkness.

"What does that have to do with Adora?" I asked, hoping she'd slip up and give away her plans. She was certainly unhinged enough to make a mistake like that.

"Adora? Adora who? Johanson?" she spat, a suspicious expression on her face. "What would we want with that monstrosity? She's the enemy, her and her brainwashed husband, why would we want anything to do with her?" Her eyes narrowed and she pursed her lips. "Has something happened to Johanson? Something nasty, I hope? I wish I could claim credit for it, but I can't. I hope she's dead, killed for her unholy rejection of our Lord God!" With that, she spun on her heel, slammed the door, and marched off, laughing hysterically.

What a nut job, I thought, *but at least I know Purity doesn't have Adora.* Of course, I needed to get the Hell out of here before that information did me any good and, even then, it left me with no leads. *Crap.*

I sighed and stood, wincing as my ribs and my head twinged. My legs and my back cramped, held still for too long, and I almost fell, catching myself on the wall at the last second. A gust of wind breezed through my cell, lifting my hair and blowing across my face and I froze. It felt familiar, like a lost friend, but that didn't make any sense, it was wind, right? But where was it coming from?

Blaming in on the heating system and putting it out of my mind, I stood again, feeling tenderly around my ribcage and stomach. Bruised, not broken, as were my fingers, thankfully. The gash on my arm was bleeding freely, making my hand sticky, but it seemed to be slowing. I put pressure on it with my right hand, wishing I had something to bind it with. I smacked myself in the forehead. *Duh*, I thought, *use your shirt.* I ripped a section off from the bottom of my shirt, tying it securely around my forearm and pulling the knot tight with my teeth. It left my flat abs open to the air, but I wasn't too concerned about it. I had bigger things to worry about than if my belly was showing.

All of her kicks hurt, but nothing was as bad as my head. Whoever had hit me, they had tried their best to make sure I didn't wake up today. Too bad for them I was too mean to curl up and die and if I found out who hit me, they'd be the ones in a world of pain.

My cell was completely dark, there didn't appear to be any light leaking from around the door, and I was exploring blind. I really, really hoped there weren't any spiders or scorpions in the corners, but the room seemed clean. No gaps, no holes, nothing but featureless sheetrock walls. In one corner, there was a small pile of what felt like twigs and a small bit of cellophane, nothing useful there. I sighed again, wincing at the twinge in my ribs. *Need to stop that*, I thought in exasperation. I leaned against the wall farthest from the door and considered. I had my pistol, but only seven shots. *Wait,* I thought, *I just changed my holster, maybe...* I hiked up my skirt and felt the edge of my 9mm holster.

"Yesss...." I hissed. "Thank you Jackson, best Christmas gift ever." My new holster had an extra magazine; I actually had thirteen shots total. Better. My stiletto, with its four inch blade, was not ideal for self defense, but would be decent for a surprise attack. The only thing to do, I supposed, was to make a ruckus, get a guard to come, and then shoot him to escape.

"*Jamie...*" the wind whistled again through my cell, seemingly saying my name. I froze, listening hard. "*Jamie... open... your... mind...*" Open my mind? What did that mean? Jackson was always telling me to open my mind, maybe... I sat down on the floor of the cell, crossed my legs, and closed my eyes. Deep, regular breaths in through my nose and out through my mouth slowed my pulse and helped me ignore the pain in my, well, everywhere. Slowly, the ethereal form of Jackson St. James formed in front of me, glowing white and pearly iridescent. His eyes were like black holes in his long, white face and his hair was like a cloud of pale mist around his head.

"Jackson," I breathed, "how did you find me?"

"Jamie. I tracked your aura when you didn't answer your phone; we knew something was wrong when Officer Gibson didn't see you come out of the Purity offices."

"Gibson? Why would he see me leave? Was he waiting for me?" Despite everything, I felt a thrill of hope. Maybe I wasn't the creepy old cougar after all.

"Yeah, Coleman told him to stay and make sure you made it out safely." Oh well, hello cougarville. "When you didn't, Coleman gave me a call and asked if I'd seen you. I decided to track your aura and found you here. What happened?"

"Ugh, I'm not even sure. I had the meeting with McBarrister, which went about exactly as I expected, but then his second banana ambushed me as I was leaving, hit me in the head and I woke up here. She's started a new radical humans first group she calls Total Purity and she plans on killing me to make an example of what they're going to do to all non-vanilla humans. They've hired a sorcerer, they think he and his demon are going to be enough to kill or drive off all the people they have a problem with. The good news is, they don't have Adora, and Phelps was so shocked when I mentioned it, I don't think she was acting. They took my 45 and my purse but they didn't find my 9mm or my stiletto. If there's not too many guards, maybe I can fight my way out. How many did you see?"

"Eight on this level, there's probably more on the other levels. You're in the basement of a downtown building, I'm not sure which one, but it's a maze up there. I found you walking through walls; you're going to be hard pressed to get out without help. Luckily, I've found some help; he'll be here in a few moments. My strength is fading so I need to go; I'll call Coleman and get him and SER down here as soon as they're able. If you can get out, do it, otherwise Phelps might make good on her threat and off you."

With that, he faded from view, slowly becoming more and more transparent until he was gone, leaving only a fading after image in my eyes. Jackson hadn't said how long his help was going to take to get here, so I busied myself stretching and trying to work blood back into my limbs. It hurt, God it hurt, but after a couple minutes I was feeling much better. My ribs hurt, and my hand was starting to stiffen, but my head was much better.

Chapter 12: Kendra

Kendra Phelps was sitting in her office in the rear of the main Purity building planning the next rally in Estes Park. She didn't go in for the ostentation of many of the higher members of Purity, she was content with a small white office with a simple pine desk. There were no pictures on the walls, no other decorations save her foot-high crucifix on the left wall, no effects on the desk, nothing but her black computer and an expensive multi-line phone. She didn't need anything else, the symbol of the Christ and her Lord was enough for her. She didn't spend very much time there, she was usually out of state seeing to business on behalf of Purity.

Kendra frowned when the intercom function on her phone began buzzing, but then her face was frequently frowning, if not twisted in disdain. George McBarrister was calling her to his office, but she really didn't have time to deal with some minor emergency right now, she had work to do. With a long suffering sigh, she rose from her desk, locking her computer, carefully arranging her papers, and conscientiously turning off the lights as she walked out.

The white painted hallway leading from her office led to a T-shaped intersection, the left leading to the main entryway of the building while the right led to a storage facility and through it, George's office. She took the right fork, preferring not to walk through the main part of the building and pretend she liked any of the people who worked there. They were insufferable know-it-alls, thinking they were making the world a better place, but they weren't. Their piddly little attempts at God's work were laughable, pathetic sops to their own consciences. Nothing they did mattered, that was why she was taking steps to advance their cause in ways that would finally make a difference. She'd found a sensitive named Carl, a repentant sinner, who believed in her cause and she'd convinced him to summon a demon.

Convincing him God would forgive him for sinning and using magic if he summoned the demon, Nefarium, and used his powers to rid the world of people like him had been simple. He'd been desperate to make up for his teenage indiscretions and had jumped at the chance to redeem himself.

Together, Kendra and Carl had found the ritual necessary to summon Nefarium in an ancient Sumerian text and performed it in a small warehouse over in Stapleton. She'd never been in the presence of true evil before and the shifting face of

Nefarium had almost made her think again about invoking its assistance in her crusade. In the end she'd prayed for God to give her a sign if her course of action was sinful, but received no word from the Lord to indicate His displeasure. She'd taken that to mean her plan of attack was acceptable.

As Kendra walked through the dim storage room, gliding between stacks of boxes with an almost instinctual awareness of the obstacles, she thought again about the shifting face of Nefarium. It most unnerved her when the thing assumed her face, but she knew it was just trying to set her off balance. It worked, but she'd never let that unholy thing know.

As she walked through the door into George's office, she realized there was another person in the office with him. She was tall, very tall for a woman, and blonde in a pink shirt and black skirt. Half her cleavage was hanging out for the world to see and if her skirt was slit any higher, it would be indecent. She looked like a hooker to Phelps' eyes. Although she was vaguely familiar, Kendra couldn't place where she had seen her. She shot the woman a glare anyway, knowing any visitor she would be summoned to see was bad news for the organization.

"Yes, George?" she purred, turning away from the woman to face her boss, George McBarrister. He looked smart today, filling his white suit with masculine strength and looking regal behind his golden oak desk. His thick, black hair looked freshly cut and styled and his presence commanded the entire room. He turned to her with a warning look, indicating she needed to be careful with this woman in the room.

"Kendra, this... person, has said some things I believe you should hear. Perhaps you would like to continue, Ms. McKinsey?"

McKinsey, which would make her Jamie McKinsey, a perennial thorn in Purity's side. Kendra's scowl deepened, as she wondered what this sinning harlot wanted, but George had continued speaking.

"You were saying about our supposed sorcerer?" he continued, spearing the harlot with a disdainful look. Kendra looked at her in a new light, seeing her arrogance and wondering how someone so deep in evil could possibly look so pleased with herself. Kendra had never met her in person, but she'd heard about her role in foiling their plans to burn the freak church in downtown Denver. There'd been more than a couple high placed members of

Purity sent to jail thanks to this Satan's whore.

"Right, your sorcerer," said the slut, shifting uncomfortably in her chair. "I know you hired him and I can prove it so we need to talk about who you have, well, illegally confined." Kendra noticed the look of relief flash across George's handsome face and knew the bitch had pushed things too far. Kendra's heart had leapt to her throat when this servant of the Devil had mentioned Carl, but George was playing things off like Carl didn't exist, so Kendra played along.

"I think I've heard enough," Kendra snapped, pushing herself away from George's desk and turning to the sinner sitting in front of him. "I think your fictional tales need to end. You have no evidence of anything, you know it and we know it, so I think you need to leave. Now, Ms. McKinsey. Follow me please," without waiting for a response she strode toward the white door she had entered through and started down the hallway toward the storage room.

I need to deal with her and soon, she thought furiously as she walked through the store room. An idea came to her, illegal as Hell, but it would serve to kill two birds with one stone. If she could capture McKinsey and offer her soul up to

Nefarium, she could serve as an example to all the worshippers of Lucifer out there and she and her accusations would be silenced for good.

Kendra grabbed a length of pipe from under the sink in the store room and quickly hit the lights before McKinsey came in, sliding behind the door to slam it shut and hit the bitch with the pipe.

She waited for a long moment, but the harlot wasn't coming quickly enough for her.

"Now Ms, McKinsey," she snapped, hefting the pipe and waiting for her to enter. McKinsey's outline filled the doorway and as soon as she walked through the door frame, Kendra slammed the door shut and struck with all her force at the back of her head. She connected with a solid blow, crumpling the sinner to the floor just as she'd hoped.

Kendra pulled her phone from her belt and quickly dialed the number for the head of their new mercenaries. Ricard Rousseau was the head of the mercenaries they had hired to backup Carl and he'd know what to do with the bitch.

"Ricard, talk to me," he answered on the third ring.

"Ricard, it's Phelps, I have a small job I need you to assist with, please come downstairs to the storage room outside

George's office. We have our first sacrifice to Nefarium and I need some help getting her out to Total Purity's HQ."

"Copy, I'll send Frank and Louie down right now, they'll help. I've got something else to deal with right now, but they'll handle it." He clicked off the line, leaving Kendra holding a dead phone. She flipped the phone closed and turned to her victim. Pulling a rag from a nearby box intending to tie McKinsey's hands together, she first pulled the bitch's purse from under her arm and tossed it into a crate at the back of the storage room. Next, she pulled off the sinner's coat and threw it alongside her purse, bending to tie her hands together in case she woke up while in transit to their other building.

As she finished, Louie and Frank arrived. Frank was completely bald, no hair, no eyebrows, no facial hair. He had a heavy eyebrow ridge and deep set dark eyes with a thin-lipped, cruel mouth and a hook nose. His body was that of typical soldier, well built and strong under his black fatigues. Louie was a smiler, non-descript brown hair and eyes with a brown goatee. He, too, was dressed in black fatigues with combat boots, but he didn't fill them out quite as well as Frank.

"What's up, boss?" asked Louie with a disarming grin. Kendra frowned at him, not trusting his cavalier attitude, but unwilling to jump his case until he'd finished moving the bitch. Both men had walked in and seen McKinsey on the floor, but neither had reacted with more than a curious glance.

"Call one of your boys," she snapped, irritated. "Get them to pull the van to the loading dock, we can't let anyone see this cow while we move her to HQ. You," she said, pointing a bony finger at Frank with a scowl, "pick up the freak and get her in the van, now. We're going to use her as an example. You," she said again, gesturing to Louie, "you run interference, no one can know we have her until it's time."

Both men saluted, Louie heading down the hallway to clear the path to the loading dock and pulling his phone from his pocket to call for the van while Frank reached down to pull a black handgun from a holster at the small of the freak's back and tuck it into his waistband. Next, he hauled the unconscious bitch onto his shoulder like she weighed nothing at all, shifting her until he found a comfortable position in which to carry her weight. Her blonde head banged grotesquely against his ass as he walked toward the loading dock, bringing a sadistic smile to Kendra's face.

They managed to get to the van and to the HQ building without anyone seeing anything. Once they arrived at HQ, Frank dumped the harlot in one of the storage rooms in the basement. Pulling the door shut, Kendra turned to Louie and Frank, about to give them further instructions, when her cell phone rang. She didn't recognize the number, so she ignored the call.

"You two, get to the guard room, you've pulled first duty to make sure that twit doesn't escape before we can make an example of her. I need to go find Carl, see if Nefarium is ready for its first sacrifice. Don't," she pointed a nearly skeletal finger between Frank's eyes before switching it to Louie's eyes, "let her escape." She retrieved a shotgun from the break room, handing it to Louie without another word. He accepted the weapon with a grin, striking a pose and eliciting another scowl from Kendra.

Irritated, she spun on her heel, heading for her office to kill a few minutes before she gloated over the sinner, when her phone dinged to tell her she had a voicemail. She pulled it from her belt to frown at the display, thinking she didn't have time to deal with it right now.

She headed up to the stairs to her office in this building, a much larger but still Spartan version of her office in the Purity building. She settled at her desk, this one a black painted particle board cheap thing. The computer was linked to the one at Purity so she pulled the schematics for the rally in Estes Park up again. She'd barely regained her train of thought when her phone rang. It was the mercenary line, so she answered.

"Boss," it was Louie, as she thought. "She's coming around I think, I hear her moving around. You might wanna come down here."

"Excellent," Kendra hissed, her eyes widening in anticipation of the upcoming confrontation with the sinner. "I'll be down momentarily."

She pulled the door to the storage room open to see the freak struggling awake, hiding her face from the sudden light. The sight sent a thrill of sadistic glee through Kendra as she watched, her rage at the injustices of life kindling into an unseeing hatred for this slut.

"So you're awake, freak. Get up! Get up now!" She screeched, wanting to kick this freak back to the ground. The bitch lay there, not moving, infuriatingly not even responding to Kendra's commands. "Get up!" she commanded. "Get up and face me, you blasphemer!" She still didn't move, curling up tighter to get away from the light. Enraged, Kendra entered the cell, hauling back to kick the freak with all her strength, right in the ribs. The bitch curled up further, trying to protect herself from another kick, but Kendra reared back to kick her again, tearing open her arm. The spray of blood sent her into a frenzy, years of getting the short end of the stick crystallizing into a rage she'd never felt before. She kicked again, hitting the freak's hand and, she hoped, breaking her fingers.

"Stop, please," the skank begged. Kendra hesitated, something resembling mercy penetrating her rage, but she remembered her first encounter with a sinner like this and kicked again with everything she had at the slut's stomach. The sinner puked on her, vomit spraying all over Kendra's legs and feet.

"You bitch!" Kendra shrieked, slipping to one knee in her vomit before heading for the door to get the shotgun and end this. "You fucking freak bitch! I'll kill you! I'll shoot you like the dog you are!"

She pulled the shotgun from Louie's unresisting fingers and chambered a round. Just as she was about to head back into the room, Henry Atkinson, her second in command, walked in through the door from outside. He was small, below average in height for a man, and slender with a sickly air about him and a nervous, twitchy smile. His eyes were strangely pale with thin, wispy white blond hair.

"What the Hell are you doing?" he demanded, nodding his head at the shotgun in Kendra's hand. "You promised this sinner to Nefarium, you can't just shoot her."

"Why the Hell not?" she shrieked, gesturing with the shotgun like she was intending to shoot her from hallway. "She's my prisoner, I'll do whatever I damn well feel like!"

"The demon will kill you if it doesn't get her soul and with you gone, Total Purity will fall apart," he replied quietly, holding his hand out for the shotgun.

Kendra frowned, her rage fighting with her reason, reason finally winning out. She handed the shotgun over to him with a horrendous scowl and marched up the stairs to take a shower and clean the vomit off her feet.

"I'll be back," she muttered darkly as she stomped up the stairs. She showered quickly, changing into black fatigues like Louie and Frank wore. After she no longer smelled of vomit, she walked back down the stairs, intending to get the better of that freak. Henry was gone, as were Louie and Frank, so she was alone to deal with the harlot.

"Awake again, freak?" she said as she opened the door once more. The bride of Beelzebub was sitting up against the wall, apparently not nearly as injured as Kendra had hoped. *Should have hit her harder,* she thought, considering doing so right that instant.

"No thanks to you, bitch," the freak replied.

"You're lucky you're breathing at all, freak. If I'd had my way, you'd be sucking air through a giant hole in your chest right now. But don't worry; you'll be dead within a few hours. We're going to use you as an example of what happens to freaks who stick their nose in where it doesn't below. Total Purity has had enough of you abominations and we're going to start cleansing the world of them, starting with you!" Her voice had risen to a triumphant shout by the time she was done.

"Total Purity?" the whore asked as if she'd never heard of it.

Kendra narrowed her eyes, wondering if she was being baited. "You've never heard of us?" She asked, her voice low and growling.

"Nope." Now she knew the bitch was messing with her, trying to make her angry again. Maybe so she could puke on her legs again. Deciding to play along, she explained.

"We are the next iteration of Purity, we are the future! We will rid the world of filth and reclaim it in the name of our Lord God!" Kendra bellowed, intending to put the fear of God into this freak, but McKinsey's face showed none of the fear she'd been hoping for.

"Think your pet sorcerer and his demon can take us all on, do you, Phelps?" the harlot said, contempt etched on her too pretty face. Kendra was momentarily taken aback as she suddenly recalled the accusations this thing had made in George's office.

"Yesss..." she hissed, "how did you find out about Carl? We were sure no one outside the organization had a clue about him and in you waltz, all arrogant and proud, and try to threaten us with him. He believes in our cause, he wants the world rid of people like him, and with his help we will succeed!" She was panting with exaltation, adrenaline singing in her ears and a nearly sexual thrill coursing through her body as she thought of all the freaks she and Carl would kill. They'd destroy them all, wipe the smug expressions off their faces as they were sent screaming to Hell where they belonged.

"What does that have to do with Adora?" the bitch asked, not nearly as cowed as Kendra had expected. Maybe she needed another kick.

"Adora? Adora who? Johanson?" Kendra spat, momentarily confused and suspicious. "What would we want with that monstrosity? She's the enemy, her and her brainwashed husband, why would we want anything to do with her?" Her eyes narrowed and she pursed her lips. "Has something happened to Johanson? Something nasty, I hope? I wish I could claim credit for it, but I can't. I hope she's dead, killed for her unholy rejection of our Lord God!" With that, she spun on her heel, slammed the door, and marched off, laughing triumphantly as she headed back upstairs to her office.

Chuckling to herself, Kendra suddenly remembered the voicemail on her phone. She pulled it from her belt again, dialing the number to check it. Her blood ran cold as she listened to the message, nearly dropping the phone in her shock.

"Kendra, this is Ricard, call me at once, we have a problem with Carl. He's become a gibbering idiot, he says nothing but 'Nefarium is gone' over and over again. Come down to his rooms right away, we have a serious problem I think." *Click.*

She ran from the Total Purity with unseemly haste, her schemes and plans falling apart around her as she raced for the basement of the Purity building, dread building in her gut and threatening to overwhelm her.

"No, no, no, it can't be, no," she grunted as she ran. She bolted down the stairs, taking two at a time, and burst into Carl's bedroom, skidding to a stop. Carl was lying on his cot, thrashing back and forth while muttering to himself. His long, black hair was tangled into a rat's nest atop his head while his gray eyes darted wildly around the dirty little room.

Kendra grabbed him by the arms, forcing him to sit up, and demanding to know what he meant.

"Nefarium, Nefarium is gone, it's gone," he gibbered, drool running down his chin, his eyes staring vacantly. She slapped him, hard, but he didn't react, just continued to repeat that Nefarium was gone. Slapping him again yielded the same result. She sat down hard on the concrete floor, her dreams and plans turned to ashes without the demon. She sat for a long time before slowly getting to her feet to return to her office and come up with another plan.

Chapter 13: Escape

I sat for a moment, wondering how best to enact my escape, when a small sound from the vicinity of the door caught my attention.

"Psst," came the faint noise from the other side of the door, "psst, hey, faerie-blood, over here!" It was coming from the floor, but I couldn't see anything. Cautiously, I knelt down, resting my face on the floor to see as far under the door as I could. I could make out a very faint light coming from the outside in the center of the door, an eerie yellowish glow with falling sparkles of greater intensity.

"A faerie," I breathed, startled. I knew faeries called sensitives faerie-bloods but I had never heard of one helping a human, even a sensitive. Usually they wanted nothing to do with us, likely because of that whole persecution thing.

"Actually a pixie," came the voice again. "Stand back, I'm going to pick the lock then I need you to open the door, it's too big for me." I stepped back, listening hard for the sound of the lock opening. After a scant couple of minutes, there was a loud click. I reached out and turned the handle, pulling the door open into the cell. Hovering at about waist height was a pixie, a petite humanoid shape with beautiful gossamer dragonfly wings. He was dressed in little pants and a t-shirt, no shoes, and his flowing green hair was almost down to his feet. I couldn't make out his face, but I knew it would look like Jackson's, long and hauntingly beautiful. He was glowing very softly, giving off enough light for me to make out the featureless hallway behind him, but little else.

"Thank you for helping me," I began, but he didn't let me get far.

"I'm not helping you; I'm using you to get my wife back. She was looking for our son when she was trapped in here and she died away from her family. If you bring her remains out with you, I'll show you how to get out. After that, you help me bring her back to our clan and I'll consider us even. Deal?" He had crossed his arms over his thin chest and was glaring at me, hatred plain in his body language, but warring with need. This was very important to him and need won out.

"All right," I said softly, "but I don't know where her remains are. I didn't..." I flashed back to the pile of twigs with cellophane. *Crap.* He zipped into the cell, hovering in the middle of the room for a moment before zooming into the corner where I had mangled the remains of his wife.

"Here she is," he said softly, almost too quietly for me to hear. "Tear some cloth off your shirt, wrap her up and we'll get out of here. Are you armed?"

"Yes," I replied, bending over to tear a square of material off the front of my shirt. I gingerly advanced on him, kneeling to approach the remains of his wife, when he turned to me and hissed like a snake. I reared back, startled, and he backed up a little, dropping a couple inches.

"Sorry," he mumbled, "you startled me, I was remembering her. Please, be gentle."

I knelt again, giving him a wide berth, and looked at the remains in the corner. In the light given off by his body, I could see that what I thought were twigs were in fact little whitish tan bones. I could see her minuscule skull and her little pelvis and the cellophane-like material was what was left of her wings. I carefully scooped as much of the remains into the square of cloth as I could, trying to be as respectful as possible, while he fussed over me, picking up little bits too small for me to see. After he was satisfied, I tied each set of opposite corners together to form a little bundle. I didn't have a pocket, so I slid the macabre little package into my bra. Ick.

"Let's go," he said, zooming for the door. I pulled my pistol, clutching it in a two handed grip, and slid my extra magazine in between my breasts. Who says boobs weren't good for something?

"Hold on," I said. "Let me get my boots off," I leaned against the wall and unzipped by boots, kicking them into the corner of the cell. I hated to leave them, but they would just slow me down and the click of the heels would give us away in an instant. Stocking feet wasn't my idea of ideal escape attire, but I really had little choice.

"Let's go," I said as I advanced into the hallway, crouched low, scuttling forward to the end of the hallway. So far so good, no guards, no one in fact. I came to a four way intersection, all four hallways stretching out into infinite blackness, the only one I was sure of was the cell behind me.

"Which way?" I whispered.

"Right," he said, hovering close to the ceiling to give me as much light as possible. I took another step, adrenaline singing in my ears, and then another. Ten paces later, there was a door, a simple white painted steel door, with a peeling brass lever handle.

"Guard station," the pixie said, "sounds like two of them in there. Can you handle it?"

"We'll see," I said, bracing myself. I took a deep breath, in through my nose, out through my mouth, and took the lever in my hand. I turned it slowly, quietly and then shoved it open with all my strength. I rammed into the room, both hands supporting my pistol, blinking away tears at the sudden light. The two guards were caught flat footed, sitting in their chairs mesmerized by a television on the left hand wall.

"Don't fucking move!" I shrieked as I leveled my pistol at the guard on the left, then switched to the guard on the right. "Hands on your heads, now, then down on the ground! Move!" My eyes were tearing badly, the sudden shock of the fluorescent bulb overhead almost blinding me.

I noticed the man on the right was bald, no facial hair, but otherwise unremarkable, while the man on the left had brown hair and a brown goatee. Both wore black fatigues just like Phelps had worn. Both men grudgingly placed their hands on their heads and went to their knees in front of the two chairs.

On the right, Baldy's expression suddenly shifted to cunning as he lashed out with a back kick with his left leg, spinning his chair into my knees. I flinched as the chair struck my right knee, the motion causing my finger to pull the trigger and jerk downward. My round tore into Baldy's back just below his shoulder blade, collapsing him with a sigh.

The sound of the gun was thunderous in the enclosed space, bringing my headache roaring to the front of my head and briefly crippling me. The other guard slammed his hands over his ears, pain causing his eyes to bug out of his head, but I was too busy trying to cover my ears to worry about him. I stumbled, disoriented, clutching my head, when I felt a crushing blow to my left arm, the arm holding the gun at this point, and my hand went completely numb, the gun spinning away. I stumbled to my knees while I felt rather than saw the second guard looming over me, his leg cocked for another strike.

Dreading the next strike, knowing it would likely hurt a lot, I watched as the faerie fell from the ceiling, stabbing at the guard's eyes with a pin-like dagger. The guard shrieked, a tinny wailing in my wounded ears, flailing at his tiny assailant, giving me a chance to lash out with a kick and take out his knee, dropping him to the ground. He screamed, the sound of his knee being crushed a grinding baritone counterpoint to his soprano cry of pain. I drew my stiletto, stabbing for his groin and scoring a hit deep enough to wrench the blade from my hand. Blood gushed over my hand, scalding hot, and he went still. Dead or passed out, I had no idea, but no one except the faerie was moving any more.

"That went well," I grunted, as the world settled to a narrow tunnel in front of me. My wrist was broken, I could tell from the grinding, my knee had been hyperextended from the chair impact, and my head was ringing from the gunshot. Nothing really hurt though, a bad sign, because I probably was going into shock. The faerie was hovering in front of me, gesturing wildly, but I couldn't hear him. People discount the sound of a firearm in an enclosed space, but they are incredibly loud. I sat back, scowling as my feet slipped in Goatee's blood, and tried to breathe.

Get up girl, I thought, *get up. You're not out yet.* I struggled to my feet, retrieving my stiletto and wiping it on Goatee's pants. It took me a minute to find my pistol, but it was undamaged so I slid it back into the holster along with the extra magazine.

I searched Baldy first, finding my 45, so I slipped it into the holster at the back of my skirt. He also had a short barrel 44 magnum and a nasty looking silver switchblade, so I swiped them too, slipping the 44 into my waistband with the folding blade going in my garter belt. Goatee had an expensive 40 and a little tiny 380 along with a high powered LED flashlight. I was starting to feel like Rambo.

Neither had my trench coat or my purse, unfortunately, but at least I was now heavily armed. Neither had a radio, something I was surprised at, but not overly concerned with. They both had cheap cells phones, Goatee having crushed his as he fell, and Baldy's was covered in blood, hopefully ruined. My hearing was coming back and I could hear the faerie shouting at me, but couldn't make out what he was saying. I squinted at him. He seemed none the worse for wear, but he was clearly frantic about something.

"Come talk in my ear," I directed him. He hovered closer to me and started shouting in my ear.

"What the Hell are you doing?" he shouted. "Why didn't you walk in shooting? They almost got you!"

"Did you hear that gunshot?" I apparently shouted because he flinched away from me. "I didn't want the whole building coming down on us so I wanted to get them to cooperate without shooting and making a lot of noise."

"And that worked SO well!" he shouted. I scowled at him, waving my hand in front of my face to make him leave. He scowled back and headed for the opposite door, apparently listening for anyone coming. I sat in one of the chairs and gingerly examined my wrist. It was swelling already, turning an ugly purple-red, and something was broken, I was sure.

I looked around the little room, looking for something, anything, to splint it with. There were two folding chairs, a little table, and a flat screen TV mounted to the wall, but nothing I really could use to immobilize my wrist. I sighed, standing to search Baldy again, bile rising in my throat. His blood was cooling rapidly and I was almost certain he was dead. He wasn't breathing and I thought my bullet had punctured a lung. He had likely bled to death or drowned in his own blood. I had killed before, lycanthropes and vampires, but never a human.

All of the sudden, the room was too hot, and it had lurched into a spin. I threw up all over Baldy or at least what remained of Baldy, and fell to my knees again, retching. I was really, really glad I had very little in my stomach after Phelps kicking me.

"Me tough Amazon, me kill," I muttered, feeling wretched.

"Help," came a soft gasp from my right, "please, don't let me die." It was Goatee, he was still alive, looking at me with pain and panic filled eyes. They were gray, I noted distantly, with a classic Roman nose. His lips were thin, almost non-existent, and twisted in a deep frown of pain. He had deep frown lines on either side of his mouth. He was strong but lean, slender in the same way a gymnast is slender. He was clutching his groin, trying desperately to staunch the red flow I had created. I frowned, uncertain what to do. I couldn't just let him die, even though he gladly would have left me bleeding on the floor, but I wasn't a doctor. He needed a hospital.

"Please," he gasped, "under the table. First aid kit. Please."

I sighed, moving away from Baldy and crouching to look under the table. Attached with clips to the underside was a simple first aid kit, nothing fancy, but maybe enough to stabilize him with until his buddies could get there. I pulled it free, flipping it open to see what was in there. Gauze, bandages, butterfly bandages, disinfectants, needles and thread, nothing I hadn't expected. I took out two stiff wood slats, placed one under my wrist and one on top of it, and wrapped the whole thing tightly with the ace bandage, tucking the end under the edge of the fabric. It hurt and I sat down hard, eliciting another spurt of pain from my ribs, and almost passed out.

After a moment, I crept closer to him, wary of a ruse, but he had passed out again. I gingerly moved his hands away from the wound, but I couldn't see anything through the tangle of ripped black fabric. I pulled my stiletto again, carefully slitting the pant leg and cutting away a square around the wound.

"What the Hell are you doing now?" hissed a voice in my ear. It was the faerie, hovering next to my head. "Forget him, let him die, he's not even a faerie-blood! You're wasting time!"

"I can't," I replied, waving my hand next to my ear to shoo him. "He's a hired gun I think, not one of those Purity assholes. I can't just let him die, he's a human being."

"You're wasting time," he hissed again, floating down to tug at my hand. I shook him off; bending closer to examine Goatee's wound. It was deep, a couple inches, but not very wide because of the thin blade of my stiletto. The blood flow had slowed considerably and wasn't coming out in pulses, a good sign I hadn't hit an artery. I grabbed a handful of the gauze and pressed the wound hard. He gasped, almost sitting up and coming fully awake.

"Fuck!" he gasped, "That hurts!"

"So does my wrist you broke, you shit, so quit bitching."

"Fuck," he said again, "am I going to die?"

"No," I said curtly, "I missed the artery, put pressure right," I shoved into the wound, eliciting a groan of pain, "here and you'll be fine as long as your friends come down and get you to a hospital."

"Really?" he gasped, "You're not gonna kill me? But you killed Frank and you broke my knee."

"No, I'm not going to kill you, and I didn't mean to kill Baldy. If he hadn't kicked that chair I'd have tied you both up and left. I'm not a cold blooded murderer, but you're making me think twice about it. Besides, you broke my wrist, I think we're even. Hey, you, pixie, ready to go?" He fluttered closer to the door.

"Wait," it was Goatee again. His eyes had cleared, still in pain but no longer panicking. "Wait, you need to listen. Go back the way you came and turn right, there's a fire exit there. It says it's wired to an alarm but they disconnected that last month. That'll lead you to the street and you can run from there."

My eyes narrowed, suspicious. Jackson had said there were eight guards on this level and these two had almost been the end of me, I couldn't handle another six much less other people who might be in the building. "Why?" I finally asked.

"You didn't hafta help me, you coulda busted in here shooting or shot me when I was out. I'm paying you back, get out, but next time we meet I'll kill ya if we're on the opposite sides of the line."

"Don't listen to him," a voice hissed in my ear, "I can get us out of here. He's lying." The pixie was hovering next to my ear again, tugging on my copper hoop earring.

"No," Goatee said, "I ain't lyin', I swear that's the easiest way out. There ain't no way you can handle the rest of the boys with a busted wrist, bad ass chick or not, they'd chew you up and leave you rottin' on the floor."

"Where's my purse? And my trench?" I asked, hoping.

"Don't know," he grunted, "don't care. Get out of here, before Ricard comes, he'll eat you alive."

"Okay, let's go," I said, headed for the door we'd entered through.

"What?" squeaked the pixie, "You're going to listen to him? Are you insane?"

"I don't like it either," I replied, "but he has a point. I'm getting woozy from pain, I've been beaten to within an inch of my life, and we're lucky no one has come running from the gunshot earlier. There's no way we can take on another six people much less anyone else in here, so we just need to be careful. Now, come on, we're killing time."

I hobbled back through the door, favoring the knee Baldy had kicked the chair into. I had the flashlight in my left hand, held gingerly in my broken wrist, with my 45 in my right hand, safety off. It was difficult to get a good grip on it, my hand had continued to swell, but I was pretty sure I could still pull the trigger if I needed to.

The pixie took the lead, hovering near the ceiling, swearing softly under his breath while I shined the flashlight at the ground ahead of me. With the high powered flashlight, I saw the moldy walls in all their moisture stained glory, as well as the water stained ceiling tiles. The floor was moldy carpet, musty and stained, but otherwise the hallway was unremarkable.

We quickly reached the intersection of hallways and turned right, just as Goatee had said. Cautiously advancing down the hallway, we passed a closed door every ten feet or so, but everything was dark, silent, and water stained. Finally, we reached a metal double door, with push levers at waist height, and a large red sign warning of the fire alarm. Taking a deep breath, praying Goatee was on the level, I pushed the door open with my shoulder, crouching low and aiming my pistol out.

Chapter 14: Streets

A surprised guard turned as I shoved the door out, bringing his rifle to bear as I spun into a hook kick, slamming him in the face and dropping him like a stone. I landed with a grunt, the shock of a spinning kick sending a sheet of fire through my ribs, a hammering through my head, and throbbing in my knee. I staggered against the railing, almost falling, but I stayed standing with a death grip on the railing. Luckily, my kick had been true and I'd knocked the guard out.

I poked the guard in the ribs with my toe, hard, but he didn't twitch. He was young, late teens, fresh faced and completely inexperienced. His freckled face was slack beneath his shock of ginger hair and I felt bad for him. My kick was already raising a large purple welt on the side of his face, but his breathing was strong and regular. He would have a Hell of a headache when he woke up, but he'd be doing a lot better than Goatee and infinitely better than Baldy.

I quickly searched Ginger, pulling a cheap 9mm from his waist holster, and appropriating his rifle as well as an iPhone. I swiped it open; he hadn't even locked it, and pulled up a map program. Amazing, I was still off Colfax. I pulled his coat off him, an expensive black Columbia coat, and I threw it over my shoulders, not bothering to put my arms through the sleeves.

It was late night or early morning, no traffic to speak of, and I knew a dirty, disheveled female wandering out onto Colfax in the dark would be asking for trouble. I had to get out of there, fast, before they realized I was gone.

"Phew, you handled that guy a whole lot better than the first two," came a voice in my ear. I jumped, having forgotten about the pixie, who was hovering near my ear once more.

"Where to?" I asked, turning to face him.

"I have no idea, faerie-blood, I just said I'd get you out, this wasn't the way I came in. We need to head toward the sun death, that's where my clan is."

"Sun death? Oh, to the west, okay," I headed off west, trying to look nonchalant, challenging with a military rifle slung across my back, barefooted, and limping. I stopped a couple blocks down from Colfax and leaned against an office building, pulling out Ginger's iPhone. *Maybe technology isn't so bad*, I thought as I looked up the number for the police department, hitting the link to dial the number as I turned down an alley.

"Hello, Denver police, how can I direct your call?" came the no-nonsense voice of a female.

"Hi, yeah, can you transfer me to Lieutenant Mark Coleman, please?"

"Lieutenant Coleman is at home right now, do you want to leave him a message?"

"No, can you transfer me to the officer of SER on duty right now?"

"Just a moment please," she replied. Bland elevator music blared from the phone as I waited.

"SER, how can I help you?" It was Gina Glasgow, one of the dispatchers for SER and not my favorite person. She saw me as competition for Gibson's attention and was very catty about it. I was about to ask if he was available when I realized who I was talking to.

"Gina, it's McKinsey, I need to reach whoever's on duty, it's an emergency," I said.

"Gibson's not in his office right now, can I take a message?"

Something had her up in a tizzy, and she was going to be difficult.

"I don't have time for this, Gina, please just transfer me to Gibson's cell, I need his help," I said, exasperated.

"Time for what McKinsey?" Gina asked, her voice dripping with sarcasm and feigned hurt. "Unlike some people, I would *never* do anything to step on your toes, McKinsey."

Grinding my teeth, I hit the end button on the phone, not willing to play catty games with Gina Glasgow right now. I called 911 instead, hoping I would get someone who would listen.

"911, what's your emergency?" a male voice responded.

"I'm on Colfax, I'm not sure where, close to Colorado Boulevard I think. There's a zombie here and he's trying to eat me!" I deliberately put a whine and a healthy dose of panic in my voice, hoping he would connect it faster.

"Calm down, ma'am, we'll have someone there as soon as we can, try to get on something high, zombies won't climb. I've tracked your cell phone, but it's an unregistered phone. What was your name? Who should we look for?"

"Uh..." My brain felt like molasses in January, and nothing came to mind.

"Ma'am? Are you still there? Ma'am?"

"Yeah, sorry, my name's... McKinsey, Jamie McKinsey and I have a black skirt and a black coat on, hurry please, he's gonna eat me!" I hung up and settled against the side of an office building to wait. SER was usually better than the regular cops about getting to a call, but they had to be, people who called them were frequently in danger of being eaten by something horrid.

Shock was starting to wear through my adrenaline high and my head was swimming. I settled to the ground, legs akimbo, with spots dancing through my vision, and tried to stay conscious. Everything hurt, especially my head, and my ribs felt like a barbeque restaurant's main dish. The urge to go to sleep was almost irresistible.

Finally, I heard the wailing siren of SER off in the distance, approaching quickly. Two maroon vans pulled up directly in front of me and I struggled to my feet to try to at least look less pathetic. Armored figures boiled out from the back of the lead van, fanning out to circle me and shouting for me to put my hands on my head. I did, fanning my fingers to show I didn't have a weapon in them, and interlacing them on top of my head. My ribs burned, a dull ache while my wrist stabbed insistently and my head felt like a bongo drum being played by a pro wrestler. My stolen rifle was under the coat behind my back, hopefully hidden from view.

"Where's the zom?" bellowed the SER figure directly in front of me, flashing his fingers to his coworkers, telling them to fan out and look. They spread out carefully, flashing powerful flashlights in the dark recesses around us.

"He left," I lied, trying to look pathetic and helpless, not truly an act. I gestured at him to ask if I could lower my arms and he nodded. I felt bad for calling in a bogus report, but I wasn't sure how close on my tail those Purity psychos were, and there really were nasty things on the street at this time of night.

"Did he bite you?" the lead SER officer asked, lowering his rifle and advancing on me, not wanting to touch me but concerned for my safety.

"No, something else caught his attention, he wandered off that way," I replied, pointing generally south down the street.

"How'd you get hurt?" he asked suspiciously, gesturing at my splinted wrist and blood stained bandage with the barrel of his rifle. He flipped his visor up, but I didn't recognize him, either someone I hadn't had contact with or a new guy on the force.

"I fell down the stairs," I hedged, not wanting to explain everything to a stranger. "Hey, look, is Gibson or Coleman working tonight, I really need to talk to one of them?"

He frowned, looking me over and probably wondering how I knew either of them. He apparently made a decision, as he turned away and pulled his phone from his belt dialing a number. Speaking low and urgently, he turned away, continuing to peer at me from the corner of his eye. Whoever was on the other end of the line wasn't listening because his voice grew more and more strained as they argued. Finally, he hung up, turning to face me, a scowl of irritation creasing his face. I didn't recognize him, although he was young with a narrow face and narrow eyes. He looked olive skinned and dark eyed in the streetlight, but his visor shadowed his face and I couldn't be sure.

"That was Coleman; he'll be here in a few minutes. I described you to him and he said knew you so he's going to come get you and take you to hospital. He said you falling down the stairs was bullshit. You want to try it again from the top?" He glared at me, willing me to tell him the truth and I had little reason not to.

I sighed, trying to decide how much I was willing to tell him. Eventually, I settled on an abbreviated version of the story. His face grew darker and darker in the streetlights as I told my tale, holding back the identity of some of the participants, but telling everything about my injuries. I desperately wanted Coleman to get here, him I trusted, but this new guy was an unknown and I wasn't sure whose side he'd be one. Some of the SER guys counted themselves among the members of Purity or one of the other humans first organizations and they didn't like people like me.

"You're telling me Purity did this to you? That's bull crap. There's no reason we'd do anything like that, we'd lose any credit we had." He scowled at me, unwilling to accuse me of outright lying but not believing anything I said. I scowled right back, hating intolerant people and feeling trapped now that I knew this new officer was a humans first nut job.

We stared at each other for a long moment in silence, each challenging the other to make a move, when a silver Kia sedan pulled up to the curb next to us. We turned in unison, me on guard and the SER officer curious, as the car idled for a moment. The windows were tinted a very dark color that looked black in the early morning light, but I was pretty sure it was Coleman. Moments later I was proven right as he opened the door and turned to lean on the roof of his car.

"What the Hell's goin' on here, Smith?" he barked, glaring at his subordinate. I relaxed, knowing most likely Coleman was on my side, when he turned his glare to me. "And you, McKinsey, what the Hell you doing out here this time a night? Last I saw you, you was heading for Purity with Gibson, but he waited for you and you never came out. He went in to look for ya and they says you never been in there. Where you been?" he pinned me with a glare, but I was totally not in the mood for this mess.

"Never was there?" I spat, my ire kindling a fire in me that cleared the cobwebs and forced me to stand up straight. "Was never there? Did you happen to call my cell phone and see if that was the truth? 'Cause it isn't, and you know it. Those assholes kidnapped me and were holding me prisoner in that building," I pointed to the building I had made my escape from with a trembling finger. Coleman's eyes widened and he put his hands out in front of him, placatingly trying to stop my tirade.

"Slow down there," he said, patting the air and looking back and forth between Smith and I, "slow down, I ain't followin' ya. What's going here?" Smith and I both starting talking at once, Smith haranguing me for making a false report and false accusations against his Purity brethren and me reiterating the events of the last few hours.

"Shut up, both of ya!" Coleman finally bellowed, losing his temper. "One at a time.

You," he pointed at Smith, "start over and keep in mind McKinsey's saved my butt more than once."

Smith scowled, glaring at me under his helmet, and started again.

"This... person, called SER and reported a zombie but when we showed up there wasn't anything here but her. Then she gives me this b.s. story about Purity kidnapping her and her busting out and then tells me to call you like she doesn't trust me or something." He finished with another glare in my direction, fingering his rifle.

Coleman laughed, a short bark of irritation, and turned to me. "Now you," he said, gesturing for me to tell my side of the story. I glared back at Smith, debating silently if I wanted to say anything I hadn't already said in front of him, and then reiterated my edited tale sprinkled with significant glances, trying to get him to understand I was holding back. His eyebrows climbed as I laid my accusations down, but he never stopped me.

"Smith, you get outta here, go find the zom she reported, I'll deal with McKinsey," Coleman finally said, turning away from Smith with a dismissive wave and giving me the once over. I realized I must look like quite a sight, filthy with torn clothes and injuries. Coleman knew I wasn't given to exaggeration, I hoped he had sent Smith off to get my whole story. Turned out, I was right.

"Now the truth, McKinsey, all of it," he said as soon as Smith was out of earshot. I told him everything, every detail I remembered, and he listened with a blank expression.

"Them's some serious accusations," he said, pulling his face with a long fingered hand and examining me. "But I don't see no reason you'd make it up, and ya look like ya been through Hell. I'll send Smith back downtown, but I think we need ta take ya to the hospital." He gripped my arm gently, leading me to his car and helping me into the passenger seat. He'd left the car running and it was wonderfully warm. My earlier anger had cooled and left me drained. Coleman had wandered off to find Smith and tell him we were leaving, but I was too worn out to care much what Smith did.

Coleman made it back to the car after a couple minutes, a grim expression on his face as he shifted into drive without a word. We accelerated smoothly onto the icy streets, heading for Denver Health, when Coleman finally spoke up.

"Gonna need to keep an eye on Smith," he advised, not looking at me. "He's got it in for you bad, no idea why, but he don't like you."

"Great," I grunted, not really caring about the opinions of the new SER officer. Right now I was more concerned with staying awake. My arm and my ribs were throbbing, a dull counterpoint to my heartbeat and the gash on my forearm was bleeding again, I could feel wetness in my sleeve. A faint buzzing in my ear I'd only subconsciously noticed was getting louder and I realized it was the pixie, he'd hidden in my hair ever since SER had shown up. He was talking to me now, tinny and high pitched, and I couldn't understand much of what he was saying. I hissed at him to talk louder, trying not to attract Coleman's attention.

"You promised," he hissed in my ear, anger making his voice thin and high. "My clan is toward the sun-death, not this way! Make the big one take you toward the sun-death!"

"I need to get to hospital," I protested softly.

"I don't care, you promised. I can't make it away from my clan much longer in this weather; you need to do what you said you would! Your bloodline walker friend swore you'd help me if I helped you!" His voice was almost unintelligible, high and very rapid with his ire. I sighed, irritated but not thinking very clearly.

"I can take you there with my car, Coleman won't understand if I tell him to go there now."

"You promised, please!" he pleaded, pulling my hair in his agitation. Dammit, I did promise.

"Hey Coleman, I'm okay, could you just drop me off at my apartment?" I asked, laying my hand on his leg.

He looked down at my hand, and then over at me. "Have ya lost yo' damn mind?" he demanded. "Ya got a hurt wrist and need stitches under that blood soaked piece of shirt, I bet. How the Hell are ya all right?"

"It's just a cut and my wrist is okay," I hedged, hoping I wasn't lying to him. "It's just bruised, I'll be okay. I need to run an errand before I come down to the precinct, it won't take long I don't think." I looked at him imploringly, willing him to understand and not ask any more questions. He stared back, a sidelong glance stretching out and out. Eventually, he flicked the blinker on and turned off the main street, headed for Stapleton and my apartment, grumbling under his breath. I sat back, slightly shocked he hadn't given me more trouble, but glad he listened to me.

The rest of the ride was uncomfortable, a strained silence developing between us, but I did my best to ignore it, knowing I was doing what I had to do. I could feel the macabre little package pressing against my breast and I knew I had to be rid of it as soon as possible.

We pulled into my apartment complex a few minutes later, how many I couldn't say for sure. Coleman hadn't said a word since I convinced him to take me home and I really didn't have much to say either. He wouldn't understand why I was risking my health for a pixie and truthfully I didn't understand it either.

"You sure about this, hun?" he asked, pulling into and parking spot and turning to face me, a questioning look in his dark eyes.

"Yeah," I said, easing the door open and flashing him a quick smile. "Thanks, I appreciate your help, don't know what I'd do without you. I'll be down to the precinct as soon as I can, count on it." He scowled, but let me go.

Just as I was about to slam the door shut, he said "Keep your head down, McKinsey. I ain't always gonna be there to get yo' butt outta the fire." He grunted, putting the car into reverse and backing out of the parking lot without another word. I shook my head ruefully, but quickly stopped when the stab of pain almost set me reeling.

Chapter 15: Chautauqua

My apartment was on the second floor of the apartment building, a brick and cement monolith looming before me, and I knew the stairs were going to be a challenge. Walking in through the garage was the easiest way in, but I didn't have my garage door opener so I'd need to go around the building. Sighing, I picked my way across the parking lot, stepping on every sharp rock in my stocking feet on the way around the building.

Reaching the white painted entry way, I headed for the door to get into the foyer for my set of apartments. My entry way was small, maybe ten feet on a side, painted a cream color with dark gray mailboxes on the left wall. Directly ahead were the two doors for my left two sets of neighbors and on the right wall were the doors for my apartment and the corner suite. I really didn't know any of my neighbors well, the hi in the hallway sort of acquaintances, and they'd likely be fast asleep at this time of night. My door was locked, as expected, so I popped it open and meandered up my stairs, frequently putting both feet on a given stair to steady myself.

I started to kick off my shoes as I got to the top of the stairs that led directly into my apartment when I remembered I didn't have any on. Sighing again, I pushed into the living room of my apartment and shut the door behind me, flipping on the lights. My living room spread out to the right of me, white walls decorated with paintings of dragons and faeries with pale hard wood floors and drapes pulled closed over the windows. My TV was hanging on the wall to the right, while my black leather sofa made a nice divider between the kitchen, lost in dimness, and the living room. Stairs led up the right wall to the two bedrooms, with a bathroom in the middle. The polished wood banister on the left was pale oak, but the stairs were carpeted with a light gray plush carpet.

"What are we doing here?" hissed a high voice in my ear. I swiped at the side of my head, startled, and the pixie took flight into my living room. "Why're we here?"

"So I can change clothes, I have no shoes," I said pointedly staring at my torn stockings. He sniffed, turning to hover in front of one of my faerie paintings, as I headed for the stairs and my bathroom. I needed a shower, but I doubted he'd give me enough time to get one before he started whining again.

Up his, I thought, heading for the bedroom and grabbing a pair of jeans, a green t-shirt, and a replacement bra and underwear from my big, dark chest of drawers. My room was not spacious, twelve feet on a side, but more than enough for a king sized bed and a dresser. I had a four post bed, real wood stained dark with a green comforter and sheets, completely messed up. I never made my bed, too lazy I guess. On the walls were more pictures of dragons and faeries, my favorite things to collect.

Next was the bathroom where I starting pulling off my soiled clothes and unwrapping my wrist. The bathroom was small, having only a single sink vanity with a large mirror on the wall and cultured white marble countertop. To the far left was the combination bath tub and shower, not great for a bath when someone is as tall as me, but good enough, a single fiberglass shell with a clear shower curtain. The floor was bone colored tile, set in a diamond pattern with dark grout.

"Yikes, no wonder Coleman wanted to take me to the hospital, I look like crap," I muttered to myself. Everything hurt, my arm and ribs a throbbing counterpoint to my aching headache and the gash on my arm was oozing thick, dark blood. I looked at myself in the mirror, startled at the Bloody Mary like reflection in the mirror. My hair was mussed with grime and dirt ground in, and I had a lovely high heel toe shaped bruise in the middle of my abs where Phelps had kicked me. My fingers on my right hand were turning purple, stiff and unwieldy while my left wrist had turned an ugly purple black and swollen to twice its normal size, long indentions from the jury-rigged splint running up and down the area.

The gash on my arm from Phelps' shoe wasn't as bad as I thought, maybe an inch and a half long, but ragged where the flesh had torn. My eyes were hollowed, deep pits in my pale, exhausted face ringed with dark bags and my lips were drawn with pain. I had new lines around my mouth, probably from stress and pain, and I looked about ten years older.

I shut the door to the bedroom and flipped the lights on, crossing the room to start the shower, and then reaching into my medicine cabinet to grab Tylenol and Advil from the shelf. I popped some of both, washing them down with water from the sink, swallowing with a grimace for my throbbing ribs.

The hot water felt marvelous, sluicing the accumulated dirt and grime from my body and hair and running red through the gash on my arm. There was a large goose egg on the back of my head, I assumed from where Phelps had hit me, and it was very tender to my touch as I washed my hair. I stood there, letting the water calm me down, until it ran lukewarm.

I awkwardly climbed out of the tub, drying off as best as I could, and then sighed once more. I wondered about how far I'd need to drive to get the pixie home as I started pulling first aid supplies from the cabinet under the sink. My wrist had been broken before, a mishap in taekwondo, so I had a nice hard brace I could use for it now. I slapped a large adhesive bandage on the gash on my arm with lots of antibacterial ointment and then pulled the brace on with a grunt. I couldn't tighten it too tight or I started losing feeling in my fingers, but I found a nice balance between tight and stabilizing and loose and letting blood into my hand. There wasn't anything I could do about my bruised fingers or my ribs, so I just let them be.

The holster for my 45 was still attached to my filthy skirt so I pulled it free, sliding my belt through the loops and securing it at the small of my back. I popped the magazine on the pistol, noting all the bullets were still there and then racked the slide. It hadn't been fired either, so I reloaded it and flipped the safety on before sliding it back in the holster.

The little package of the pixie's wife's remains I placed carefully in one of my backup purses along with my backup wallet and ID. I'd need to call and cancel the credit cards and report my gun stolen, but that could wait 'til morning. I'd stowed my appropriated weapons in my gun safe in the extra bedroom, spinning the dial to lock them up. I might turn them in to the cops, I might not. You never knew when an unregistered firearm could turn out handy and I had technically stolen them.

As I dressed, my head had already started to feel better from the medicine and I thought about the growling in my stomach. I was ravenous, much hungrier than I had been a few minutes ago, so I headed downstairs to cook a bagel with some cream cheese. The pixie was nowhere to be found, but I knew he'd make himself known as soon as he realized I was out of the shower.

I liked my kitchen, average sized with oak cabinets and dark granite countertops. The stainless steel appliances complemented the light gray ceramic tile quite well, I thought. I toasted a bagel, slathering it with cream cheese and chugging a Coke along with it, hoping to finish eating before the pixie decided to make his appearance.

My bagel was half gone before the pixie made his entrance into the kitchen, floating quietly into the room without a word. I eyed him warily, waiting for the tirade, but he just hovered there, waiting.

I finished the bagel, dropping the plate into the sink and downing the rest of the Coke, and turned toward him. "Ready to go?" I asked, only slightly sarcastically.

He floated over to my shoulder, landing lightly and grabbing my hair to support himself. I took that for a yes and strode down the stairs, locking the door as I left, and pulling my white snow boots on as I opened the garage door. My little black Honda Accord sat in her parking spot just as I had left her, so I hit the switch to open the door and climbed in, careful not to squish the pixie.

"Where to?" I asked.

"Toward the sun-death, I'll give you better instructions when we're closer. You apes call our land Chautauqua park, if that means anything to you."

It did, so I headed for I-25 to get to US36 and head for Boulder. I was glad there was no other traffic, I wasn't making good decisions and nearly veered off the roads several times. I figured I likely had a concussion, and it was pretty stupid to be driving with one, but I didn't think I had a lot of choice.

After about half an hour, I pulled into the snow covered parking lot of Chautauqua Park. We climbed out of the car, the pixie burrowing into my hair to stay warm and still be able to talk to me, and I headed for the trailhead.

"Where to?" I asked.

"Take the path to the left, toward the Sky Ribbon of stone, and I'll guide you from there."

"Up the trail?" I demanded, astonished. "It's freakin' dark, I'll break my ankle trying to head up there. Besides, I have a concussion, I can't hike that far!"

"It's not too far," he said, unsympathetic, "and you promised." I sighed in irritation. *Me and my big mouth,* I thought. I trudged toward the trail he indicated, pleasantly surprised to find it wasn't knee deep snow but in fact hard packed snow bank, easier to walk on.

After ten minutes of walking, the pixie tugged on my ear, telling me to turn right into the trees. I shook my head, looking around for forest rangers, and plunged into the pine trees, slogging through the knee deep snow. After about a hundred yards, I found a titanic Douglas fir, wider around than my outstretched arms with a hollow spot some fifteen feet from the ground.

"This is it, faerie-blood, you've done as promised. Give me my wife and I'll consider us even." He took flight from my shoulder, hovering in front of my face with his arms outstretched. Gingerly pulling the sad little bundle from my purse, I handed it to him gravely, making sure he had it before I let go. He zipped out, up into the tree, returning a moment later empty handed.

"Thank you. Your help and your honor has rekindled some of my trust in you big ones, but you need to leave before my family wakes and finds you here. They won't be happy. Farewell." He lifted off once more, leaving a trail of sparkling light as he ascended to his home. I turned toward the trail, tramping through the high snow and feeling lightheaded from the exertion. I needed to get home and to a doctor, soon, or I'd be sorry.

The trail here was ice, slippery and steep, and I climbed back on with care. Futile care, it would seem, because as soon as my foot struck the icy surface, it went out from under me and I fell, slamming my hip into the ground and stunning me for a moment. I lay there in the snow, marveling at the spinning stars, when I heard a voice hissing in my ear.

"Faerie-blood! Faerie-blood! Get up! There's trouble, get up!" It was the pixie again, he was pulling at my copper earring and trying to get me to stand up. I swatted at him, lazily swishing my hand by my head, trying to shoo him without hurting him.

"Get up, there's a corrupted one coming, get up!" he tugged hard enough to hurt me, and his words finally penetrated my fog. *Corrupted one? What was that?* I turned my head slowly to the right, seeing a pretty young woman walking toward me. She was dressed in jeans and a simple dark t-shirt with black Uggs, her long brown hair braided in an asymmetric plait that fell to her right side. She wasn't wearing a coat but she didn't seem cold, walking along casually without a care in the world. At two in the morning. Alone. In Chautauqua Park. Something was wrong, very wrong. She stopped, threw her head back, sniffing the air like a dog, and then snapped her head around to stare directly at me.

My blood ran cold as I realized what a corrupted one was. "Vampire?" I muttered, "Shit, shit, shit!"

Chapter 16: Vampire

Jordan Rockensuess sat atop Flat Iron number one, gazing out at the twinkling lights of Boulder, Denver, and the rest of the metro area. They lay like a great sea of cold fireflies, a rich reflection of the crystalline blackness of the winter sky. It was very cold and clear, the night air shimmering. She liked it best when the Aurora Borealis could be seen, but that wasn't the case, not tonight. She came here to think, to contemplate her existence, and sometimes to think about jumping to the ground far below.

She'd remember her life before Erick, her Master before she'd been given to her current Master, and wonder where she would be if he'd never bit her. Maybe she'd be a grandmother, maybe she'd be someone, instead of a nearly nameless vampire servant wandering the mountain trails of the west. Before she'd met him, she'd been a sorority girl, working charity with her sisters, going to class to study as an engineer, drinking too much. She'd worked nights at the college radio station, playing the best new music, going to sleep curled up with her fat dog. Then she'd met him and her life had been destroyed, spiraling into the cesspool it was now.

When her Master or Erick beat her, abused her, or forced her to service them, she came up here to think and wonder why she hung on. Was this half life really worth the pain and misery? She feared death, feared it enough that she had put up with her vampire existence for almost fifty years, but sometimes it became just too much. She'd tried alcohol, other drugs, but her vampire metabolism destroyed the drugs and made her vomit the alcohol, lending no relief. There was no such thing as a vampire therapist so the cool night air was the only solace she found.

After a time, she descended to wander through the night, prowling through the darkness like a great cat. Sometimes she'd meet a lover up here, but not tonight, tonight she didn't want the touch of another person, vampire or human. After last time, she didn't want to tempt the anger of her Master, she who was so very jealous of her pet.

Jordan loved nature, she hadn't complained at all when they had been moved here from Oregon, and this forest was nearly as good as her native Cascades. Chautauqua was empty this time of night, too early for the hardcore hikers and too late for the drunks, so it was all hers. Sometimes she found a hiker here, usually camping deep in the forest, a perfect snack to tide her over for a while. In the summer, the homeless sleeping on the trail were a perfect meal, able to keep her fed and away from the rest of the vampires for months at a time. Eventually, though, her Master would call her home, force her to feed with the rest of the family, and bind her tight with sex and sustenance.

Descending back to the parking lot, nearing the end of her hike, she grieved for the end of the night, but she knew she needed to get back to Denver and into the Sanctuary before the sun rose. She'd spent many days burrowed under leaves, hiding from the sun, but they'd been mostly sleepless days, full of apprehension and fear because this time of year her usual daytime resting places were inconvenient. She never knew if some scavenging animal or curious hiker would accidently uncover her, setting her body alight like oil soaked wood.

Still, sometimes better than dealing with her Master, but not tonight. Tonight she was too hungry to stay out here, away from her family. She snorted, thinking there couldn't be a less accurate moniker for their group unless maybe they were a tiger family.

Skipping down the trail, she breathed the frigid air in and out in great lung filling breaths, trying not to think about the reception when she got back to Denver. She wasn't cold, one of the many advantages to being a vampire, nor was she worried about slipping on the icy trails, she knew her quick reactions would keep her from falling.

As she descended, a faint scuffling caught her attention, leading her down the left hand trail rather than the right she was about to take. *Probably a deer,* she thought, *but you never know.* Maybe she'd get lucky and find an early hiker out to see the sunrise from the Flatiron. If she could find a meal, she wouldn't need to go back to Denver.

Struggling through the trees and knee deep snow was a lone hiker, oddly enough coming from the faerie nest and heading toward the trail. Jordan paused, waiting to see if she was alone and easy prey or with someone and not worth messing with. The hiker slipped on the icy trail, falling and lying still for a long moment. She smelled good, wounded, like she'd been in a fight or something, easy prey. She was a sensitive, a faerie blood as Erick called them, and would sustain Jordan's hunger for several nights. With a feral grin, she broke into a run, eagerly anticipating her feast.

I struggled to my feet as quickly as I could, fumbling with the 45 in my waist band, but my bruised fingers wouldn't close on the butt of the pistol. The vampire caught my gaze, her startlingly blue-green eyes boring into mine. She grinned a fang-baring feral smile, and broke into a run straight toward me. As she ran, her true vampire visage was revealed, long skeletal face with black almond eyes and a large fanged mouth. I stumbled back, tripping over the edge of the trail and falling again into the snow, and she was on me, pinning me to the ground with the full weight of her body. She landed on top of me, trying to pin my arms to the ground so she could get a better shot at my throat. Her distended fang-filled maw snapped at me, clacking with painful force every time she missed.

I struggled, striking her across the face with the back of my hand, but I hit her with my left hand instead of my right. My arm exploded in pain as the strike twisted my wrist against the brace, eliciting a scream from the depths of my body. The vampire grinned and grabbed my chin with her right hand, slamming my head into the ice packed surface with all her force, exploding the world in a cascade of purple stars. I pushed with all my strength, trying to keep her snapping jaws from me with my left hand when she bit me, tearing into my left forearm with savage ferocity and worrying it like a dog. I bellowed, fear and pain giving me strength beyond anything I had experienced before.

The fingers of my scrabbling right hand closed on something solid, rough and round with a good heft to it, likely a branch, and I slammed it into her head with as much force as I could muster. My arm exploded in a fiery wall of pain as her mouth was ripped from my flesh, but the vampire rolled off me enough that I could roll to the side. She was slumped against the railing, mewling softly and clutching her skull where I had slammed the branch into it, her face back to its human form. Blood leaked between her fingers, black in the darkness of the forest, and flowing freely, staining her shirt with splotches of inky darkness.

I rolled to a crouching position, keeping an eye on the vampire as I finally succeeded in pulling my 45 from my waistband with stiff, clumsy fingers. I flicked the safety off, aimed at her chest and shot her, point blank, but apparently my hands were shaking worse than I thought and I missed her core. My bullet tore through the muscle of her right shoulder, exploding out the other side in a fountain of black gore, throwing her to the ground.

She rolled, much quicker than I thought possible, and reared back, crouching and hissing at me, fangs bared and glistening in the white light of the almost full moon. Her face was once more her vampire countenance and her right arm hung uselessly while she supported her weight with her left hand, crouching like a mountain lion. Hair was matted to her face by the blood continuing to flow from her head wound, lending her a macabre air. Her shoulder was bleeding freely, but she looked ready to pounce, a very faint white light shining in her wide eyes as she ran a long forked tongue over her razor teeth.

Pointing my gun at her head with shaking hands, I started to pull the trigger when a warm wind, smelling of lilac, slithered softly down the trail. Confusion marred the vampire's suddenly human face, quickly replaced with fear, and then she was gone, fleeing down the trail like the Devil himself was after her, leaving a black spotted trail in her wake. I fired twice at her fleeing form, missing both times. I shuddered, pulling my finger from the trigger, and leaning against the railing. Adrenaline still sang in my veins, but it was fading, leaving me shaking and scared. I'd been bitten, chewed on like a piece of rawhide, and now I was at risk for Stoker-Dracul syndrome. SDS was rarely transmitted through a bite from a servant, but it had happened before. *Shit*. This had to be the worst day I had ever had in my whole life.

Examining my arm in the darkness of the trail didn't lead to much information. I could tell I was bleeding, fairly badly it seemed from the level of slipperiness up and down my arm and the wet sensation gathering around the cuff of my jacket, but I had no idea how bad it was. My hand still worked, albeit with pain, and I hoped that was a good sign. My appropriated coat was torn to ribbons, smashed into the wound, and poking through it just made me hiss in pain.

Dragging myself to my feet and gripping the pistol in my right hand, I headed back down the trail, putting pressure on my arm to try and stop the bleeding and keeping a sharp eye out for the vampire. By the time I was back at my car, my head was swimming again and I was having trouble putting one foot in front of the other. Sitting in the warmth of my car helped, but I knew I needed to see a doctor. I started my car, heading back to Denver, thankful for the early hour.

Chapter 17: Intruder

My apartment looming into view was one of the most welcome sights I had ever seen, and I had made it without hitting anything. I pulled into my garage and killed the car, letting out a sigh of relief. I didn't remember the trip upstairs, but I found myself at the door to my living room a moment later. I pulled the door open, fuzzily alarmed as I realized I had locked it when I left, my blood running cold.

"Hello, Jamie," came a soft voice from my dark living room. I screamed, slamming my hand into the switches next to me to turn the lights on just in time to see the vampire who attacked me hurtling toward me, fangs bared in her vampire countenance, her dark brown braid whipping around her head as she lunged. I stepped aside reflexively and slammed my forearm into her back as she rammed the door, denting the steel. Snarling, she whirled on me, quick as a cat, but this time I was ready for her, adrenaline singing through my veins and clearing my head. My crescent kick struck her in the face, snapping her head back as my next side kick pinned her to the door again by her stomach.

She collapsed, gasping from the severe blow to her diaphragm, as I landed a stunning forearm strike to the side of her neck, the metal plates in my brace added extra force to the strike. Her eyes rolled back into her head as she nearly passed out. I pulled my 45 from my belt, thumbing the safety and pointing it at her head, finger tensed over the trigger.

"No, please, don't kill me!" She gasped, "I was sent to get you, my Master wants to talk to you. She recognized your scent on me and wants to talk to you! Please!" Her blue-green eyes were huge in her ashen face. She was pretty, young with wide round-shaped blue-green eyes and thick, curled lashes, a pert nose, and a mouth accustomed to smiling, maybe late teens to early twenties when she had been converted. She was wearing a t-shirt similar to the one she had worn on the trail, this one red, and jeans with the same black Uggs. Clutching her stomach, her face already swelling and turning dark from my kick, she looked young and vulnerable. I pulled the gun back, pointing at the ceiling, thumbing the safety back on, and taking my finger off the trigger as she pleaded with me through her teal eyes.

I didn't know why I stopped, wasn't sure why I didn't just shoot her, but I found myself staring at her. I'd killed vampires before, even face to face, but something about this one disturbed me. Maybe it was because she was the first one to get the better of me, maybe I was more rattled by my near-brush with death, but I found myself listening to her.

"Why'd you attack me then? How'd you get in, anyway?" I asked warily, gun at the ready but no longer trained on her.

"You smell... good, like a really fine steak used to," she said, holding her hands out in front of her and sniffing the air.

"Stop it," I said, retraining the gun on her. "I'm not a snack so quit talking about how I smell like a steak. How'd you get in here?"

"My Master has your landlord, she's made him give her the keys to your apartment, and she let me in to wait for you. I was supposed to bring you to her by any means necessary, but you took so long to get back from the park I thought I was going to need to leave before dawn. When you came in, I thought I could take you by force 'cause I knew you were hurt." She finished, confusion warring with pain on her delicate face.

"Why didn't she just stay here if she wanted to talk to me so badly?" I asked, suspicious.

"She was afraid your warlock friend would be with you, she didn't want to tangle with him and knew I could slip out a window if he was with you. I'm no threat to him, unlike her. Please, you gotta come with me, she'll hurt me if she finds out I failed." Her voice was plaintive, almost begging, and her eyes were huge with pain. I found myself almost agreeing with her before I shook myself out of it.

"I have nothing to say to your Master, I hunt predators like her," I said, thumbing the safety back off and pointing the gun between her eyes. She cringed, putting her hands in front of her face and starting to cry.

"Please, please, no!" She begged, tears streaming down her face as she held her hands out to me, her face crumpling. "She says you have unfinished business, something about Oregon and you'd know what she was talking about, please!" She was sobbing now, her body wracking in great shivers of distress. Irritated, I pulled my gun back up, thumbing the safety back on for the second time and glaring at this little wisp of a girl who'd caused so many problems.

"Fine," I heard myself say, wondering what the heck I was doing. "Lead on," I said, gesturing toward the door with the gun. I wanted to change clothes, I was soaked through from falling in the snow and covered in blood, but I didn't trust this little bitch as far as I could throw her so I had to make do with what I had.

Her eyes lit up, and she wiped her nose with the back of her hand, standing awkwardly, still obviously in pain. I noticed her earlier wounds were gone, a cute trick considering I used silver ammo. The shoulder wound might have killed her; instead it was gone like it'd never been there.

"You could've just asked you know," I grumbled, gesturing for the door.

"You would've come with me if I had?" She asked, confusion again mingled with astonishment on her face.

"Hell no, but you could've anyway. I don't even know why I'm going now. I shot you, how are you using your arm again?" I asked, curious. She grinned her feral, fang baring grin and winked at me.

"My Master healed me," she said simply. "It's one of her many gifts. She'll tell you more when we get there." She turned and opened the door, passing through and waiting for me in the hallway. I kept the gun trained on her, locking the door behind me, and followed her down the stairs. She moved like a kid heading toward the park, swinging her arms and smiling at me like I was her best friend in the world. I scowled back, getting a really bad feeling about this, but following her anyway.

"Where are we going?" I demanded. It would look odd if I walked down the street with the gun pointed at her while she wandered ahead of me so I put it back in the holster at the small of my back.

"Not far," she replied blithely. "You'll see." We walked down the street in a line, heading toward the outskirts of Stapleton, taking about five minutes to reach a small warehouse. We entered through a side door into a dark, cavernous area with a plain concrete floor and little else I could see. The vampire turned to me and giggled, and then dashed into the darkness without a backward glance.

"Hey!" I shouted, spinning to reach the door we had entered through, but it slammed shut in my face. In the center of the warehouse, a single light bulb began to glow very softly. I awkwardly pulled my 45 and walked toward it, pointing the gun at the floor but ready to shoot anything that moved. It was dark, cold, and smelled faintly of musty old death and something else, something I couldn't identify, but which raised the hackles on the back of my neck. There didn't seem to be anything else in the warehouse that I could see.

"Hello?" I hazarded, my voice swallowed by the blackness all around me. "Hey, get back here!" I shouted, my voice reverberating through the darkness and fading to nothing.

"So eager to die, Jamie?" came a slithering voice from behind me, sliding up my spine and raising goosebumps all over. Her voice was low, husky, with a slight accent I couldn't place, but it had all the power of a Master vampire. I turned slowly, the way you turn when you know the monster is behind you, but you have nowhere to go.

"Hello?" I tried again, hoping to pinpoint more accurately where the voice was coming from. Her voice was familiar, but I couldn't place it, remembrance on the very tip of my mind.

"Hello?" she mocked, again from behind me. I spun, relaxing into a shooting stance, trying not to wobble with my exhaustion and pain. Her mocking laughter swirled around me, coming from all directions at once. Switching tactics, I stood up straight, throwing my head back, my arms loose at my sides, and emptied my mind. She was playing her mind games with me, but I had the power to stop her if I tried hard enough. Her laughter faded, narrowing to a point on the left, and I knew where she was. I turned to face her, opening my eyes to darkness, but calm and relaxed, the gun pointed where I thought she was.

Slow, mocking clapping came from her direction, along with a low chuckle which made my stomach clench.

"Very good, your warlock angel friend has taught you to use your blood well. Not many hunters can shield their mind from me. Tell me, why were you in my alley earlier this night, talking to the police?"

"First tell me who you are," I fished, hoping she wasn't too irrational. She was a Master, of that I was sure; no servant possessed the power she had, not on a sensitive like me. Her voice was familiar, but the memory slid through my mind like a fish through water, leaving no trace.

"You don't recognize me?" she asked, pique making her voice crackle with frost.

"How can I? I can't see in the dark like you can,"

"Of course," she chuckled, a good natured sound, turned spine chilling for being completely out of place.

The bulb over my head brightened, faint phosphorescence in the inky blackness, slowly glowing brighter as my eyes adjusted. The warehouse was perhaps thirty feet high with the seamless concrete floor as I had seen from the street, but the walls were lost to the darkness. I knew one wasn't far off and I sensed the others weren't too far off either, maybe thirty yards in each direction. Other than the

196

glowing fluorescent bulb, there was only the crisscrossing I-beams overhead. I frowned, feeling something not right, like I was staring at a lifelike painting with something missing. Softly, almost unheard but there, was a slithering noise, something akin to snakes moving through underbrush. It scared me, raising my flesh to goosebumps again.

On the edge of the light, fading in and out of the luminescence as the bulb swung slightly, was a woman, almost as tall as I was, with flowing waist length blonde hair, eyes like pools of darkness, and lips the color of the finest garnet. She was very pale, ghostly white with not a hint of color, and slender. She was dressed in a shoulder-baring, flowing dress of simple fabric, the color of freshest blood. It trailed behind her into the darkness as she stood, still as stone, soft breathing lifting her well endowed chest. Finally, she lifted a long fingered pale hand with nails the color of a midnight sky and gestured toward the ceiling. A graceful gesture, turning her palm toward the light, and looking up at me expectantly.

"Shit," I said, wondering how this day could get any worse. "Svetlana," I breathed, panic rising in my throat and threatening to choke me.

Chapter 18: Svetlana

The last time I had seen Svetlana Gregorova had been in Portland, Oregon, four years ago. Another hunter had killed her Master for the death of a family outside Corvallis and she and the six servants in her family had gone on a killing spree in retaliation. I was one of three hunters hired to deal with them along with heavy Portland SER support.

We had finally cornered them in a house in the suburbs, but they had dug themselves in and weren't coming out. Our lieutenant in charge of the operation, against our recommendations, had decided to storm the house with guns blazing; reasoning the family in there was already dead. His officers had stormed the front and back doors simultaneously, hoping to pin them in and catch them in the cross fire. Svetlana had been too powerful, though, or one of the officers had let his fear get to him, because she had grabbed his mind and forced him to start shooting his comrades.

We'd eliminated all the servants, but Svetlana took her officer hostage and walked out, bold as brass. She told us if we followed her, she'd tear his throat out. I'd followed anyway, as far from her as I could get and still track her, not willing to let her get away, and I had cornered her again in a downtown bar. After a battle of wills, I had her at gunpoint when my gun jammed. She'd disarmed me, bending the barrel of my pistol like a rubber toy and shattering the polymer frame, advancing on me with a sadistic smile. I was saved by another hunter, Kris Delaroux, shooting her twice from behind. Hissing, she blew past me and disappeared into the night.

Svetlana was old, three to four hundred years, and powerful. She had created several Master vampires over the last hundred years and she was that much harder to resist because of it. Originally from Russia, she had contracted Stoker-Dracul syndrome as a late teenager and been converted after a very short battle with the illness. Consequently, she was not a pure psychopath, but hundreds of years of survival had hardened her to the point where she would not hesitate to use anyone around her. She was never, ever to be trusted.

"*Very good, Jamishka,*" she replied, her lips not moving as she spoke, her accent much thicker in my mind. Jamishka. *Oh shit,* I thought. Not her, please not her. Jamishka was the diminutive name given to me by a Master I'd had a run in with at the beginning of my hunting career, a condescending way to make me feel like a child, and Svetlana had adopted it to intimidate me. My fear, and something else, had let her back into my mind, something that panicked me further. I closed my eyes, something very challenging to do with a Master vampire not ten feet from me, and tried to think of something to relax me.

"Polar bears," I muttered, "big, white, polar bears with black noses." I relaxed, emptying my mind again, until I felt breath on my face from too close, far too close. I opened my eyes to stare directly into her black gaze, falling into her eyes. I hated vampires, especially Masters, I really, really did.

"So you remember me, Jamishka. So tell me, why were you in my alley talking to your police? My girl bit you, this I know, but you do not smell like a vampire, you smell... different. Explain this to me." She demanded in a curious tone.

"I didn't realize it was your alley," I hedged, trying not to look in her eyes but unable to break her gaze. "And I don't know why I smell different to you."

"Hmm," she replied, turning away in a swirl of lilac perfume and blonde hair, releasing her hold on my mind and taking a step to the right. "I am believing you are telling the truth, mostly, and I am thinking you are very lucky, because you did not contract our gift. But I ask again, why were you, my hunter, skulking in my alley?" She breathed into my ear, running the outside of her right index finger down my cheek. I shuddered, trying to keep my mind calm, but I knew if she wanted to, she could rend me limb from limb before I made a move against her. It was like staring a female tiger in the eye as she decided whether or not she was hungry.

"I had a run in with Purity," I replied, resorting to the truth basically because I had no choice. "They kidnapped me and were threatening to kill me. I escaped and was trying to get my friends to come help." The police were my friends, right?

"You smell like... blood," she breathed, "and pain." She sniffed my hair, her breath hot on my neck, her forearm braced across my chest. I could smell her perfume, cloying flowery lilac, and underneath that was the smell of blood, coppery and sharp. "And death," she finished. "Were you having a good time with Purity's new mercenaries? They have moved many in recently. Fine feeding for my family, no one misses a mercenary or two. You do not smell of evil, though. You did not play with their pet demon?"

She had pulled back, looking me in the face again, but I was careful not to look her in the eyes. Out of my peripheral vision, I saw that her eyes had reverted to a pale blue-gray, the color of an angry, stormy sky. This close to her, I could see her face more clearly. Her skin was flawless, like the finest alabaster, and her cheekbones were high and sculpted. Her lips were full and stained dark maroon. She could have been the model for Helen of Troy, if Helen had been a Nordic goddess.

"No," I replied, taken aback. She was quite well informed, but I guess it paid to know your enemy. I had to get to SER, tell them about Purity and their associations with sorcery, before Phelps and her cronies unleashed their evil on the world.

"Why were you playing with the mercenaries, Jamishka? Why were you talking with the people of Purity?" she asked, walking around me slowly, her heels making a slow *click-click* on the concrete floor.

"Adora Johanson has been kidnapped," I replied, closing my eyes and trying to ignore her hand trailing across my right breast, fingers lingering on my nipple. "I thought they might have something to do with it so I went and interviewed McBarrister. They threw me out but I guess I hit on their sorcerer secret so Phelps decided she was going to eliminate me as an example. I broke out and was waiting for the police in your alley, that's all, I swear."

She grabbed my nipple, twisted hard, and forced a gasp from my lips. "What do you mean Adora has been kidnapped? She was with Erick last night! Who has taken her captive, tell me!" Her eyes had gone jet black, inky pools of power. She grabbed my chin in her right hand, jerking my gaze to hers, her hand like a warm steel vice. I struggled, so she squeezed, ever so slightly. It felt like my jaw was being pushed through the top of my head. "Tell me," she demanded.

"I don't know," I gasped, "please, that hurts!"

"It's supposed to hurt, Jamishka. Look me in the eye, tell me what you know." She forced my gaze up to hers and I fell, down, down, down, into her endless gaze.

"Someone powerful," I heard myself say, "they left a ransom note for her husband but even Jackson's Arts couldn't reveal who it was. They're powerful, enough to conceal their aura from him. He said he could sense demon, angel, or Master vampire powers but he wasn't sure which because Adora's aura was obscuring it. I don't know who kidnapped, her, please," I begged.

"When was she taken?"

"We don't know for sure, somewhere between Wednesday night and Friday morning," I gasped out.

She released my face and my breast suddenly, causing me to stumble backwards, almost falling.

"Stupid girl, she was not kidnapped. Her idiot husband does not know of what he speaks. Drop the case, you have no idea what you deal with," she said, a sneer on her lovely face.

"Not kidnapped? Are you sure? How do you know?" I asked, rubbing my jaw. In response, she slapped me, casually with the back of her hand, but it was enough to send me sprawling. I hit the concrete hard, skinning my knees and my palms, stars swirling through my vision.

"Do not question me, Jamishka. I say she was not kidnapped, you are to believe she was not kidnapped. Drop the case, you will live longer. It does not concern you," she replied.

"You present me with problems, Jamishka. You say you were talking to your police because of running from Purity, but bringing you here has attracted the attention of your angel friend. Even now, your friends gather outside and we must make plans to leave as soon as feasible. Your friend, the divine one, he has told them you are here in my house, but he cannot contact you because I will not allow him to. He grows worried, soon he will try to enter my realm and I will be forced to expose him as a practitioner of the Forbidden Arts. His divine blood will make it difficult to defeat him, I am not sure I would prevail.

"So, am I to be taking you with me, as my plan was originally, or do I leave you here to tell your police where I have gone? They did not know I was here until you came." She was staring at me, not trying to control my mind for once, just staring with a puzzled expression on her perfect face.

"If your girl hadn't jumped me, I'd be home in my bed right now," I pointed out.

"Da, this I know. Jordan saw an injured faerie blood and wanted to bring you home to feed us. Your kind's blood is much sweeter than an ape-blood, we much prefer it. I can feed more of my kin in one feeding with a faerie blood than with ape blood. Once I realized it was you, I thought we could continue our last meeting so I left her with instructions to bring you here to me. Tell me," she glided closer to me, gently pulling me to my feet and gathering me into her embrace. "Why did you not shoot me in Oregon? You could have, perhaps you wanted to, I do not know. But you did not. Why?"

"I... uh, well, I..." I stuttered, uncomfortable in her very intimate embrace. I was straight, not interested in women, but I sensed Svetlana didn't really care what my preferences were. She placed her manicured finger to my lips, silencing me.

"No lies, Jamishka, you know I can tell when you lie to me. Tell me why you did not try to kill me. Is it because you are interested in me as I am interested in you?" she breathed, her breath warm and smelling strongly of cinnamon. Her lips were very close to mine, almost touching. How do you tell a psychopathic, ancient, lesbian who can bench press a car you aren't interested, and you didn't kill her because your gun jammed? Damned if I knew, but, all the sudden, it was a very pertinent question. Honesty, thou hast slain me.

"My gun jammed," I admitted softly, bracing for impact. She shoved me away, violently, sending me skidding across the floor like a skipping stone across a lake. The impact against something unseen some ten feet away knocked the breath from me and I lay stunned, the world swirling in a nauseating spin.

I heard the clatter of her heels on the concrete, quickly approaching, but there was nothing I could do. She leaned over me, face to face, and hissed, her face morphing into a bizarre cross between human and animal, her true vampire face. Her eyes narrowed, becoming much more almond shaped and as dark as the deepest night while her face lengthened to a caricature of a human face, hollow cheeked and almost equine with a large fang-filled mouth. Her skin thinned, revealing a shining blue-white light under her skin as she stretched her jaws wide and bared her fangs to tear out my throat.

I watched in fascinated horror as her mouth descended, thinking I knew what a deer in headlights felt like, when, inexplicably, she stopped, snapped her mouth shut, and reached down to grab the front of my shirt, her face reverting to its earlier ethereal beauty. One armed, she lifted me from the ground like I weighed no more than a feather, pulling me into her for another embrace.

She gingerly pulled my arm up, the one Jordan had bitten, and sniffed it delicately, grabbing the hem of my jacket where the sleeve met the body. With a violent motion, she tore the sleeve completely away, baring the bandaged gash and the bloody mess that was the bite. Dried blood and torn fibers split, ripping the embedded threads from the bite and eliciting a cry of pain from my diaphragm.

She sucked delicately at the still bleeding wound; probing it with her tongue, making me cry out in pain once more and try to jerk my arm away. Her grip was inexorable; I might as well have tried to shift the Earth on its axis. She smiled up at me, a wolfish baring of her fangs, and thrust my arm away. If I wasn't infected before, I more than likely was now.

"Why do you lie to me, Jamishka?" she whispered, her blood stained lips a fraction of an inch from my ear. "Why do you lie, when you know I will kill you for it? You say your gun jammed, you deny your interest in me is akin to my interest in you, but your body says otherwise. Your heart, she beats like a captured bird when you are in my arms. Your breath comes in gasps when I hold you. How can you deny you are attracted to me, too?"

"I'm afraid of you," I admitted, "I don't want to be a vampire and I don't want to be a ghoul. I don't want to lose my ability to love, to understand when I hurt people, I don't want to be a servant, not to anyone." There, I said it. Now she'd kill me, but I didn't lie to her.

"What if I made you a Master?" she whispered, licking my earlobe and making me shudder, only partly in terror I admitted privately, very privately.

"I'd still be a vampire, I'd still lose my ability to connect with other people. I enjoy being with other people, talking with them,

I can't do that if my very existence puts a target on my butt."

"My attention would not be enough for you?" she asked arching a plucked eyebrow, pulling away. "The love and affection of your Master wouldn't be enough for you to give up your so-called friends? Where are these friends of yours now? Do you mean so little to them they do not try to rescue..." She stopped, her head cocked to the left and up as her hold on me slackened. She was listening to something I couldn't hear, cocking her head left and right as if tuning in.

She let go of me abruptly, causing me to stumble back and trip over the same object I had slid into that I still couldn't see in the semi-darkness. I sprawled to the ground, head over heels, as she turned and shouted something in Russian into the darkness. I sat up to see what was happening, but she was gone, just gone. No flicker of movement, no fleet figure through the darkness, just gone.

As I watched, the warehouse around me brightened, harsh industrial lighting glowing to life to illuminate a fully furnished living area being frantically packed up by a half dozen people, including the vampire who'd jumped me, Jordan. Svetlana had been blocking my perception of them, even blocking my hearing and preventing me from seeing them. Her power made me whimper in fear. Jordan turned to me and hissed, fangs bared, pure hatred burning in her eyes, but she was a servant and I could hold my own against her just fine. I glared back, blaming her for my whole situation.

The object I had been thrown into and stumbled over appeared out of the dimness, coalescing into the body of my land lord. He'd been bitten at least six times, probably drained completely, and left to rot on the warehouse floor. I recoiled, scrabbling crab-like away from the horror show uncovered by Svetlana's redirected attention, bile rising in my throat as I tried to put distance between me and his unfortunate remains.

Svetlana appeared in front of Jordan, just freaking appeared, and slapped her hard enough to spin her around and throw her to the ground. Jordan climbed to her knees, crawling and mewling in front of Svetlana like a kicked puppy. Her face, already a lurid red from my kick, was reddening on the other side from Svetlana's slap, but Svetlana ignored her, shouting in Russian at the other vampires. One of them, a very large dark haired man, had to be a Master, he was carrying a massive armoire alone, but I couldn't tell how many other vampires were in the room. Right before my eyes, things were being deconstructed and hauled through a double door in the back of the warehouse. They'd have the place cleaned out within a couple more minutes.

Svetlana appeared again right in front of me. It scared me, I had never seen a Master powerful enough to move like that, and I knew anyone gunning for her would be in deep trouble.

"Jamishka, I must go, and I cannot take you with me. Your angel friend knows you are here, and were I to take you with me, he would follow. Things as they are will test my powers to the limit if I am to get away. I will find you again, Jamishka, and we will explore the answers I wish to know. Think about them, think about them long and hard, because I get whatever it is I want or someone will die. I have infected you, Jamishka, and the only way you will live is as my servant. Think about your life, think about those you love, and decide if you truly wish to die. Call out into the night, and I will come to you."

She leaned down and kissed me, an ephemeral caress across my lips, and then she was gone, leaving nothing more than a few dust bunnies and my dead landlord in the warehouse and a swirl of her lilac perfume. I sighed, wondering who I had pissed off to deserve this day.

I walked out the double doors, pausing at the street, and finally slumped to a half crouched position against the outside of the building. I sat there, thinking SER should be here any second if Svetlana had been telling the truth, and hoping they would get here before something else happened.

Chapter 19: Recon

Jackson was awoken by a biting sensation on the left side of his chest. He rolled to the right, trying to escape the unpleasant sensation, when reason penetrated his sleep fog. Snapping his eyes open, his hand darting to the amulet resting on his chest, he sat up completely in the bed. The triangular knot amulet suspended on a slim silver chain was alternately burning and freezing, indicating Jamie being in extreme danger from a supernatural source and injured to boot.

Jackson looked over at his slumbering wife, hoping his movements hadn't awoken her, but she slept on, her eyes closed and her mouth slightly open. She looked peaceful. For the third time today, he needed to enter the aetheric, but if Akane woke and found him apparently asleep in his sanctuary, she'd ask questions he didn't want to deal with. He frowned, not wanting to use his Arts on her, but knowing it was easier than dealing with the alternative. He pulled air from without and water from the plumbing around him, weaving a simple sleep net and cast it over the house. Everyone would sleep until he released it, freeing him for his journey on the aetheric.

He rose stiffly, very tired from his earlier adventures, and wandered into his sanctuary. He'd neglected to secure the circle from his dinner time jaunt and all the candlesticks remained in the floor where he'd left them. Lighting them required a flick of his mind as he settled into the recliner, relaxing and allowing himself to enter a trance. His corporeal form released with a sudden lifting motion and he repeated his earlier steps to locate Jamie. This time, he flew toward her apartment, veering off at the last minute to approach a small warehouse on the edge of the Stapleton property.

The structure glimmered dully in the moonlight, streaks of red and black forming a netted dome over the entire structure. He frowned, staring at the structure as he floated closer to inspect it. Someone powerful had built a shield of fire and earth around this warehouse and he sensed the fire stained presences of several vampires, one very powerful.

As he probed the net, sending seekers of air and water through the filaments, fire alarms began to blare inside the structure, alerting the occupants to his presence. He sensed the attention of the most powerful vampire, a baleful flare of fire that almost sent him reeling. She was powerful, more powerful than he was at the moment, truth be told, and he wasn't sure he wanted to tangle with her right now.

Jamie was in there, of that he was sure, but how to get her out? Vampires usually went to great lengths to avoid the attention of the establishment, maybe it would be worthwhile to summon SER and allow them to deal with it. He hated doing that, someone was likely to be killed with a vampire this powerful, but if he provided support on the aetheric maybe he could occupy her long enough for them to get Jamie out.

He made a decision, rocketing back to his sanctuary to settle back into his corporeal form. As soon as he opened his eyes again, he reached for his phone, dialing the number for SER and tapping his fingers impatiently as it rang through.

"SER, this is Gina, how may I direct your call?" a woman's voice picked up after a couple rings.

"Hi, Gina, this is Jackson St. James, I need to talk to the officer in charge, please."

"Certainly, Mr. St. James, I'll connect you to Lieutenant Gibson's phone right away, please hold." The line clicked over to bland elevator music, a slow paced rendition of Don't Stop Believing. He rolled his eyes, impatient, but only a few moments passed before Gibson picked up.

"Gibson, how can I help you?"

"Hey Terry, it's Jackson, I think I have some information you might find, uh, enlightening."

"Oh yeah? How so?"

"I may have a lead in on that vampire activity McKinsey and Coleman uncovered. There's a warehouse in the Stapleton area you might want to check out and soon. Someone's in trouble and I'm sure she'd appreciate a little SER assistance." He gave Gibson the address and said his goodbyes, settling back into his recliner to reenter the aetheric and hopefully engage the vampire long enough to prevent her from killing anyone from SER.

The warehouse was just as he'd left it, surrounded in its fire and earth cocoon. This time, as he floated closer, he noticed a very fine gossamer web of fire, probably the source of the earlier alarm, so he floated higher to avoid it, but it was a complete dome. An inspection revealed little helpful information until he reached the apex of the dome. Reaching from the black and red protection shield to the gossamer red alarm shield was a tenuous connection. Most likely, any break in the alarm shield traveled through the monofilament and activated the alarm he'd heard earlier.

"Maybe I can bypass it," he thought out loud, hovering as close as he dared to inspect the connections. The alarm shield

wasn't pure fire, there was air mixed in to create a finer filament. Air was his, he was a master of its use, so maybe he could...

Drifting to the ground, he focused air into the strands intersecting the ground and gingerly pushed the strands upward a little at a time. After a few minutes, he had an opening about the size of a doorway and hadn't heard the alarm so he advanced through the shield to inspect the fire and earth shield. He'd never seen anything like it. Usually protection shields included air or water to help defend against more than one other element and to act as a binder, but inclusion of earth in this shield had created a matrix he wasn't sure how to unravel. Whoever this vampire was, she was very powerful.

Abruptly the shield began to writhe, the filaments twining around themselves like a nest of vipers, thinner strands reaching out to snap in his face. He backed away, uncertain what was happening, when the shield suddenly exploded, fire shrapnel flying in all directions. The shockwave blasted Jackson through the aetheric, tumbling him like a leaf in a hurricane, until he righted himself a short distance from the warehouse.

Inspecting his aetheric form, it seems he was undamaged, but when he made it back to the warehouse, all traces of magic were gone save the lingering smell of smoke. Puzzled, Jackson decided to take a risk and pass through the walls of the warehouse.

Inside there was nothing, simply an empty warehouse, but the auras remaining spoke of a large family of vampires who had been here for several months. There was no other trace of them now, nor a trail to tell him which way they had gone. Jamie was gone, too, but her aura trail led out to the street where SER had just arrived. Satisfied that she would be taken care, he allowed himself to be drawn back to his sanctuary and his warm bed with his wife.

Chapter 20: SER

I stood on the street for only a few minutes before red and blue lights streaked through the semi-darkness of the street, casting eerie glowing shadows on the buildings and the sidewalk, as SER screamed toward me, both vans tearing through the frigid air. They screeched to a halt in front of where I leaned heavily against Svetlana's former residence, four men in heavy riot gear pouring from the back of the first van, their maroon jumpers looking black in the frigid night. All four stopped about ten feet from me in a semicircle, leveling their rifles at me and shouting for me to put my hands on my head. I gaped at them, my mouth working silently like a fish struggling to breathe out of the water.

"McKinsey?" asked the second man from the left, looking like a square caricature of a person in his heavy body armor, his face mask an expressionless mirror. "McKinsey, what the fuck are you doing here?"

"Trying not to get shot," I gasped, leaning on the edge of the building and trying my best to put my hands on my head. My left arm screamed in protest, hot blood pooling in the cuff of my jacket, seeming to congeal and cool as I stood there. My head was swimming and shock was making me nauseous. Second from the left dropped his rifle, allowing it to slide on the sling to his side as he walked carefully toward me, pulling his riot mask up and revealing the heart shaped face of Sergeant Gibson. His blue eyes were crinkled in confusion, wariness warring with concern as he advanced slowly on me.

"Are you okay? Jackson called and told us the vampires you uncovered were here, but we didn't expect to find you. What happened?"

"Long story," I said as I sat down hard. All three of Gibson's men flinched, riding up on their triggers, and then relaxing as they realized I wasn't going to attack them. "Can we go to the doctor now, please? There's a vampire lurking around here and she bit me, I need to get to the hospital."

Gibson inhaled sharply, his breath hissing through his teeth as he realized what I said, his eyes flicking side to side like he expected the vampire to leap out of the darkness. All three of the others backed off a step, raising their M16s to point at me as if expecting me to grow fangs and go for their throats any second now.

"Sure," Gibson said, exchanging an unreadable look with the middle SER officer. Gibson advanced on me, warily, but I could tell he was trying. He helped me to my feet and led me limping to the maroon van with its lights still flashing red and blue in the darkness, careful to avoid my still bleeding arm. He helped me into the passenger seat of the van, barking at the driver to sit in back with the rest of the men, as he climbed into the driver's seat, shifted into drive and started down the street.

"What happened?" He finally asked after a couple minutes of silence. I was drifting in and out of consciousness, trying to keep from throwing up and starting to shake even worse than before. Oh, yeah, shock was great stuff.

"What hasn't happened today," I asked drolly. "I've been attacked by a ghoul, human purists, a servant, and a Master vampire in the last twenty four hours. This has to be the worst day I've ever had. I don't want to talk much about it, I have a feeling legal troubles are in my future and I don't want to talk without a lawyer present."

Gibson shot me a wounded look, but didn't reply, just grimly heading down the streets toward University of Colorado Health Sciences. They were the vampire experts in the area and right now, the vampire bite was my most pressing problem.

We pulled into the ambulance-only round about after a few more minutes of strained silence, pulling up to the covered entrance and gliding to a stop. Gibson got out and walked around the van, opening my door and helping me out with only a little wince when my bloody hand touched his. He knew Stoker-Dracul syndrome was less contagious than HIV but, when faced with the reality of contracting a deadly disease, a lot of people tend to forget what their head knows and go along with the fear in their hearts.

I was wobbly, probably resembling a baby giraffe, as I stumbled through the automatic double doors into the hospital ER. Gibson sat me down in a hard, navy-upholstered armless chair as he went to the desk to check me in. I looked around at the pale colored wallpaper and dark green Berber carpet, everything feeling unreal, as I tried to hold pressure to my bleeding arm.

There were two other people in the waiting room, a mother and daughter from the look of them. The mother was mid thirties, bleach blonde hair flat and unkempt from being woken up in the middle of the night by her very pale daughter. The daughter looked about like I felt, ashen with a confused look on her face and her hands twisted in a knot in her lap.

Her pink faerie pajamas were wrinkled, her blonde hair tangled, but she didn't look like she'd slept in a while. When she looked over at me, her eyes grew very large in her little face and she quickly buried her face into her mother's lap. Mom absently patted her head as she filled out a clipboard of forms, frowning at something in them and then scribbling something down.

I could hear Gibson talking in a low, urgent voice to the bored looking nurse behind the counter, but otherwise the waiting room was silent. The nurse was older, plump and motherly looking with her graying dark brown hair pulled into a severe bun on the back of her head. She was wearing green scrubs a size too big for her with no makeup, her face round and unremarkable. She listened to Gibson with a polite expression but her eyes widened as he explained what he knew about my injuries. She paled, her mouth slackening as she half rose to peer over the counter at me.

She picked up the phone and spoke urgently into it, gesturing wildly with her hands, as Gibson walked back to me with a grim expression on his face. He stopped about midway, a faint beeping coming from his belt, and a spasm of annoyance flashed across his beautiful blue eyes. He pulled his phone from his tool belt, scowling at the message, and replacing it in the holster as he resumed walking toward me.

"She's calling Dr. Schmitz," he explained, leaning over me and looking into my eyes with a worried expression. "She'll be in as soon as possible to see what she can do. In the mean time, she wants to admit you and see to your other injuries. I think you'll be at the head of the line, not too many people survive vampire attacks with only a bite," he said with a sardonic smirk. "I gotta run, apparently your vampire friend attacked someone else, they've called us back to the same area where we found you. I'll be back later to check on you, so don't do anything stupid like die before I get back. You think you'll be okay in the mean time?"

"Sure thing," I said thickly, my arms and legs feeling like lead and my eyes drooping. "Do me a favor, though, call Jackson and let him know I'm here, maybe he can call my mom for me."

"Sure thing," he replied. "Give me a ring if you're not in there in the next few minutes, I'll call Coleman, see if he can get down here and stir things up." He walked out, pulling his phone from his holster again and breaking into a light jog toward his van.

"McKinsey?" A new nurse was standing in the door to the right of the admittance window, this one young and fresh faced. She was blonde, average height and pretty but her bright smiled was strained, tugging at the corners of her eyes as she held the door open, looking at me expectantly. *Everyone thought I was already dead*, I realized as I dragged myself to my feet and started for the door. *Maybe they were right.*

She led me through the winding halls, getting my height and weight as we walked past the machines and then seating me on one of the beds and getting my blood pressure. She pulled the curtain closed with a last look of sympathy and walked off.

I struggled out of the remains of my coat, hissing as the elastic pressed on my bruised right fingers, and examined my left arm. In the harsh fluorescent lighting of the ER, it didn't look nearly as bad as I thought it would. Jordan's teeth had glanced off the splints, causing four long, shallow scratches leading to four deep punctures with some tearing around them in the muscle of my upper forearm. Most of the scratches had stopped bleeding, but the punctures were still leaking lurid red blood and my broken wrist had swollen to the size of a baseball. Vampires had an anticoagulant in their saliva so I knew the punctures would be bleeding for a while yet, especially after Svetlana sucked at them.

I hoped, prayed, begged I hadn't contracted Stoker-Dracul syndrome, but I knew it was very contagious from a bite from a Master. I'd heard rumors that a Master could infect or not infect a victim at will, and if that was true, Svetlana had infected me on purpose.

There really wasn't too much chance of me not contracting it, but there were isolated cases of people receiving antibody treatment in time to prevent the syndrome. No one knew if they wouldn't have contracted the syndrome with or without the antibody treatment, some people were naturally immune, but I'd never heard of a sensitive who was immune. Maybe I was the first. Yeah, and maybe I was the Queen of Sheba. I leaned back, intending to close my eyes for a minute, but I must have fallen asleep.

Chapter 21: Hospital

Soft white light spread across my world, turning the inky blackness a pearlescent gray, finally fading to a pure, white glow. I opened my eyes, stared at the white ceiling, listened to the soft beep of a heart monitor, and wondered what the Hell I was doing in a hospital. Everything came rushing back to me and I groaned.

I sat up quickly, too quickly, and my head started spinning again. I grunted, falling back to the mattress and closing my eyes again. After a moment, I opened them again, slowly sitting up this time. I was still in the ER, a white curtain pulled around my hospital bed, but someone had put an IV in my arm and a heart monitor under my gown while I had been sleeping. *Gown?* I thought, confused. I must have passed out, out cold enough for someone to stick me with an IV and change my clothes. There was something in the IV because I wasn't in very much pain any more, but the world was fuzzy and vaguely unreal. They had bandaged my arm, too, as well as put a temporary splint on my wrist.

A white sheathed arm was thrust through the opening in the curtain, pulling it back enough for a young man in a lab coat to slip through. He was in his early thirties, with copper red hair and grass green eyes; tall and handsome, with a shy smile and high cheek bones. Built like a swimmer, with long, strong limbs and a slender waist, he moved like a dancer, or would have. His right leg was twisted with his foot pointing out and he walked with a cane and a limp. Under his lab coat, he wore slacks and boat shoes, but his pants were well tailored and fit just right.

"Hey sleepy head, I'm Dr. Winston, how ya feeling?" he asked, flashing a shy smile and looking at the heart monitor. He frowned, bending down to get a better view of one of the machines, finally making a note on his clipboard.

"Ugh," I groaned, sticking my tongue out. "I fink dis is de ony ting dat doesn't urt." I said, making a face. Yeah, definitely something good in the IV. He laughed, a quiet chuckle, and limped a little closer to my bed.

"Tell me what happened, as much as you remember," he directed, pen ready. I told him as much as I could, as much as I thought I was allowed to without giving away too much of my case, as he diligently asked questions about my injuries.

"Has SER been called to the Purity building yet?" I asked anxiously, remembering there was a sorcerer on the loose.

"I don't know, I'll see if I can find out for you. Right now I'm just worried about you, I need to examine you, okay?" He shined a light in my eyes, in my ears, and down my throat, telling me to say ahh.

"Breathe deep," he said as he placed his stethoscope on my chest.

"Cold," I gasped.

"Hush," he replied. I inhaled as much as I could, squeaking when my injured ribs protested. He made me do it three more times with his stethoscope on my chest and then three times with it on my back. Next came my fingers, which involved flexing them over and over until I wanted to smack him in the head.

"We need to get you to x-ray," he said, making another note on the clipboard, "check your fingers and those ribs. I don't think you have a skull fracture, but we'll check it just to be sure. You definitely have a concussion, not too bad though, considering how many times you've been smacked in the head in the last couple days. I wish you'd been here sooner so I could stitch up that gash on your arm, but it's too late now, it's swollen too much. Your knee is okay, I think just bruised, stay off it for a couple days and it'll be fine.

"That bite is the major worry, I think, but there's nothing I can do about stitching it up or anything, it's too ragged and not deep enough to bother with. We'll test you for Stoker-Dracul syndrome, of course, but you know the results aren't always reliable. Otherwise, you seem to be in great health." He stood, patting my knee and smiling again as he made his way back through the curtain. I sighed, lying back onto the flat pillow and closing my eyes.

I must have drifted off again because the next thing I knew, they were wheeling me to x-ray. I suffered through their rearranging and fussing over me, still loopy from whatever was in my IV, and found myself back in the urgent care a little later.

"You're one mostly lucky girl, Jamie," it was Doctor Cutie again, leaning over the side of my bed and smiling at me. I hadn't heard him come in. Whatever was in that IV, it was great stuff. "You don't have a skull fracture and your ribs are just bruised. Your wrist, though, is broken, a fracture in your ulna. We're going to need to cast it."

"Great," I muttered.

His face fell, growing long and grim. "The bad news is we tested you for Stoker-Dracul and..."

"Shit," I breathed softly, my heart sinking into my toes. "What about antibody treatment?" I asked dully.

"Dr. Schmitz will be in a little later, you'd need to talk to her about it, she's our resident expert on vampire bites. We don't see them often, there's no standard technique we use but she didn't seem too worried, maybe she has a trick or two up her sleeve."

"Allison? Allison Schmitz? She's coming in?" God I hoped she had some good news for me, but I hadn't heard anything about it from her over lunches in the recent past. Maybe she couldn't tell me, maybe she didn't think I'd care, but right now it was on the very top of my list of things I was interested in.

"Oh, by the way," he said, "there's someone here to see you, I'll let him in if you're up to it?" he looked me in the face, staring me in the eyes and apparently making a decision. "I'll get him for you."

"Can you take out the IV first?" I asked, not liking the loopy feeling any more. I didn't fancy the idea of being a drooling idiot in front of anyone I knew.

"Sure," he reached over and turned off the machine controlling the drip and then reached down to start peeling the tape, shifting the needle in my vein. It didn't hurt, but it was a grinding, bizarre sensation, and it made me squirm. Gingerly, he pulled out the needle, quickly slapping a cotton ball over the wound, and then pasting a bandage over it. "There you are, no more needles. Do you want some ibuprofen, something stronger? I had them give you Demerol, but you'll come down off that pretty soon and then you'll be hurting, I think. I'll have them bring you a couple options, you can decide once you're off the Demerol and a little less loopy."

"K, thanks Dr. Cutie," I replied. My eyes widened and my face burst into flame as I realized I had said that out loud, instead of in my head. *God, I'm such a goober*, I thought. He smiled, flushing, and started for the slit in the curtain without replying.

Dr. Cutie passed back through the curtain, returning a minute later with Jackson. Jackson was wearing his usual tan Dockers and loafers, but with a royal purple t-shirt this time. His solemn face cracked into a huge smile as he saw me sitting up in the bed and he took my hand in his. I hadn't realized how big his hands were; they swallowed mine like a baseball glove, a very pale baseball glove. His other hand was behind his back, hiding something.

"Jackson! What are you doing here?"

"Checking on you, sister, glad we found you in time. I didn't think you'd get out and wander the streets, why didn't you call me? Or Coleman? Heck, your mom would've come to get you."

"I did, I called Coleman, but I needed to finish helping the pixie you led to me. Besides, I lost my phone," I mumbled.

"What was that, hun?"

"I lost my phone," I said more loudly, looking up at him, "and I couldn't remember anyone's number. That's what I have my phone for, you know?"

"Oh, you mean this phone?" he asked, pulling his other arm from behind his back. He was holding my purse, the black leather scuffed and dusty, but otherwise unscathed.

"You found it! Awesome!" I reached for my purse, pulling it from his hand and rummaging through it to see what they'd taken. Nothing seemed to be missing, even my revolver was in the back pocket. Phelps had apparently taken my purse and simply tossed it in the corner without searching it. Sloppy.

"We found your coat and boots too; I knew they were yours because your aura was on them. By the way, Coleman is waiting to talk to you. Phelps has made some really nasty accusations against you; you might be looking at some legal trouble." He moved his hand to my knee, probably unconsciously, a sympathetic expression on his long face.

"What?" I gasped, flabbergasted. "They kidnap me and I'm facing legal trouble? What the Hell?"

"Coleman knows her accusations are bogus, but Purity's pretty powerful, they have a bunch of lawyers on retainer and you may have a fight on your hands. She's accusing you of murder, witchcraft, all sorts of stuff. We caught her sorcerer red-handed, Coleman cuffed him personally and he's awaiting trial, but Phelps is denying any knowledge of his activities. She claims he was doing everything under her nose.

"McBarrister and Phelps claim you threatened both of them, accusing them of witchcraft and pulling a gun on them and then shooting two of their employees, killed one and wounded the other fairly grievously. The body of the one was contaminated, the crime scene is no longer viable so they aren't sure of what happened, but the wounded one isn't backing up Phelps' story. His story doesn't match yours exactly, but it's close enough you might be in the clear on a self-defense technicality. They're all in custody on my testimony of kidnapping, but McBarrister swears he knew nothing about it."

"McBarrister may not, I think it was Phelps who was behind it. She's formed a new group, a sub-group of Purity she calls

Total Purity. From what she said while I was in her, uh, care, they're pretty well off the deep end. She thought her pet sorcerer would be able to kill all the non-vanilla humans and she was going to kill me as an example to others like us."

"Hmm," he said, his arm crossed over his chest as he rested his elbow on his forearm and raised his hand to his mouth, resting his index finger on his upper lip, thinking. "Well, she's severely overestimated her pet sorcerer then, an old Master could handle a demon, much less what a King or Queen would do to it. I'm shocked she was willing to consort with a demon to achieve her ends. Guess that whole ends justifies the means idea was her modus operandi."

"Splendid," I grunted.

"Excuse me," it was someone outside the curtain, a woman from her voice. "I'm here to cast Ms. McKinsey's wrist. All visitors need to leave, she'll be released soon enough." An older latino nurse pushed her way through the curtain, giving Jackson a look calculated to hasten his departure. She was short, around five feet tall, with graying black hair and a wide, olive skinned face. Jackson left with a wry expression, using his hands to signal that he would be back when she was done.

"Here you are, dear, ibuprofen and acetaminophen or I can give you some Percocet. What would you rather have?" I didn't like opiates, they made me throw up and I'd done plenty of that in the last few hours. They didn't really do a whole for my pain anyway.

"Ibuprofen and acetaminophen please," I said. "Can I get a Coke too? It helps if I take them with caffeine."

"Of course dear. Let me get your wrist cast and then I'll see if I can track one down for you." She busied herself with wrapping my wrist with linen and then fiberglass resin impregnated linen. She hummed softly, her hair flopping as she applied pressure to the cast until it set. "There we are, mija, let me go see if I can find that Coke for you. If I can't find a Coke, is Pepsi okay?"

"Sure," I replied, flexing my fingers and wishing they'd put a metal plate in the cast. Then I could hit people with it if I needed to. I sighed, starting to feel every little bruise as the effects of the Demerol faded. People discount bruises, but they really hurt in a draining, soul grinding sort of way.

The nurse came back a minute later, bearing a nice cold Coke. I popped the top with a sharp hiss, swigging the soda down with all four pills, grimacing at the burn of carbonation. Bolting back the rest of the soda, I swung my legs off the side of the bed, wanting to stand. My nurse clucked at me, pushing me back onto the bed and shaking her finger.

"No, no," she admonished, "not until Dr. Winston says it's okay. Stay in the bed please." She split the curtain and left with a final look of reproach. I sighed again. Great. I sat back, waiting for Jackson to return, but when the curtains parted once again, it wasn't Jackson, but Coleman instead.

"Hey kiddo," he said, looking me over from head to foot. "How ya feeling?"

"Like I imagine your punching bag feels after a workout," I quipped.

He chortled, a white grin splitting his dark face. "You look better than my punchin' bag, ain't really much to see. Heard you got another good conk on the head, how many fingers am I holding up?" He held up two fingers, then three, then back to two, smirking.

"Which one of you?" I asked. He laughed, shaking his head. "Okay, I gotta get your side of the story, we're holdin' Phelps on kidnapping charges but she's made a lot of accusations 'gainst ya I need to clear up. I already reported what ya said before I dropped ya off at your place, you're gonna have to tell me what the Hell that was about someday, but right now we gotta get your side of things. I brought SER's lie detector, but I gotta have your consent to bring'em in. We tried it with Phelps but she said she ain't gonna be near a freak like him, much less let'em touch her. That okay? If so I gotta have you sign this paper," he slid me a single page paper with small print and a pen. I read it through, seeing it was standard release form, and signed it with a flourish.

"Wouldn't work on her anyway," I grumbled. "She's not a sensitive, he wouldn't be able to read her well enough to say for sure if she was lying or not."

"True, but don't tell her that," he replied. "Be right back, sit tight." He left, returning a few moments later with a heavyset Asian man. He was short; around five foot two, and heavy at about one hundred sixty pounds with a round face and a heavy epicanthic fold to his eyes. His thin, almost lipless mouth was set in a hard line, while his eyes darted back and forth constantly. His black hair was shot with gray, receding, and he was clean shaven. I noticed his gray collared shirt was clean, starched, and ironed and his black slacks were clean and lint free over his shiny black shoes.

"Jamie, this is Thomas Teung, he's on our payroll for his psychic talents. I'll let'em take over from here," Coleman ducked out again, disappearing through the curtain.

"Hi Thomas, how are you?" I asked, not extending my hand. Offering to shake hands with a known psychic was very rude.

"Good," he replied shortly, taking a deep breath and letting it out in a rush. "Let's get started." Thomas reached out with his right hand to touch my right hand, gently at first then harder, pressing as much of his flesh to mine as he could. His hands were clammy, cold and slippery. It could be very trying to use psychic talents like Thomas' from what I understood, so he needed to work up to it. He shuddered, snapping his eyes open.

"Relax your mind," he instructed. I settled back on the hospital bed, trying to think about soothing things. I felt him enter my mind, sliding in like a lover, and I stiffened. *Don't fight me,* said a thought in my head. I relaxed, knowing I could throw him out with a thought, and allowed him to do what he needed to do.

"Okay, I'm ready. Please reiterate everything you have experienced, no matter how trivial, over the last few days and I will ask my questions as things progress." I repeated my experiences, glossing over nothing and trying my best to be completely truthful. He asked pointed questions periodically, some of which made me squirm, but I knew he was trying to help. Finally, he starting asking me questions pertaining to the accusations made by Phelps and I answered them as truthfully as I remembered.

After what seemed like hours, he began to withdraw his mind from mine with a feeling similar to the sensation of the needle coming out of my arm. He dropped my hand with a sharp motion and I opened my eyes to look at him. He looked the same, but the tightness around his mouth had gone and he was more relaxed.

"Thank you, Jamie, you have nothing to worry about I think. All the accusations against you are without merit, you were acting in self-defense, and the police department will handle things from here. You may be called to testify, but Ms. Phelps will be looking at significant jail time. Mr. Stevens and young Mr. O'Leary were acting as mercenaries, their actions were illegal in the US and their charges are bogus. Let me just add, I don't ever want to be on your bad side, Jamie. Good day to you, I'll be in touch." With that, he walked through the curtain and was gone. *That was abrupt*, I thought, laying back once again.

Chapter 22: Allie

"Jamie?" came a soft voice from outside the curtain.

"Allie?"

Allison Schmitz pushed through the curtain, shooting me a tremulous smile and gliding over to lean on the edge of the bed. Allison was tiny, not more than five feet tall and slender with huge dark eyes and an oft smiling face. Her smile was her blank look, not really meaning anything, but it tended to put me at ease most of the time anyway. Her oval face was flawless, smooth and lovely framed by her waves of chestnut hair. She never wore makeup, too practical for that mess, but she didn't need it. Her lips were full and red and her nose petite with a slight upturn. But her eyes, her eyes were what drew the boys in, large and dark as night, they grabbed your attention and made you think she could read your deepest thoughts. Unfortunately for her suitors, she wasn't interested, not just in men, not in women either; she lived for her work and didn't care about much else. She was not a sensitive, although her mother and her younger sister had been, probably why a Master had targeted her family.

Tonight she was dressed casually, expensive jeans and a fitted blue t-shirt under her black leather waist length coat with knee high black leather riding boots. I envied her easy style, but knowing I didn't have the natural gifts to pull it off, I didn't even try. She looked me over from head to toe, patting my leg softly and then knitting her fingers together in front of her waist.

"Finally got the worse end of the deal messing with the monsters, huh?" she asked, arching a shapely eyebrow and looking me in the eye. Reaching over to the med cart on the wall, she pulled a pair of purple gloves from a small bag and slipped them on with two deft motions. They were too big, wrinkling around her little manicured hands.

"Yeah," I sighed, grinning ruefully. "Problem is, this whole mess started when I went to talk to the humans first whackos. Most of this is their handy work. Seems I'm lucky to be alive, I wouldn't be if Phelps had her way.

"I don't know where the vampire came from, Denver's usually pretty good at keeping families out of the city, but she wasn't shy. Hungry," I shrugged, raising my arm up for her to see, "but not shy."

Allison grabbed my arm, not replying, and peeled the bandage back to get a better look at the bite wounds. All but one puncture had quit bleeding but the whole area was an angry red and was starting to swell. Not a good sign. She poked into one of the punctures with her finger, squeezing until it started to bleed a little again, and then stretching the skin away from the puncture. Pursing her lips, she put her hands on either side of the wounds and slid the skin together, creating a mound of swollen flesh between her hands. I hissed in pain and she flicked her gaze to mine, quickly returning it to the wound. Black-red blood was oozing from most of the wounds at this point, but she didn't seem to notice it. Finally, she slapped the bandage back over the wound and slid up onto the bed, peeling the gloves from her hands and throwing them into the biohazard bag by the bed. Wiping her hands on her jeans, she gave me a sympathetic look.

"And your tests came back positive?" she asked, examining her fingernails and not looking into my eyes.

"Yeah," I sighed, "but they said you'd have options. If anyone can do something, you can, right?" I asked, putting my hand on her shoulder and turning her to face me. She wouldn't meet my eyes and my heart plummeted through the floor.

"So I'm dead, then?" I whispered, starting to tear up.

"No..." she drawled, looking at the floor. "There's other options..."

"But..?" I prompted, slightly irritated and getting more annoyed with her. It's not like we were talking about what options I had for dinner tonight.

"I need to clear it first," she said mysteriously, still not looking at me. "You've got a little time before things get desperate, so hang tight, I may have options."

"What the Hell do you mean, hang tight?" I yelled, my voice shrill with ire as I leveraged myself to a half sitting position. She shushed me, finally looking me in the face and raising a finger to her lips in silent warning.

"It's experimental and if I give it to you without their approval, I'll lose all my funding and you might lose your life," she hissed lowly.

"Whose approval? What are you talking about?" I said, grabbing her arm and trying to pull her closer. She twisted against my bruised fingers and I let go with a hiss of pain.

"I need to go," she said, detangling herself from me and picking up her purse. "I'll have an answer soon, before there's any damage, you'll be okay for a week or so. I need to contact them," she concluded, walking out through the curtain without another word.

"Contact who?" I shouted at her retreating back but she didn't answer. I lay back in the bed, scared and irritated, but I knew Allie wouldn't leave me hanging if she had any other option. Svetlana's option was there too, lurking at the corner of my mind like a stalker in the night.

I laid back, thoroughly drained, and promptly fell asleep again.

Someone was shaking my arm, softly calling my name, as I struggled awake. It didn't feel like I had slept long, but I felt better for it. Jackson was standing on the edge of the bed, dangling a paper in front of me tauntingly with a grin on his solemn face.

"Know what this is?" he asked as I reached for it. He pulled it away, smiling.

"Come on Jackson, gimme the release papers, I need to go home and sleep," I complained, making a grab for it and missing again. He chuckled and handed it to me along with a pen. I signed it and passed it back to him, shifting around so my legs dangled from the edge of the bed. Everything hurt, but I wasn't going to let that stop me, I had a case to solve. Glancing around, I realized I had no clue what they had done with what remained of my clothes and I sure as heck wasn't walking out of here in the hospital gown with my butt on display for everyone to see.

Jackson saw me looking around and raised a finger without saying a word. He disappeared through the curtain, returning a moment later with a pair of jeans and a t-shirt. They were my spares from the office, I kept a set of clothes there just in case. I grinned at him, thankful for good friends, and then gave him a pointed look. He laughed, raising his hands in surrender and leaving once more.

Dressing myself was a challenge, I never realized how much I used my core until I couldn't and my left arm was almost useless. Even my right hand wasn't completely usable so it took almost three times as long to get dressed as it should have. Zippering up my boots, I slipped on my trench coat, and grabbed my purse to limp through the curtain. Jackson was waiting for me at the door, jangling his keys in his hand. He saw me coming and fell into step with me, sticking close to me in case I fell, but I was doing better than I thought I would be.

Jackson led me out to the parking lot and his blue Volvo parked near a street lamp. It was still dark, a frigid knife's edge breeze blowing from the east, as we eased out onto the main street and headed back to my apartment. I used the time to tell

Jackson everything that had happened, down to the vampire waiting in my living room and Svetlana's offer to convert me. After I finished, he stayed silent for a long moment, apparently thinking.

"So what are you going to do?" he asked softly, eyes intent on the road, purposefully not looking at me.

"I haven't decided," I said, equally softly, startled at the truth in my statement. If I'd been asked forty eight hours ago, I'd have said unequivocally I'd never choose to be a vampire, but staring death in the face had cast doubt on that decision. I didn't want to die, especially not slowly and painfully as I would with Stoker-Dracul syndrome.

"What did Allison say?" he asked gently. I felt my anger rising at her mysterious behavior, but I smashed it down with all my will power.

"She didn't say much, just something about she needed to talk to someone and she'd let me know. She was really mysterious, it kinda irked me."

"Nothing else? No experimental treatment or anything?"

"Nothing, it was really odd, not like Allie at all."

We'd reached my apartment by now so Jackson pulled into the handicap parking spot in front of my apartment building. He flipped on the blinkers and came around to help me out of the car, but I waved him off. I'd do it myself or die trying. I finally managed to lever myself up by the time he lost patience with me, so he went and opened the door to the foyer as I made my way gingerly up the stairs.

"Wait," he called, pulling the door closed behind him and then closing his eyes. He hummed a tuneless melody as I stared at him, confused. After a moment, he opened his eyes and gave me a thumbs-up.

"All clear, no vampires this time," he said, turning to leave. He paused, turning back to me and shooting me a quizzical look. "You going to be okay alone?"

"I'll be fine, shoo. I need some sleep and I'm not likely to get it with you around. Get!" He grinned good-naturedly, pulling the door closed and locked behind him. My front door was still locked, I noticed, as I fumbled with the keys and finally got it open.

I dropped my purse on the shelves to my right, struggling out of my coat and hanging it on the back of the door, as I bent stiffly to unzip my boots, kicking them off in the entryway. I eyed the stairs, wondering if my bed was worth the effort or if I should just crash on the couch. *Bed, totally the bed*, I thought as I walked stiffly up to my bedroom, turning on every light on my way up. I could afford to leave the lights on, much better than having someone waiting for me again. Paranoid, yes, even if Jackson had said it was clear, Svetlana might be powerful enough to keep him from sensing her.

Fortunately, there was no one, I was alone. My bed was a mess, I never made it after I got up, so I just crashed down in the middle of it, clothes and all, pulling the covers up over my shoulders. I was out within a couple moments.

Chapter 23: Dead Cows

I woke without really knowing why, groggy and unsure as to where I was, in a lot of pain. My ribs ached with every movement and my right hand was a twisted claw of bruises. My head felt like a piñata at a birthday party. I groaned, rolling over and catching the afternoon sun full in the face. I cursed, curling into a fetal ball under my covers and hating my life. I sighed, struggling out of the covers and staggering like a drunk to the bathroom. My knee almost gave out more than once, but eventually I made it to the bathroom. Four Advil and two Tylenol later, I crawled back into bed and tried to go back to sleep.

I gave up after half an hour, feeling better with the pain medicine, and decided to have a shower, which went much better than I thought it was going to. Clean, awake, and in less pain than a few minutes ago, I glanced over at the clock and realized it was mid-afternoon and I was ravenous.

Another thirty minutes later, I had dunch (linner?) consisting of two French bread pizzas and a Coke as I sat down on my couch to eat. Halfway through my second pizza, the very faint sound of my cell phone ringing from my purse caught my attention. I thought seriously about letting it ring, but I knew anyone who knew my number would be someone I probably wanted to talk to. Grunting, I retrieved my purse and pulled the phone out in time to take the call. It was Kristen from my office and I didn't know why she'd be calling.

"Hello?" I said, cradling the phone against my shoulder so I could finish my pizza.

"Hey, Jamie, it's Kristen. Listen, I've got Mr. Bateman on the phone, he says he's going out to the pasture where his cow was killed and he wanted to know if you want to go with him. Should I tell him you're busy or do you want to go? Full moon's in a couple days, might not get another chance to go." Her voice was strained, almost like she was forcing cheer for my benefit.

"Shuwe," I said through a mouth full of pizza, not willing to dwell on things the way they stood.

"How's that again?" she asked, confused.

I swallowed hard, almost choking on the bite. "Sure," I replied again. "Tell him I'll be up there in about half an hour if that's okay."

"He said he'd wait for ya, take your time, I'll let him know you're on your way. And Jamie?" Her voice was sad and it almost sounded like she'd been crying, "I'm really sorry, I hope something comes up for you, some treatment from Dr. Schmitz. You can't have SDS, you just can't!" Now she was crying for sure and I didn't have any idea what to say to reassure her. Tell her I was seriously thinking about letting Svetlana convert me, even though it meant servitude and doing things I didn't want to do? I couldn't tell her that, she'd never understand, and besides, I hadn't made any decision yet.

"It'll be okay," I said awkwardly, knowing it wouldn't but not sure what else to tell her. She snuffled and hung up without another word, the phone just going dead in my hand. I shrugged, uncomfortable with her sudden emotion, and stuffed the rest of the pizza in my mouth, chasing it with Coke. I had to get dressed if I was going to make it to Brighton in my self-allotted half an hour.

I pulled on some bootcut jeans and a long sleeved black round necked t-shirt along with a pair of black hiking boots, ran a brush through my hair, and added a little powder to even my skin tone. Nothing too complicated, I was going to a farm after all, but I didn't want to look like a complete disaster. I caught a glimpse in the mirror and jumped at the stranger staring back at me. Pain and abuse had aged my face ten years, deep lines around my eyes and mouth making me look like my mother. I was pale as a sheet, lurid circles under my eyes and a drawn look to my pale pink lips. I sighed, pulling out my concealers and doing my best to cover the dark circles. After a few layers and a nice dark lip stain, I looked almost human.

I made sure to lock my door, consciously turning the key, grabbing my short leather jacket from behind the door as I left. I headed to my car, checking to make sure my revolver was in the back pocket of my purse and my 45 was secure in its holster in the small of my back before I started the engine.

Twenty minutes later, I pulled into the driveway of the address on Mr. Bateman's card. Driving had been interesting with a bruised hand, a broken wrist, and a fading concussion, but I'd managed. Mike walked out to meet me, dressed in his working clothes, basically the same outfit I'd met him in but much more worn. Broken in and faded blue jeans, a faded red and white flannel under his heavy black canvas coat, tan work boots stained with mud (I hoped). He had the same green and yellow John Deere cap on and was grinning a welcoming smile. He approached my car with his hand outstretched, intending to shake my hand, when he noticed my cast. His face fell and along with it his outstretched hand, concern replacing his smile.

"Dang, girl, what happened to you?" he asked, eying me up and down.

"Rough night," I replied, trying to shrug it off. I really, really didn't want to explain everything that had happened; afraid I might break down into tears if I was forced to meet my situation head on. "No worries. You ready to head out to the pasture, or's there something we need to do first?" I asked, forcing a casual atmosphere.

He looked at me for a moment, not sure if he wanted to push things, and deciding to take my false joviality at face value.

"Let's get a move on then," he replied cheerily, turning to head for his barn, a huge red structure straight out of the movies. Parked inside was a Honda MUV with the canopy removed, ready for us to head out. I climbed stiffly into the passenger seat, but Mike had enough sense not to try and help me, instead climbing into the driver seat and cranking it up. It was quieter than I thought it would be, not even loud enough to block our conversation.

"Anything new happen?" I asked as he eased the MUV out of the barn and then hit the gas once we were on the trail.

"Nope, not on my land, but my neighbor says one of his cows had the same thing happen to her, real similar kinda thing. He didn't think about it being a werewolf so he just wrote it off as a puma or somethin'. When he heard about mine, we thought maybe they was connected. I'll take you by his place, too, see if you can get anything from that kill." I sat back in the seat, trying not to show how much the jostling from the rough trail was hurting my ribs, and closed my eyes.

"You sure you're okay, darlin'? We can do this another time if you're in a bad way," he said, looking at me from the corner of his eye.

"I'm good," I lied, not willing to go home and mope. I needed to be out and doing something, not pining away alone in my apartment, and I had no idea where to go with the Johanson case. So, here I was, trying to find out what had killed Mike's cow.

We rode in silence for a while, me because I was hurting, Mike because he didn't know what else to say. Eventually, we reached an isolated field, grown high with winter grass due to lack of use and layered in a thick blanket of snow. The stench of death was strong, even in the frigid January air, and I knew something big had died close by. We rode next to the fence for a few yards then cut left into the field, the stench getting stronger the closer we got to the left end of the field.

As we approached the site, a small dog-like animal took off running from the carcass. *A coyote*, I thought, startled. Mike didn't react so I figured it was likely not out of the ordinary out here. We stopped a couple yards from the grisly scene, Mike climbing out and holding a hand to his nose and coming around to offer me his other hand. For once, I swallowed my pride and allowed him to help me out of the MUV, gasping at the pain in my, well, everywhere.

He'd been right; the cow was torn to mutilated bits. I didn't want to get too close, I didn't need to see the whole thing to know if something supernatural had done this. I pulled a compact with a silver backed mirror from my purse, flipping it open and turning my back to the carnage to get a better view of the scene through the mirror.

"There's definitely an aura," I said, slightly surprised there was anything left after so long. The aura swirled around the scene, a faint green phosphorescence like the blush of a new spring, laced through with smoke-like darkness throughout.

"Definitely lycanthrope," I commented distractedly, turning to see if I could tell what direction it had come from. Mike stiffened as I said it, turning to look apprehensively at the nearby copse of cottonwood trees. I couldn't tell what direction the aura led from, the lycanthrope had spent a lot more time mutilating the cow so the aura was much stronger here.

"You said there was a trail when you first found her, what direction was it from?" I asked, snapping the mirror closed and turning to face him.

"There," he said simply, pointing at the copse of cottonwood trees a dozen yards away. I turned to head for the little glade, keeping an eye out for any tracks or broken twigs along the way, but there was nothing. I suspected I wasn't on the trail he had found, but he did nothing to change my course as I struggled through the high, snow covered grass, my head, knee, and ribs screaming and a grim expression on my face.

I reached the copse of trees, and realized the trees were much larger than I had suspected, ranging from twenty feet to probably close to sixty feet tall. A small creek ran gurgling over round rocks through the center of the trees, clear and cold as ice. Standing amongst the trees, their leafless limbs stretched toward the sky like skeletal fingers rattling in the slight breeze. I shivered, suddenly cold.

Pulling my mirror from my pocket, I flipped it open again and spun to take in the small glade. I didn't see anything, no aura, no tracks, nothing interesting. Grunting, I turned to Mike straggling behind me, seeing the apprehension in his face as he approached the trees.

"Did you come this far over to look for tracks?" I asked, searching the area between the trees and the field.

"Yep, didn't find nothing else."

I spun in a circle, holding the mirror high and low, but there was no aura. Either the lycanthrope hadn't come through right here, or the trail was too old for me to sense anything.

"What about there?" Mike said suddenly from behind me. I jumped, spinning, and then wobbling, to see him pointing into a very large tree on the edge of the field. One of its branches, big enough to be a tree unto itself, was hanging out over the edge of the field, drooping to within ten feet of the ground. I frowned, spinning again to put my back to the limb and bringing my mirror down to waist level and angling it so I could look up into the tree.

"Bingo," I said, excited. "You're a genius, Mike, he must have climbed through the trees and then taken off into the field to grab your cow."

"Yeah," he replied absently, pulling on his chin with his left hand. "Also explains why he only got one of 'em here, the rest would've run at his scent, I bet. Let's head back, you ain't lookin' so hot and I got a pot of coffee brewing back at the house, we can warm up there."

"What about your neighbor's cow?" I asked distractedly, surveying the area for a good vantage to set up my rifle when the full moon arrived in a couple days. There was a small hillock about one hundred yards from the copse of trees, enough I could hide behind and set up my tripod to shoot from. If this was the lycanthrope the sheriff had set up the bounty on, it'd be a nice bump to my bank account.

"You can see it if you want, it's gonna be the same as this one. I just thought maybe you'd had enough tramping around my fields."

"I'd better," I said, not looking forward to the trip. We climbed back into the MUV and headed through the field and across another before arriving at another grisly scene. This one was very similar to the first, the smell of barnyard death strong on the wind. I found the aura again, green and black, and that was enough to convince me it was the work of the same lycanthrope. HBV sufferers were rare enough that having two different lycanthropes kill two cattle this close together was very unlikely.

We headed back to the MUV, my head and ribs spasming almost continuously, and drove our bumpy way back to his house. Mike didn't say much on the way back, apparently deep in thought, and it gave me time to think about my situation. My mind kept shying away from the reality of the situation, but I knew I'd need to make a decision and soon.

Svetlana's option hung heavy in my mind, a black cloud of temptation I wanted to ignore, but couldn't. I hoped Allie had an option, but she had been so mysterious about anything she could do that I wasn't sure I wanted to count on it. She said I had a week, but I knew of cases where the symptoms of SDS had started cropping up within a couple days. One of the first was moral erosion, the ability to choose between right and wrong. SDS ate at the areas of the brain responsible for empathy and sympathy first, hence the reason so many vampires were complete psychopaths. They didn't see their prey as anything but sheep and they didn't care about them in any meaningful way.

I wasn't sure I wanted to live like that, but I knew I didn't want to die. I wondered how long I would remain a good person, if I was even now, if I didn't have something in my head telling me right from wrong.

"Here ya go," Mike said as we pulled back into his barn to park the MUV. I climbed stiffly out, wondering if it was time for more pain meds, and followed him into his house. We kicked our shoes off at the door, a painful process for me, and entered his foyer.

"Can I get ya some coffee? Hot chocolate?" He asked, leading me into his living room and inviting me to take a seat. He had a lovely home, rustic rough-wood couch and loveseat upholstered in blue canvas and dark oak hard wood floors with a well-worn Lazyboy by an old CRT TV set. Pictures on the walls showed two young men, spitting images of their dad, and a lovely brunette woman who'd have to be their mother, among other family members. I levered myself down onto the couch, digging through my purse for my painkillers.

"Hot chocolate, please," I said, pulling my Advil out and shaking some into my hand.

"Marshmallows?" he asked, disappearing around the corner.

"Sure."

He returned a moment later, bearing two white coffee cups, one with black coffee the other with my hot chocolate. He handed mine to me, cautioning that it was hot, and sank into the rocking chair. Blowing across the surface, I waited for it to cool, as Mike sipped his coffee.

"What kind of were-beastie you think it is?" he asked, glancing over the rim of his cup at me.

"Can't say for sure, but I'd guess werewolf or coyote, maybe mountain lion based on the tree climbing. More than likely something native to the area, so probably not tiger or lion or something," I said, taking a sip of my hot chocolate and burning my tongue. It was good, though, not from a mix, I didn't think. Taking a swig after it had cooled a little more allowed me to swallow my pills with a grimace, but I sipped the rest slowly, savoring the sweet cocoa taste.

Mike grunted, sipping his coffee, and staring out the window.

"How did you want to take him out?" he asked at length, not meeting my eyes.

"There's a hillock in the first field we went to, I'm going to set up my rifle there and take him when he comes back. Can you drive me out there in a couple nights? He won't return 'til the full moon, but he had a good enough meal last time that he's likely to come back."

"Sure thing, you just give me a buzz when you want to head over and we'll go set up for it. Should I leave a cow out there, like as bait or something, or just leave it empty?" he asked thoughtfully, his glance flicking to me and then out the window again.

"Yeah, that's a good idea, he's more likely to come back if there's prey in the field. We know where he came from, I promise I'll get off my shot before he gets one of the cows and if not, I'll pay you for it," I offered, staring forlornly at the bottom of my empty cup.

"No worries there, covered by insurance, I ain't worried about it too much."

I stood, wobbling a little before I got my balance back, and pulled my jacket back on.

"I should get going," I said, turning to pick up my purse. "You've probably got stuff to do, milking or feeding or something, and I've taken enough of your time."

He stood along with me, taking my empty cup from me and putting it on the coffee table in the middle of the room, as he guided me to the door. He thanked me for coming out to look at the cow and promised to be on the lookout for my call, shutting the door quietly behind me as I walked to my car. I pulled out of his driveway, heading back to the interstate, thinking of what I should do next. It was already getting dark and I hadn't heard from Allie or Jackson, but I really didn't have any other leads on the Johanson case so I was at a loss for where to go from here.

Chapter 24: Revelation

I was restless, nervous energy and worry making me antsy as I made my way through rush hour traffic back home.

"Purity is innocent when it comes to kidnapping Adora if not many other things," I mused out loud, waiting in I-25 traffic on my way home. "So who...?" I trailed off, thinking of something Svetlana had said and going cold. "Stupid girl, she was not kidnapped. Her idiot husband does not know of what he speaks. Drop the case, you have no idea what you deal with," Svetlana had said. She'd seen Adora with someone named Erick, maybe her Master, on Saturday, the same day the note had been delivered. Had she been rescued and no one told me? Irked, I pulled out my phone and fished through my bag for Harold Johanson's card, dialing with one hand and driving with my knees.

"Hello, Harold Johanson's office, how may I direct your call?" came a soothing female voice. I jerked back, expecting to reach his phone directly, momentarily startled.

"This is Jamie McKinsey, may I speak to Mr. Johanson please?" I asked, politely.

"One moment Ms. Mckinsey," she replied, the line going dead for a few moments. "He's expecting your call but he's on another business call right now, would you like to call back or may I put you on hold?" she asked. I snorted, wishing our secretary was as professional, but then decided she'd get walked all over in our business if she was.

"I'll wait," I said, with nothing better to do while sitting in traffic.

"Certainly," she replied as the line cut over to poorly performed cover music. I rolled my eyes at the muzak cover of Eye of the Tiger and waited. Finally, after what seemed like years, Johanson's smooth voice came on the line.

"Jamie, nice to hear from you, I heard you ran into a little trouble dealing with Purity, is everything all right?" he asked, concern in his voice. *How the Hell did he know that?* I thought, astonished.

"Uh, sure, yeah, everything's fine," I stuttered. Marshalling my thoughts, I managed to get back on track just as he spoke again.

"I'm certainly glad to hear that," he was saying, "and if you need some legal council, I have some excellent lawyers on retainer, I can include their services as part of your finder's fee. You wouldn't have been there had it not been for me. Now tell me, your good news. It's good news, right?" I could almost hear the arched eyebrow over the phone and I exhaled loudly.

"Actually, no, I don't, you just answered the question I was calling to ask you. So you haven't seen Adora?" "No, I have not. Why? Have you found something?" he asked, voice suddenly tense.

"Maybe, it's just... I'm not sure how things fit together yet, an old... acquaintance I ran into mentioned seeing Adora on Saturday night. She swears Adora hasn't been kidnapped, and she was shocked I would even suggest it." "An acquaintance?" he asked, sarcasm thick in his voice. "Just who is this mysterious acquaintance? It wouldn't have anything to do with the vampire who bit you last night, would it?" My mouth flapped like a fish, shock temporarily stealing my words.

"How the Hell did you know about that?" I demanded, starting to get angry.

"My associate, Dr. Winston, informed me when you were admitted to the ER," he replied, matter of fact. "I take an interest in any Illegal activity in the city and a vampire bite is a strong indicator of vampire activity in the area. He reports to me whenever a case involving an Illegal crosses his path."

I snorted again, really irritated at how much Johanson apparently knew about me, and wary. If he was so well connected, why had he hired me to find Adora? Surely he could do better with his contacts than my bumbling had so far.

"Has Adora ever mentioned someone named Erick to you?" I asked, switching tactics. This time it was his turn to remain quiet, apparently thinking things through before he answered.

"Yesss..." he said slowly, drawing the ess out and hesitating again. "She mentioned an Erick she met at the Denver Art Museum gala, an exhibit of some local artist. She seemed quite taken with him, talking at length about their common interests." I could hear the frown in his voice as he continued. "Why? Does this Erick have something to do with her kidnapping? Who is he?" he demanded, his voice heating.

"I don't know for sure, I need to make some calls," I hedged, thinking quickly. I didn't want to tell him my budding suspicions, not yet, not until I had some proof. "I'll be in touch, and probably soon. Is there a better number I can reach you on?"

"No, this is the best number," he replied curtly, apparently irritated with my dodging his questions. "I look forward to hearing from you soon, Jamie, remember time is of an issue," and he hung up. I stared at the phone, thinking *how rude* as traffic began to break up, and I eased off onto the exit for my apartment. I needed backup for what I was planning, I couldn't handle Svetlana and her Master by myself in any known universe. Hopefully, I could reach another hunter I'd worked with in the past and have him come back me up.

As I pulled into my garage, killing the engine and gathering my things, my phone rang. It was Allie, her pert face grinning back at me from my screen.

"Allie? Hey, what's up?" I answered, juggling my purse and my keys to unlock the door and head up to my apartment.

"Jamie, thank goodness, I have an answer for you, and I need you to come down to Colorado Health Sciences right now."

"What?" I asked, bewildered. "An answer to what? Why do I need to come down to the hospital? It's rush hour!" "I know," she snapped, "but you need to come down here now, I've got approval to try an experimental therapy on you, but I need you in the hospital in case something goes wrong."

"Whoa, whoa, whoa, I didn't give you approval to try an experimental therapy on me, what kind of experimental?"

"Just meet me down here, as soon as you can, please? I'll tell you more when you get there, I need to prep the treatment," she said and promptly hung up.

"What the heck is with rude people today?" I mused out loud, shaking my head and walking into my apartment. I needed to call Kris Delaroux before I went to the hospital, I wanted to get moving on my theory as soon as possible. I had his phone number in my phone, but sometimes he took a while to get back to me. I thumbed through my phonebook, finding his number and hitting send as I kicked off my boots and wandered to the kitchen to get a Coke.

He picked up on the third ring, surprising me. "'Ello, this is Kris, how ken I help ya?"

"Hey Kris, it's Jamie, you got a minute?"

"Sure, darlin', anythin' for you, what's happenin'?"

"I think I've got a line on a vampire nest here in Denver, but I think there's going to be at least two Masters in there and I need some help," I said, straight to the point. He whistled, low and soft, but didn't reply immediately.

"Jamie, darlin', you always did like pokin' de gator's snout, I'm in, but I need more info. Come ta think of it, hun, with at least two Masters you should call van der Slavv, he the one you need in a scrape. I be dere for you with my skills, but two Masters is a tough one."

I hmm and hawed, not really wanting to call Morgan van der Slavv, he really creeped me out.

"Nah," I said, making the decision. "We don't need Morgan, we'll be okay I think. I think I'm gonna call SER, give them a piece of this action too, and with their firepower they'll never see us coming. Here's what we're going to do..." I outlined my plan, getting his input and finalizing the directions.

"Where are you?" I finally asked, hoping he was close.

"I ain't far, darlin', I ken be dere tomorrow morning. Ya sure ya don' wanna call van der Slavv? We work well together, him and me and you, darlin'."

Kris and I had met Morgan van der Slavv on a hunt in Tampa, Florida. Originally from Denmark, Morgan had made quite a name for himself as a hunter in Europe before he decided to move to the US. He was one of the few non-sensitive hunters I had ever met, and he made up for his lack of sensitive ability by shooting first and last. He was also one of the extremely rare individuals immune to SDS and fortunate enough to have reacted well to both the *Reanimagus* vaccine and the experimental military vaccine for HBV. He was resistant to all the pathogens the rest of us worried about so he took much bigger risks for much bigger payoffs.

He was ex-military, trained with just about any weapon you put in his hand, but he specialized in automatic weapons and demolitions and I'd never seen a better sniper. He had a reputation for the cold-blooded killing of his hunts, a fact I had seen first hand when he gunned down a child vampire without so much as a twitch in his face. He shot first and asked questions later, a policy that made him unpopular with the police and myself alike.

"No, the less people the better I think. Besides, if you and I can't handle, it can't be handled."

"Suit yourself. You come get me at de airport, or I should I rent a car?"

"I'll come get you, just text me your flight and arrival time so I know when to get there. DIA's a bit of a drive from here."

"Course, darlin', I let ya know when I know, I better go plan. You be good, now, keep ya head down 'til I get dere," he said, hanging up. I sighed, gathering up my purse and heading back down to the car to go to the hospital. This time of night it might take me an hour.

It took me more than an hour, closer to an hour and a half, but when I walked in, the nurse on duty took my arm and led me to a room with a single bed in it. She left without a word, giving me a mysterious look as she shut the door. Allie walked in moments later, dressed in a lab coat with jeans and a chenille sweater underneath.

Chapter 25: Treatment

"Hey Jamie, thanks for coming, I know this is hard and I kinda left you in the lurch, but trust me when I say I had a good reason," she said, suddenly awkward. I stared at her, confused. Allie hadn't been awkward around me since we first met and hit it off and I didn't understand her consternation now. "I've contacted my funders and they green-lighted this treatment I'm about to give you, if you agree to it. But there's strings attached and I need you to agree without knowing what they are.

"It's a treatment I've been working on for most of my career, but I've never tested it on a human, only monkeys," she said softly. "Once you agree to the strings, there's no going back on your word, you don't want to go there, trust me." She impaled me on her gaze, eyes hard as flint and sharp as obsidian all the sudden, trying to tell me something without telling me.

"Come again?" I said, confused. I had thought she was my friend, we'd known each other for years and years. Why was she being so cryptic and why wouldn't she just give me her treatment? Why did she need to ask her funders? This was turning into something from the Twilight Zone.

"I have a treatment," she reiterated, "but it's experimental and the people who control it require payment in the form of something other than money. If you agree, I can tell you what you have agreed to, but not until then. I'm not sure it's worth it, the price is high, but you're young, maybe you'd be okay with it. Wait, I'll get someone else for you to talk to, he'll be able to offer an alternate perspective." She stood and pushed through the door, violently thrusting it open and disappearing down the hallway with sharp clicks from her boots. She came back moments later, a very tall, thin shadow behind her.

"Jackson?" I said, really confused now.

"Hey, sister, how are you?" he asked, sliding through the doorway and standing at the foot of the bed, as far from me as possible. He wouldn't meet my eyes, either, and seemed flushed, hands like great white nervous butterflies flittering about.

"Jackson, what the hell is going on here? You people are acting like secret agents or something. What's with all the cloak and dagger crap? And how do you know Allison, I didn't think you'd ever met her." He flushed deeper, his ears and neck turning a lurid red as he coughed nervously.

"That's what we wanted you to think," Allison replied, striding back through the door and closing it firmly behind her. I was getting crowded in my little space and I really didn't like all the secrets and lies that were being exposed.

"What the Hell, Allison, I thought I was your friend, what's going on here?"

"The people who fund my research aren't people to mess with and I won't do anything to go against their wishes, even for you." She replied, her face a mask, completely unreadable. "I'll tell you one more time, I have a treatment, it's experimental so I don't know if it will work, but it's not free. You need to agree to their terms before I can tell you what their terms are, but I caution you they are steep. Jackson, what do you think?"

"I've been watching you," Jackson said softly, turning his huge eyes on me and putting his left hand on my left knee. I could feel the warmth of his hand through my jeans, and I could tell he was anxious from the tension in his long fingers. "Ever since we met on our mission to find the family of vampires in Colorado Springs, I've been watching how you handle yourself, how you react to pressure and stress. You're a powerful sensitive, you could be an amazing practitioner if you wanted to risk that path. All things considered, I think you'd be a good candidate for, uh, the strings Allison mentioned. But you need to realize it will be very demanding and you may need to do things you don't agree with. You are stubborn, headstrong, and that's frankly the reason I haven't approached you earlier. I'd hoped you would grow out of it, leave this childish disrespect for authority behind as you grew up, but we're out of time."

"Out of time for what? I don't understand, why can't you tell me what's going on here?" My voice rose to a shrill near shout as my gaze darted between these two strangers I had thought were my friends. I was getting scared, scared and frustrated with the two people in the world I trusted more than any others. Starting to hyperventilate, I scrutinized their faces, hoping, searching for some clue as to what they were talking about. Maybe I was hallucinating, having some kind of awful dream. I pinched myself, hard, on my thigh and jumped. That hurt! I obviously wasn't dreaming. *Maybe I have fallen into the twilight zone*, I thought hopefully.

"There's no other treatment for Stoker-Dracul syndrome," Allison said, her voice barely above a whisper. "The cases you have heard of with antibody treatment weren't effective long term, the people treated with the antibody therapy developed an autoimmune disease similar to lupus but much more virulent. They died horribly a few months later. We didn't release the results because people are terrified enough of Stoker-Dracul, releasing those results wouldn't have accomplished anything. But you need to decide now, the prion is already beginning to affect your system and soon we won't be able to reverse the damage."

She looked at me earnestly, her face still a mask but with a strange pleading in her eyes, and I realized she desperately wanted me to agree so she could try and save my life and tell me the truth. I looked over and Jackson, startled when his gaze pierced me to my very core, willing me to decide to save my own life even at this mysterious price. I'd never seen him so cold, so earnest and it scared me. *Do it*, a voice whispered in my head, feeling like a warm wind on a cold winter night.

My eyes widened further, threatening to pop out of my head as I realized it was Jackson speaking to me mind-to-mind. I had no idea he could do that, he'd never done anything like it before when he wasn't in his ethereal form. I recoiled from him, pulling my leg out from under his hand.

"Who are you?" I whispered, staring at him and really seeing him for the first time. He was throbbing with power, his aura creating a heat wave like effect around his head. I could almost feel heat emanating from him, but it was cold at the same time, making me break into a sweat and shiver at the same time. Allison didn't seem to notice anything, standing there cool as a cucumber.

"I'm Jackson," he said, his voice flat and cold with a strange resonance. "The same person you've always known." *Do it*, his voice echoed in my head, *it's worth it, if you're strong enough.*

I looked at him, seeing the power waver around his head, and making a sudden decision.

"Do it," I said. Both of them relaxed, a horrible tension draining from them as they both smiled and came forward to touch me, Allison touching my face with a gentle hand and a brilliant smile and Jackson patting my knee like my father used to, but with a strange melancholy smile.

"Put this on," Allie said, handing me a hospital gown. I shrugged, disappearing into the bathroom to change and returning a moment later.

"Now tell me why I just apparently sold my soul to the Devil," I said, exasperated and still uncomfortable with these now-strangers I thought I had known as I sat back on the bed.

"Later," Allison replied, "when there's no people around to hear. Right now, we need to get going on your treatment." She snapped her fingers, pulling her cell phone from her belt and turning away. She spoke low and urgently into it, too low for me to hear, and then slipped out the door again.

Jackson was still patting my knee, looking like a father at his daughter's wedding, and staying silent.

"Okay, you tell me what the Hell's going on them," I said, grabbing his wrist and pulling it toward me, forcing his eyes to mine. He smiled, but didn't say anything else, gently pulling his arm out of my grip. Just as I was about to get huffy and push it, Allison pushed back through the door with a small saline IV bag in one hand and a kit for another IV in the other. I sighed, dreading getting another IV in such a short span of time. Of course, if the alternative was dying in a dementia filled horror from Stoker-Dracul syndrome, they could stick me with a hundred IVs.

She pulled a chair away from the wall and levered it higher so she could reach my arm. Her hands were deft and gentle, guiding the needle into my vein with only a small pinch, but when she pulled a length of plastic wrapped wire as long as my arm from the package, I stiffened.

"What is that?" I said, raising my eyebrows and making my displeasure known.

"A PICC line," she replied. "We need to get the protein into your central cardiovascular system as soon as possible and a peripheral line's too slow."

"Of course," I said faintly, experiencing a twinge of doubt and wondering what I had gotten myself into. "A little more information would be highly appreciated," I grumbled, squirming as she began feeding the tube into my arm. I'd never felt anything like it, I could actually feel the tube threading up my arm. It was a horrible sensation, causing bile to rise in my throat so I closed my eyes and tried to think of anything besides the procedure.

"PICC line," she replied, her voice a pedantic lecturing tone, "peripherally inserted central catheter. Used for chemotherapy, TPN, etc, anything where it needs to stay in place for a while or where the drug being administered would cause pain to a peripheral site. We're not going to leave it in very long, but the sooner we can get this modified version of Stoker-Dracul into your system, the sooner it will spread and eliminate the wild type currently causing your dire situation."

"Modified version of Stoker-Dracul syndrome?" I asked, my voice rising in a new bout of panic.

"Yes," she replied absently, concentrating on threading the wired tube into my arm. "We modified a version of Stoker-Dracul so it takes the place of Sonic Hedgehog Homolog, SHH, and prevents the conformational changes in SHH by Stoker-Dracul syndrome. Our studies in rhesus monkeys show a ninety percent prevention of infection from SDS, but we don't know what side effects it will have in a sensitive. No monkeys are sensitives," she finished, looking me in the eye and arching her left eyebrow. "I did warn you it was experimental. Besides, you've already contracted Stoker-Dracul, what are you worried about?"

She swiveled something around from overhead, a white plastic screen attached to a prehensile boom arm, and positioned it over my heart. The screen lit up briefly, showing an x-ray of my chest and the wire she had inserted as a white line ending above my heart. She grunted, a smile tugging the corner of her mouth as she switched the x-ray machine off and rotated it back to its position on the ceiling. Next she pulled a set of padded leather cuffs from her the bag I hadn't noticed.

"Kinky," I gasped, trying to be flippant and failing as my panic threatened to choke me.

"Relax, it's just for your safety," she said, bending to attach them to my wrists and ankles and then securing the chains to the bed. "Based on how the monkeys react to it, I think this is going to hurt like Hell," she finished with a sardonic smile.

"No, no, no, wait, what do you mean hurt like Hell?" I yelled, abruptly changing my mind about this whole thing and pulling hard on the restraints. They didn't budge more than a couple inches. "You didn't say anything about hurting like Hell!"

She smiled the same sardonic smile and hooked the IV bag to the line, punching a high feed rate into the pump and stepping back. I struggled, yelling at her to stop, I'd changed my mind, but she and Jackson just looked at me. Jackson fastened a ball gag around my mouth, whether to quiet me or to stop me from biting my tongue I didn't know. Probably both.

Liquid fire began in my chest and spread through my core with astonishing speed. I could feel every nerve, every neuron in my body as the fire spread like a venom. Then it began itching, then freezing. When the crushing pressure started, like a whale landing atop me, I started screaming. I screamed, screamed through the gag, screamed like my soul was being torn from me, as fast as I could draw breath, arching my back and pulling with all my strength against the restraints.

The pressure from the cuffs on my broken wrist was a spark next to the sun when compared to the itching, freezing, crushing molten steel flowing through my nerves. Finally, mercifully, I passed out.

Chapter 26: Miracle?

I wandered through a dark hallway, walls covered in slimy mold, a light in the distance and nothing but darkness behind me. There was something in the darkness, something that promised pain, but running was like moving through molasses. Tripping and stumbling over unseen things, most soft and moaning, I struggled toward the light. Just as the dark thing was almost on me, a door yawned wide in the wall to my left and I slammed my shoulder into it as the dark thing's fingers grazed me, leaving a searing pain in my left forearm where it had brushed against me.

White light blasted around me, my eyes tearing up, purple shadows flickering as after images in my vision, before I realized I was back in the hospital. All the curtains in the ER were drawn, moans and cries of pain emanating from behind most of them, some dripping crimson blood on the white linoleum floor. A petite, dark haired nurse stood near one of the curtains, and I put my hand on her shoulder to turn her around, intending to ask where I was.

It was Allie. She turned and lunged at me, fangs bared with a twisted vampire countenance, snapping and snarling like a wild beast. She latched into my forearm and worried it like a dog just as Jordan had, knocking me to the ground. Struggling and kicking, I tried to fight her off, but she was too strong. The wounds closed as fast as she made them, my flesh stretching like rubber as she pulled at the piece in her mouth. A scarecrow figure loomed over her, pulling her off me and almost lifting me from the ground. Jackson stood over me, offering me a hand, so I took it, pulled to my feet with a sharp jerk. Jackson's eyes were filmed with death, his face a pallid gray with a slack jaw, and I recoiled, tripping over something behind me and going sprawling but never hitting the floor.

I fell, screaming, fell through a whirling storm, gray clouds whipping around me while purple lightning flashed, closer and closer. I struck something soft, bouncing through the storm into a star filled sky and coming to rest afloat in emptiness.

"Jamie?" came a soft voice from the darkness.

Go away, I thought sullenly, comfortable in the warm supporting emptiness. I floated there, serene, no thoughts broaching the ebony velvet I had retreated into.

"Wake up," came the voice again, a soft female voice. "We're done, it's over," she said.

No.

"Help me Jackson, she's retreated into her subconscious."

Jamie, came a male voice from the darkness, more insistent than the female voice, more real.

Go 'way, I thought back at him.

No, I won't, you need to wake up, he insisted.

Don't want to, I whined. *It hurts out there.*

Something grabbed my mind, twisting it like ribbon through someone's fingers and I shrieked, fighting the force for all I was worth. I fled, fled from the darkness and whatever had grabbed my mind, running toward a bright light, quick as a thought. My eyes snapped open, white light spearing into my head as I tried to roll away from the offending pain. I couldn't move, my hands and legs were still shackled to the bed, but I struggled all the same, screaming.

After an eternity, I calmed down, breathing deeply and trying to remember where I was. It came back to me in flashes, the hospital, the treatment, my friends acting like nutcases. *What a nightmare*, I thought, finally relaxing. Opening my eyes this time was easier, the lights still too bright but manageable. Hovering in my field of vision were two blurry faces, one long and pale and the other oval and dark.

"Jackson? Allison?" I croaked, my throat feeling like a desert in summer. "Water?"

Allison's face slid away, coming back a second later with a white Styrofoam cup half full of water in her hand. She pressed it to my lips so I could drink, greedily slurping at the lip of the cup and spilling most of it.

"More," I said, sounding somewhat less like a toad croaking and more like myself. She refilled the cup, guiding my hand to take it, and pulled away. I drank deeply, managing not to spill too much this time, and tried to sit up. Agile hands unbuckled the restraints while another set of strong hands grabbed my elbow and helped me sit up, pulling away as I settled against the pillow behind me.

"What happened?" I croaked.

"You lived through the treatment, thank God, but your reaction was much stronger than any I've seen in my monkeys. We need to wait to see what kinds of effects it will have on you, because you're a sensitive, but they may take time to develop. I'm having them run another screening for Stoker-Dracul, but I'm confident it'll come back negative now. If I'm right, if you responded to the treatment the way our rhesus monkeys did, you'll be completely immune to Stoker-Dracul from now on."

"Neat," I said, realizing it hadn't been a nightmare at all, just a nightmarish few hours. "Handy trick to have for a hunter."

"Yeah," this distractedly from Jackson, frowning at me and reaching down to touch my arm where the bandage covered my vampire bite. "What happened here?" he asked, touching the bandage lightly and jerking away as if stung.

"I got bit, remem...," I trailed off as I looked down and gasped, recoiling from my own arm. My bite had apparently opened, bleeding all over the bed, but it wasn't red. It was black, like a puddle of oil spilled on the bed and the bandage was completely soaked through, smelling strongly of decaying meat.

"What in the Hell is that?" came the shocked gasp from Allison.

"You tell me, Dr. Schmitz!" I snapped, horrified.

"None... None of the monkeys had that happen," she stuttered, recoiling from the mess spreading on the bed next to me. I retched, the smell making my head swim, scooting as far from the stain as I could on the single bed. Finally, Allison rallied herself and her scientific curiosity took over. She turned to the med cart against the wall and pulled a pair of latex gloves from the box in the left drawer, sliding them on with two deft motions. She pulled a urine sample vial from another drawer, along with a package of sterile gauze.

"Hold still," she ordered gently, "I need a sample to analyze." She pulled my arm closer to her, trying to avoid the slick of darkness around the bandage with her hands but wiping the gauze through it, absorbing as much as she could, and then sealing it in the specimen jar. Carefully, she pulled the bandage back and gasped, turning huge eyes on me.

"What?" I snapped, "What now?" She turned my arm so I could see under the bandage and I echoed her gasp. Under the slick of black goo, my skin was pink and whole, not a mark on it where Phelps had torn it with her shoe nor where the vampire had bit me. Nothing.

"What. The. Hell," Jackson said, towering over Allison and peering over her head, his mouth and eyes wide with shock.

"I don't know," she said faintly. "None of the monkeys healed from the treatment, otherwise their IV sites would have healed over too. Maybe it's a side effect of being a sensitive," she mused, pulling my arm closer to poke at the IV site. I hissed, trying to pull my arm away, but she held on with surprising strength. "Your IV's healed too," she said, pulling on the tube and eliciting another hiss from me. "Your skin's healed around it; I'm going to need to cut it out. I've never seen anything like it; even people who have PICC lines for years don't heal over them like that."

She rummaged through the med cart again, coming up with a disposable scalpel and looking at my arm with a strange expression. Pulling the outer plastic away, she gripped the blade in a surgeon's grip and pulled my arm closer.

"Allie, she needs anesthesia if you're going to do that," Jackson said, laying a hand on her shoulder and pulling to turn her away from her task. She blinked at him like she was seeing him for the first time, and then shook herself, comprehension returning to her face.

"Sorry," she mumbled, "got carried away. Anesthesia, let me go find some lidocaine or something." She wandered back out the door, scalpel still in hand, as Jackson looked at me with a bemused expression which quickly shifted back to concern. He, too, rummaged through the med cart and came up with some saline and more gauze. He started wiping the black goo, which had thickened to a tar-like consistency, off my arm, but it was a bigger task than he expected. My cast was soaked, and the smell was getting worse from the bedding. Exasperated, he gave up, throwing the fouled gauze into the biohazard bag on the med cart and crossing his arms across in chest in irritation.

Allison finally returned, baring a syringe and a small vial.

"This'll sting a bit," she said, pulling the fluid into the syringe and tapping the side to remove any bubbles. Four injections around the IV site numbed the area enough for her to gently cut the skin from around the IV, but when she started pulling the tube out I felt my gorge rising.

"Stop, stop, stop!" I blurted. "Get me something quick, I'm going to be sick!" Jackson grabbed the red plastic bin from the med cart, dumping the contents on the floor and thrusting it under my head. I heaved, spitting up bile and acid, and my hot chocolate from earlier. I hadn't eaten for a while, so thankfully there wasn't a whole lot to come up.

"You okay?" He asked, concern written on his face.

"Yeah, that smell and pulling the IV out was too much, can we maybe get me cleaned up, then worry about the IV? Whatever that black stuff is, it reeks."

"Sure," he replied, "right on, sister, let me get some clean linens."

"Don't bother," Allison spoke up. "I'll just have her transferred to another bed; someone else can deal with this." She pushed the nurse call button, requesting a new bed when the nurse's voice came on over the intercom, the door opening moments later with two wide eyed orderlies and another bed. They looked at me, looked at the bed, and looked at me again, both deciding they didn't want to know and motioned for me to stand. I stood up, shockingly steady considering, as they wheeled the soiled bed out and another identical one into its place. Sitting gingerly, keeping my arm elevated to keep from contaminating the new bed, I looked around for Allison.

"Where'd she go?" I asked Jackson.

"To find a nurse and a cast saw, that needs to be replaced," he said, gesturing at my fetid arm. I grimaced, trying not to gag any more, and not really succeeding. Allison returned moments later, the petite nurse who originally cast my arm in tow and a strange looking rotary tool in her hand. Without a word, Allie flipped the thing on, creating a high pitched whining noise, and began to cut the cast from my arm. The smell of the cast being cut and the black goo burning almost made me throw up again, but I held my nose with my right hand and tried not to breathe. Jackson couldn't handle it, ducking through the door leading to the bathroom where retching sounds almost sent me back over the edge.

The cast fell away into the red bin the nurse placed under it, landing with a wet splat. I scowled, amazed at how much black goo was still on my skin, but the nurse was already wetting some gauze and sponging it off. She got as much as she could and then took the plastic bin away through the door with a grimace.

"Jamie," Allison said distantly, "flex your wrist."

"Why?" I asked, wary.

"Just do it, please," she said, eyes focused on where it had been broken. Looking where she was looking, I bit back another gasp. There was no swelling, no discoloration now that the black goo had been swabbed off. I frowned, catching on to what Allison was getting at, and flexed my wrist. Nothing, no pain, no stiffness, it was completely healed.

"Amazing," she breathed, taking my arm in her hands and flexing my wrist to full extension and back again. Her gaze snapped to mine and she stared hard into my eyes, looking at them rather than me. "Your concussion is gone too, your eyes aren't dilated differentially any more. What an amazing effect, I need to document this," she said, reaching into her purse and pulling out a scuffed notebook. She scribbled notes for a few minutes, asking how I felt, examining and turning my former injuries until I was ready to slap her.

"IV?" I prompted, tired of feeling like a test subject.

"Right," she said, stashing her notebook back in her purse and pulling my arm back toward her. I braced myself, dreading the sensation of the tube coming out of my arm, and I was right, it was ten times worse than the smaller IV had been. I shuddered, contemplating being sick again, and then she was done, stuffing the used line into the biohazard bag. Blood welled from the IV site, thick and thankfully bright red, smelling faintly of copper, not dead meat. She slapped a cotton ball and a bandage over it, putting pressure on to stop the bleeding while she peeled her fouled gloves off and tossed them in the biohazard bag.

"Can I go home now?" I asked plaintively, suddenly very tired and wanting my bed.

"Probably," she said, looking me over and apparently making a decision. "I see no reason to keep you here, you're not injured anymore through God only knows what mechanism and there's nothing else I can learn here. Let me find Dr. Winston, maybe he'll have those SDS results too. Besides, he's gotta see this," she commented, turning to go through the curtain and disappearing through the white cloth. I sighed again, laying back on my bed and marveling at everything that had happened in the last few minutes.

Jackson returned a couple minutes later, looking a little green, but otherwise none the worse for wear. He was holding a manila folder about half an inch thick with a strange expression on his face.

"Jamie," he said, with a bemused half grin, "With all the excitement, I forgot you sold your soul to the Devil to have this treatment. I'm sure you're wondering what you've gotten yourself into." My shock must have shown on my face because he quickly wiped the bemused expression off his face, surprise replacing it as he realized what he had said.

"Not really, not really," he said quickly, moving to pat my hand, trying to reassure me. "Figure of speech, you haven't really sold your soul to the Devil. Although sometimes I think the Devil might be less demanding," he trailed off, a sly, amused glint in his eye. I punched him in the arm, not finding any of this funny, but he laughed and shrugged it off.

"Here," he said, handing me the folder. "All you wanted to know about who's beck and call you're now at. I can tell you more when we're someplace more private, this area is too exposed."

I took the folder gingerly, eyeing it like a cat eyes a feral dog. I flipped it open to the first paper in the stack, but Jackson quickly reached over and closed it before I could read anything.

"Later," he admonished, giving me a stern look. I scowled up at him, nearing my bull crap limit and about to give him a piece of my mind when Allison returned with Dr. Winston in tow. In his hand was a slightly crumpled piece of copier paper but he seemed to have forgotten about it. Shaking his head, he looked at me with something close to fear.

"I have no idea how, Ms. McKinsey, but I ran the test three times. Your Stoker-Dracul syndrome is gone. I thought maybe your first test was a false positive, so I tracked down your blood sample from the first test again and ran it too. It came up positive two more times," he finished, staring at me in expectation, his left eyebrow arched.

I looked over at Allison, wondering how much I could say, when I noticed the minute shake of her head. Apparently I couldn't say anything.

"I don't have a clue, Doctor, how would I know?" I asked, trying for my best innocent expression. It worked, for once, and he turned to Allison for support. She shrugged, an innocent expression on her face as well, and he turned to Jackson, exasperated.

"Fine," he said, piqued, "if someone happens to remember, please let me know, I know a couple patients a year who'd really like to know." He spun on his heel, pushing through the curtain and limping out in a huff.

"I'll tell him later, somewhere less public," Allison whispered to Jackson, but I heard her anyway.

"Why would you tell him later?" I asked, suspicious. Her eyes widened as she turned, face flushing.

"Uh, I'll tell you that later," she replied, blushing. "Now let's get you out of here," she said, switching subjects to cover her gaffe. "Get changed and we'll get out of here."

I looked pointedly at Jackson and he raised his hands with a good natured smile, leaving through the door, softly closing it behind him and allowing us girls to be alone. Carefully, I reached up to untie the hospital gown from around my neck, but even my ribs were now pain free. I stretched, pulling my arms over my head and pulling. No pain from my ribs interfered and I breathed a deep, deep sigh of relief.

Allie helped me untie the tie around my back and I slipped it off, noticing my underwear was still intact. Quickly and miraculously pain-free I was dressed, pulling my boots on and sliding my arms through the arm holes of my coat. Allison pulled the door open so we could head for the sign out desk as Jackson fell into step next to us. They walked on either side of me like the most mismatched pair of bodyguards in the history of time, but I felt strangely comforted by their presence.

"I had Jackson take your car home," Allison commented, idly. I turned and stared at her, offended she would do such a thing without my permission, when I caught her embarrassed look.

"Why...?" I asked, preparing to get angry.

"I didn't know what kind of shape you'd be in after the treatment and I was just going to take you home myself," she squirmed, aware I was angry. I decided to let it go, vowing to myself to talk about this later.

Allison signed the papers for my release, we gathered my equipment and personal things, and headed out to her car in the staff parking lot. Jackson said his goodbyes, heading off toward the visitor parking lot, promising to let me know what I had gotten myself into after I had some sleep. Allison's red Lexus IS350 was parked under a streetlight, but we walked around it to check anyway. You never know what kinds of nasties might be wandering Denver's streets this time of night, as evidenced by my rough last few days.

Satisfied, I climbed into the passenger side as she started it up and we headed out. It was close to midnight, 11:30 PM from the clock on her dashboard, and traffic for the day had exhausted itself long ago, so we were almost alone on the icy streets. Hulking gray office buildings with the occasional brightly lit gas station passed by swiftly as we headed for my apartment, but the growling of my stomach distracted me from any sightseeing.

"Good God, Jamie, is that your stomach?" Allison asked, half turning her body to glance momentarily at me.

"Yeah," I replied, "she's hungry. You mind stopping at that McDonald's?" I asked, pointing to a sign a few blocks away.

"Sure," she replied, easing the car down the drive through. I ordered two quarter pounders, two French fries, and a large Dr. Pepper, paying with my debit card.

"Spill it in my car and I'll beat you senseless next time we spar," she warned me. I grunted, mouth full of fries, and gave her a thumbs-up. I ate it all, picking at the wrappers for crumbs as she pulled into the parking lot of my apartment.

"Give me a buzz when you're up," she said, leaning over the passenger seat to meet my eyes. "Jackson and I will come over and we'll talk about what you have committed yourself to. I want you to keep an eye out for any new symptoms, anything out of the ordinary so I can document it. And Jamie?"

"Yeah?"

"I'm really glad you're okay,"

"Thanks," I smiled softly, leaning down to give her a hug and then closing the door. She waved as she pulled out of the parking lot, heading for home I guessed, as I trudged up the stairs toward my apartment. Dragging myself up the dark gray carpeted stairs, I finally arrived at my dark blue door and, fumbling with the keys, managed to get it open. Right inside my door was a set of triangular corner shelves where I usually dumped my purse and tonight was no exception. Kicking the door closed and locking it with along with sliding the chain, I leaned against it and sighed, drained.

I needed a shower, I could still smell that black stuff on me, so I wandered upstairs, brushed my teeth, showered, and headed for my bed, still marveling at my lack of pain. My healing had taken a lot out of me, though, as I crashed asleep almost immediately.

Chapter 27: Strings Attached

My cell phone woke me, an incessant buzzing from my nightstand, and I answered it already hostile.

"Yeah?" I demanded, never opening my eyes and pulling the phone under the sheets with me.

"Are you up, Jamie?" It was Allie. I vaguely recalled her saying she'd come by after I woke up to talk about her mysterious strings. I grunted, wanting to say not really, but I knew I'd need to face the music eventually. I sat up, looking at my alarm clock. It was 10:00 AM, so I'd been asleep for a while, at least for me.

"Yeah," I grunted again.

"Good. Jackson and I will be over in about thirty minutes, is that okay?"

"Sure," I said, not looking forward to this conversation.

"See you then!" she said brightly, hanging up the phone. Mornings weren't my favorite time of day to begin with, and the rough last couple of days had drained me. I didn't feel like getting dressed just yet so I threw a robe on and wandered down the stairs in search of a Coke. I hated coffee, so to get my caffeine fix I usually drank tea or a Coke, especially if it had been a late night.

Popping the top, I took a healthy swig and flopped down on my couch to wait for the two strangers I had thought I knew. Just as I got comfortable, my phone rang again. This time I didn't recognize the number, but I answered it anyway.

"Hello?" I said, sounding grumpy.

"Good mornin' to you too, darlin'," Kris retorted, a smile in his voice.

"Kris? Hey, what's up? Did you get a flight?"

"I sure 'nough did, I'll be on United flight 979 out of Nawlins, I call you when it lands if'n ya just wanna wait in the cell phone lot dere. I'm on ma way now, shug, and I'll be landin' right about one o'clock your time. With all the security bullshit, I ain't gonna be able to bring ma arsenal, but you got weapons I can borrow, eh?"

"Course I do," I replied. "Anything you need firearm wise, plus plenty of silver plated ammo. I don't mess around with explosives, we'll need to see if we can find that stuff here if you want it."

"Nah, I'm thinkin' your plan go better without any big booms, I don' usually use them anyhow. I gotta run, we taking off an' de stewardess tells me I gotta shut off de phone. Bye for now, shug."

The phone went dead in my hand as I yawned. I wandered into the bathroom before Allie and Jackson got there, finally giving a thought about my appearance. My hair was a fright, completely screwed up after being slept on, but there was a healthy glow to my face I hadn't seen for a long time. I looked five years younger. Smirking, I thought, *maybe it's worth the price they're going to tell me about.*

A knock at my door heralded their arrival. Jackson and Allie were waiting at the door, but two people stood silently behind them to either side, looking like another pair of mismatched pair of bodyguards. The one on the left was African-American, a few inches taller than Allie with skin the color of the finest dark chocolate. His dark eyes were sharp, missing very little, with a heart shaped face and dark lips. His head was shaved with a pencil thin mustache decorating his upper lip. He was dressed in simple blue jeans with a red hooded sweatshirt and brown leather Birkenstock clogs.

On the right, a petite blonde waited. She was well-dressed in tailored gray dress pants and a black leather waist length coat with a red chenille scarf around her throat and slim black leather gloves. Her face was round with a warm smile, a petite nose, tawny eyes and large silver hoop earrings.

"Hi Jamie," Allie said brightly, turning to introduce her companions. "This is Joshua McClellan, one of our heavy hitters," she said, gesturing toward the man. He advanced on me with a large white smile, extending his hand and almost crushing mine in his grip.

"Nice to meet you, Jamie," he said, eyeing me up and down. Suddenly I wished I'd taken time to get dressed, but I hadn't known they were bringing other people.

"Uh, nice to meet you," I mumbled, not meeting his gaze.

"This is Lindsey Burns," Allie continued, oblivious, gesturing toward the woman. "Also one of our heavy hitters, but in a different way." Lindsey didn't offer to shake hands, instead nodding at me with a small smile. I'd unconsciously extended my hand, expecting her to shake it, when an unseen force seized it and made my hand move up and down as if there was someone shaking it. Her smile turned to a smirk as I stared at her open-mouthed.

I'd heard of telekinetic individuals who were this powerful, but I'd never met one, they were exceedingly rare. Most people capable of telekinesis experienced a surge of their power during puberty that disappeared once their hormones calmed down. A select few gained sufficient control over their powers to have them remain into adulthood, but it took work and their powers were usually fairly weak. Every once in a long while, a sensitive was born powerful enough and controlled enough to keep their full powers, and Lindsey was apparently one of those people.

"Come in, come in," I said, remembering my manners.

Inviting them to sit and offering tea or soda, I took Jackson's brown pea coat and Allie's black leather jacket along with Lindsey's leather coat and Joshua's hoodie, hanging them in the coat closet under the stairs, and then sat on the couch. Allie and Lindsey accepted a cup of tea, wandering into the kitchen to make it, while Jackson, with a gravid air about him, sat down on my couch. He was wearing his usual tan Dockers and t-shirt, this one a bright orange, with brown loafers. Joshua also wandered into the kitchen, raiding my refrigerator for a Coke and leaning on the counter with a smirk.

Joshua was ripped and built, the kind of body that came from hard work and lots of time in the gym, his six pack visible through his thin white t-shirt, arms bulging as he sipped the can of soda. I caught myself staring and shook my head, but Joshua had caught me staring too and he flexed his arms with a waggle of his eyebrows. I blushed, turning to focus on what Jackson was saying, and pointedly ignored Joshua.

"You start," Allie said, gesturing at Jackson and settling back into the couch to blow across her tea. She, too, had her usual jeans on with a thick sky blue sweater, but her shoes were expensive designer flats I hadn't seen before.

"Jamie," Jackson began, abruptly, taking my hand and pulling it toward him. "We've known each other for, what, four years? In all that time, I've not been completely truthful with you. See, our meeting wasn't accidental. I saw you in action in Boulder and I was curious about you. By a weird coincidence, you also knew Allie so I had her introduce us. When you tracked Svetlana alone and faced her down in that bar, I thought you might be suitable for the organization we all work for, but I needed to observe you. You're headstrong, sometimes impetuous, and you pull the trigger a little too easily. All of these characteristics aren't necessarily bad, but they are when you work for the government as we do. We're all members of a small cadre of unusual people referred to as Division 99.

"Division 99 was created in the aftermath of the September 11th bombings, an adjunct to the Department of Homeland Security. We're paid for under the black budget, essentially unlimited funding, but we do answer to the head of Homeland Security. We're a group of sensitives, scientists, and agents whose purpose is to protect the population of the US from supernatural threats. I was exposed as a practitioner in 2002 when they gave me a choice: join them and put my powers to use helping them, or be severed, so guess which I chose. Joshua and Lindsey were recruited a few months before I was. You've seen Lindsey's gifts, she can lift a car with her mind, but she doesn't like to touch people, a side effect of her telekinesis ramped up her touch reading abilities. I'll let her tell you about it.

"Joshua is a lycanthrope, a werewolf to be specific. He's a primary, do you know what that means?"

"Nope," I replied, eying him with a touch of unease. HBV wasn't very infectious, it usually had to be spread with blood to blood contact, but it still scared me. He scowled back at me, catching my uncertainty, so I turned back to Jackson.

"Again, I'll let him tell you about it when I'm done. Back to Division 99, Allison has been a member since its inception, that's where most of her funding to find a cure for SDS comes from. Similar projects are under way to find cures for the *Reanimagus* plague and HBV, but they haven't been as successful as our little doctor here. She had to clear it with our boss, the Director, before she was allowed to treat you, but it opened the door for us to recruit you.

"I'd hoped to wait to see if you matured a little, but when you were infected, our hand was forced. The price of your treatment was working for Division 99. Not always, but any time your services as a hunter are needed, you'll drop everything and help us. Because you'll be on retainer, Division 99 will pay you for your services at your standard rate, but you aren't to mention our existence to anyone, even your mother."

My eyebrows had risen higher and higher in disbelief, not willing to believe in some shadowy government organization, but I hadn't ever known Jackson to exaggerate. His face was deadly serious, his dark eyes stone hard and boring into me with an intensity I had never seen in him. Allie was watching us with cool, dark eyes, not speaking, sipping her tea with her knees curled to her chest. I glanced over to her, looking for support, but she returned my gaze with a level stare. Lindsey and Joshua were engaged in a private conversation, their heads bent low, not paying any attention to us.

"That's it? I just have to jump when the government says jump? And I get paid for it? What's so bad about that?"

"What's so bad," interjected Allie, "is that the call for a job can come any time, day or night, and you need to drop everything and respond. You'll likely be flown somewhere in the world where your services are needed, but sometimes you'll need to drive. No questions asked, you do as you're told, even if you object to it on moral grounds," she finished, her hard gaze shifting between Jackson and me.

"I've experimented on children, teenagers, any vampire I could get my hands on. Some of them begged me, begged me," she almost shouted, her face twisted in pain, "to help them, to stop, but I couldn't. If I can rid the world of SDS or come up with a cure, I'll sacrifice a thousand vampires. Anything to keep another family from ending up lunch to those bloodsuckers." Her face was so warped with hate and loathing I scarcely recognized her. As I watched, she got a hold of herself and relaxed back into the couch, sipping her tea and staring holes in the wall.

Jackson cleared his throat, looking at Allie with a disconcerted expression and turning then back to me with a shrug. "That's about it. You're at their beck and call to do whatever they need without questions or else. You do not, I repeat, do not want to know what or else means. We'll introduce you to the rest of the Division when you receive your first assignment; it's not important right now."

"I can handle that, I think," I said slowly. "Better than dying of SDS, right?" Both Jackson and Allie grinned, nodding in an eerily synchronous way. "What about you two?" I asked, nodding at Lindsey and Joshua. Joshua had sauntered over to lean on the wall, idly inspecting my red dragon poster, picking at the peeling paint around the thumbtack. I turned to him, one eyebrow arched, and waited for him to notice.

"What's a primary?" I finally asked. He grinned that ready white grin of his and gestured at himself, ending with his hands in the air.

"I am," he replied, with a slightly mocking smile. "We're the leaders, the badasses. Me, I'm gangsta, and I am who I am."

"What he means to say," cut in Jackson with a warning look at Joshua, "is that primaries are the lucky lycanthropes. The have HBV, but their symptoms are more benign. Joshua will turn into a wolfman at the full moon and also whenever he chooses, but he'll remain in control at all times, keeping his human mind and human thoughts. He's one of the leaders of the local lycanthrope community. He makes sure his people are away from humans at the full moon and keeps them from killing people."

"Plus I can bench press a thousand pounds, heal from even your silver rounds, and run faster than a horse. How's that for gangsta?" Joshua added, the smirk on his face supplemented with an arrogant posture. Joshua was hot, and powerful, and he knew it, but underneath was a need, a yearning for people to understand and accept him as he was, werewolf or not. I saw his need in his eyes, so I smiled back at him.

"Totally gangsta, remind me not to piss you off," I replied, winking at him. He laughed, a good, rich sound, and relaxed into my recliner.

"Can I see?" I asked, hoping I wasn't being too rude. He didn't reply, simply closed his eyes and breathed deeply. As I watched, his skin sprouted thick, wiry black hair, his face elongating into a canine muzzle. He grew an easy foot, maybe more, in height, thinning as he did, and his fingers grew spidery, tipped with vicious looking black talons. His canines were at least two inches long, glistening white in his black muzzle. I gulped, my eyes wide and staring while he grinned a wolfish smile.

"Wicked," I breathed, shocked and impressed. His black human eye winked at me as the hair began to recede, flowing in reverse back into his skin, his face shrinking and his height reducing back to its previous level. Within a few moments, he'd returned to his previous appearance, sitting with a big grin on his face. I'd never seen anything like it, and doubted I would again.

"And you're a telekinetic and a powerful touch psychic," I said breathlessly turning away from the werewolf toward the telekinetic. She bobbed her head, turning to set her cup in the sink and walking in to sit next to Allie. She had a pretty flowery patterned tunic style shirt on, black with blue and green flowers. I noticed she made very certain not to touch anyone as she walked past, giving any exposed flesh a wide berth.

"Touching other people draws me too deeply into their psyche and it takes me a long time to rebuild my own psyche. It's hard, and I don't always rebuild myself properly. Sometimes their memories are accidently integrated into mine and I don't know which are mine and which are someone else's. That's hard," she finished with a sad smile. Her voice was soft with a strong southern accent, her eyes wide as she recounted her history. My heart went out to her. She had a great gift, but the price seemed very high.

"My powers showed at a young age when I threw a classmate against a wall when he picked on me. I dislocated his wrist and bruised one of his kidneys. After that, the other kids left me alone, but people kept egging or teepeeing my house. Eventually we had to move, and my parents put me in a private school for psychics. Puberty was Hell, that was when my powers really took off, and I accidently absorbed some of my first boyfriend's memories. After puberty, I gained control of a lot of them, but I'm still working on the touch thing."

"How... powerful are you?" I asked, morbidly curious. She turned large eyes on me, catching me with her gaze.

"Look out the window, at your parking lot," she said, her voice hollow with concentration. I stood to look, peering out the window into the bright morning sunlight. Hovering a foot above the ground, a dozen cars were floating above their parking spots. As I watched, she set them down, as light as a feather. I gaped, shocked, turning back to her smiling at me.

"Okay, I'm impressed," I said, the queen of understatement. I had no idea what people like this could possibly want with me, I wasn't anywhere near as powerful as they were. Allie stood a moment later, heading for the kitchen and picking up her black leather purse.

"I need to go, Jamie, I have an experiment ending soon and I need to get across town. If you have any questions, feel free to ask Jackson or myself, but try to do it in private. Keep track of any new symptoms or side effects that develop, please? You're my first human guinea pig."

She hugged me as she left, whispering in my ear how glad she was I was okay, and then turned for the door. She winked and gestured for Jackson, Lindsey, and Joshua to follow, then headed out the door, back to the Allie I knew. He hugged me, too, reminding me to ask him any questions, and trailed out the door behind Allie as Joshua shook my hand and welcomed me to the team. Lindsey took my hand in her mind again, moving it up and down in the same shaking motion and welcoming me as well. If I'd closed my eyes, I could have sworn I was holding someone's hand, that was how complete her psychic grip was.

Chapter 28: Kris

After they left, I snorted, wondering again if I was in the Twilight Zone, as I headed upstairs to get ready for the day. I pulled my nightclothes off and pulled on some bicycle shorts and a sports bra. My place was a two bedroom and I used the other bedroom as an exercise room/weapon storage. I preferred a stationary bike, but sometimes a hunter had to run away so I kept a treadmill along with my bike and punching bag.

Today is a punching bag day, I thought, needing to blow off some steam. I pulled the Wavemaster to the center of the room and proceeding to wail on it until I was drenched and my knuckles and feet were red. My martial arts had already saved my life more times than I could count and I found it gave me a confidence I wouldn't otherwise have.

Next was the shower as I rewashed my hair, knowing it would be much easier to start fresh than try and style my sweaty mess. Makeup, a curling iron, and a spritz of perfume later, I was sliding into my skinny jeans and a long sleeve boat-neck black t-shirt. Next came my riding boots, calf high black leather and I was ready for the world.

After breakfast, I decided, as I popped a couple waffles into the toaster and poured a Coke. Still hungry after finishing them, I toasted another pair, humming tunelessly to myself. It was about time to head for the airport, so I wandered down to my car, making sure to grab my phone and secure my 45 in its holster as I walked out and locked the door. DIA was a ways off, but I knew I'd have plenty of time.

Kris' plane was on time and he called shortly after it was scheduled to land. He didn't have baggage so he was ready as I pulled up to the curb, smiling slightly to myself. Kris was Cajun down to the bone, occasionally outrageous, always fun to be around. He was shorter than I was, a fact that affected him not at all, and a cheerful lecher. The first time he slapped my ass in fun I'd about fed him his hand, but we'd come to an understanding since then. Hands off, or we'd see who was the better martial artist. His poison was hapkido, another Korean martial art, and he was an excellent practitioner. I was pretty sure I'd win, because I was taller with a longer reach and because he'd likely underestimate me, but he was a better shot with a sniper rifle. Part of the reason I'd called him.

He was standing on the curb, carry-on bag at this side, whistling loudly. He was about five eight, a trim hundred and fifty pounds with olive skin and startling blue eyes. His oval face was handsome, as he knew all too well, his lips full under a thin mustache with a Roman nose and a wide forehead. Dark, almost black hair peeked out from under his Saints cap as he waved at me. He was wearing jeans and a black Saints t-shirt under a heavy black Michelin man winter coat with heavy combat boots, well worn.

"Hey darlin'," he greeted as I pulled to a stop. I grinned back, wondering in the back of my head how such a cute guy could be such a good hunter. I popped the trunk and helped him with his bag, pulling away from the curb moments later.

"How was your flight?" I asked, pulling onto I-70 and heading for my place.

"Good," he replied, "dere was a lovely young thang in a very short skirt across de aisle, so I just put on ma sunglasses and just looked for de whole trip." He arched his eyebrows suggestively, waggling them up and down at me with a leer. I rolled my eyes, punching him in the knee and earning myself a chuckle.

"You hungry?"

"Nah, I ate in Nawlins, I'm good." We chatted most of the way home, about this and that. By the time we got back to my place, we'd run out of things to talk about besides work.

I led him upstairs, making sure the door was still locked, and into my apartment. He declined an offer for a drink or a snack, instead inviting himself up into my extra bedroom to take a peek at my gun collection. I had firearms in most calibers, Sigs being my favorite, with a smattering of other brands. Nothing cheap, it was worth my life to invest in higher quality. He cooed over most of the semiautomatics, turned his nose up at the revolvers, and almost wet himself at my favorite rifle. It was a bolt-action .45-70 Government, an old round used on American bison, and a very effective anti-vampire round with the right ammunition. Smaller calibers designed for armor penetration weren't great when used on a vampire or lycanthrope, they tended to punch a hole through and blow out the other side. Damaging, but not devastating. My money was on a big bullet moving slower so that all the energy went into the target. Hollow points were even better, especially ones that disintegrated as they mushroomed, because they imparted all their energy in the target.

"Hoo, darlin', you have amazing taste in rifles, if no' in men," he said, winking at me and pulling the rifle closer to him. It was blued with a black stock, no shiny parts to give away his position. I handed him a box of silver plated frangible hollow points with a flourish, which brought another grin to his face.

"Damn," he whistled, pulling out a round and holding it up in the light from the window. It was as long as my thumb, about as big around, with a polymer aerodynamic tip. It would make a nasty hole in anything he shot. In like a pencil, out like a pizza was the saying.

"What else you got?" He settled on my 10mm Colt with hollow points as his backup which made me laugh, it was too big for me to carry as a primary much less a backup. "What should I do if you inside?" he asked suddenly. I hadn't thought of that. That bolt-action rifle was great if there was a clean shot at the target, but if he had to shoot through something, say a window, the .45-70 wouldn't penetrate well. I grinned, pulling another sniper rifle from the back of the safe along with another box of silver ammo, handing them both to him with a another flourish.

I thought his grin would split his face in two as he gingerly took the rifle.

"Oh, darlin', I haven't seen one of dese for years, .338 Lapua will do de trick." He grinned at me again, turning the rifle around to familiarize himself with the workings as I headed out the door.

"I'm going to call SER," I said, "see if we have their support before I set this thing into action. We'll need to wait 'til dark anyway, I can't contact Svetlana until then anyway."

"You sure you wanna contact dat ting? She'd've ate ya if I hadn't shot her dat one time in Portland."

"Yeah, we have unfinished business. Plus, I checked, that bounty from Oregon is still open, maybe we can collect on it at the same time. I need to talk to this Erick, something Svetlana said keeps pulling at my brain, and I think he knows what's happened to Adora Johanson. Svetlana seeing her with Erick after the note was delivered is ringing alarm bells for me, and she warned me very strongly to drop the case. I think she knows more and I need to get it out of her."

He snorted, shaking his head and working the bolt action of the rifle. "Get it outta her, ya say like you is plannin' on interrogatin' a human. She's a Master, cherie, ya interrogate one o' dem with a bullet, not questions."

I shrugged, having no answer, watching him work the action of my rifle. Within a few minutes, he was smoother with it than I was, working the bolt with a fluid grace born of long training. Kris as backup was ideal; I only hoped I could get

Svetlana within range of the rifle before she tore my throat out. I didn't think she'd take it kindly when she realized I was pulling her tail, using her to get to talk to Erick and see if I could make some progress on the Johanson case.

"I'm hungry," I said, turning to leave the room as a not so subtle hint for him to follow. Placing the rifles back into my safe, he shut the door and spun the dial with a last forlorn look for his new babies. If I could get another one of either of them, I might need to buy them for him for Christmas, but I'd never seen another .45-70 exactly like mine and the .338 Lapua was hard to come by.

Mid-afternoon had come and gone, so I suggested we order some Chinese takeout. Kris made a face but didn't argue so I ordered for both of us. We ate mostly in silence, both of us thinking about what was going to transpire tonight, nerves thick on the winter air.

I'd called Coleman and he'd agreed to have SER ready to go when I confirmed the location of the meeting. I'd found a GPS at the store that we could link to Kris' cell phone and he would know where I was at all times. His job was to follow me without giving himself away and set up the sniper rifles near wherever I ended up, providing some back up. He'd also be responsible for calling SER and giving them the location so we'd have their backup when we needed it. Coleman had already agreed to give him a ride, so I wasn't worried about outrunning them. I called Kris on my cell, intending to keep the line open so he would know when I needed help.

As a last moment thought, I put a bandage on my arm where the vampire bite had been, making it look like I was still injured. Darkness had fallen, so I nerved myself and went outside, staring into the frigid dusk for a few moments. I didn't know what Svetlana had meant, call out into the night, so I stood in my parking lot under a streetlight and simply called her name, feeling stupid.

Chapter 29: Svetlana Once More

I don't know how long I waited, but it wasn't nearly long enough for my peace of mind. A warm wind suddenly blew from my right, smelling of lilac, and I turned into it to see Svetlana standing just outside the light cast by the streetlamp, still as stone. I hadn't heard her come up. Damn she was powerful. She was dressed all in black, skin tight black jeans with thigh high black leather stiletto boots and a black flowing long sleeve blouse. Her face was lost in shadow, her pale hair blowing around her face in the warm wind of her creation.

"You have made your decision, Jamishka?" She asked, lifting her head up so I could see her face. There was a scar on her chin, a small line on the left side, but it looked old, probably from before she became a Master. I was startled, curious why I had never noticed it before, but it wasn't important right now.

"Yes," I replied simply. "I don't want to die. But I have a favor to ask before you, uh, convert me. I need to talk to Erick about the Adora Johanson case."

Rage flickered across her face, immediately quelled, but suddenly I wasn't so sure about this whole plan. She stalked toward me, moving like a great black cat, stopping a couple yards from me. I could see her face better now, and I was shocked to notice her eyes were blue-gray, not the endless black I had been expecting.

"I told you to drop the case, Jamishka. Adora's husband does not know of which he speaks or else he misleads you on purpose, I do not know which. Adora was not kidnapped; she does not need your help."

"I believe you," I said cautiously, unnerved by her proximity and trying not to meet her eyes. "I've been offered a lot of money to find her, and if you're going to convert me, it leaves my mother completely alone. I wanted to talk to Erick, get the whole story so I can tell Harold and get the money for my mother. You understand that, right, Svetlana? I need to take care of my family. Before I go." I was begging, but I knew anything less than an Oscar worthy performance would get me killed really quickly. Kris was covering me from my apartment with the rifle, but she was more unstable than I remembered.

Svetlana stood there, a thoughtful expression on her beautiful face, her head cocked to the side as she considered.

"Very well, Jamishka, I require his permission before I convert you in any case, we shall ride in your automobile, it's too far to walk. Follow," she said, brushing past me and walking toward my garage. I found myself envying her seductive sway, shaking my head hard as I realized I was staring. Grimacing in irritation, I followed, hitting the button on my key fob to unlock the car. She slid into the passenger seat and beckoned for me to sit on the driver's side. I took a deep breath, steeling myself for a dangerous and tense ride, as I climbed into my little Honda.

We set off, her giving me directions periodically, heading toward downtown Denver. She was quiet other than the periodic directions, sitting still as stone next to me, only the soft rise and fall of her breath giving away her presence. By the time we arrived at the address, I was as tense as a piano string, nerves frayed. I was about to walk into a powerful Master vampire lair along with another powerful Master at my back with only a sniper and SER as backup. I was having severe second thoughts about this whole thing, but I'd come too far to turn back now.

We pulled into the parking garage of a downtown high rise, parking in one of the visitor spaces. If this Erick was Erick McBean, and I strongly suspected he was, it meant he was here in Denver, which was bad, bad news for us. I'd heard he was on the front range of the Rockies, but to have him here was really disturbing. That SER hadn't had an inkling of his presence until that ghoul attacked me worried me even more.

"What now, Svetlana?" I asked, killing the ignition and turning toward her. She turned her blue-gray eyes on me, but didn't say anything, just stared at me.

"You will call me Master from now on," she finally retorted, a stinging rebuke hidden in her words. "Erick will test you, you must answer him truthfully or he will have you killed. If he does not like your answers, there is nothing I can do to save you, so weigh your answers carefully." She pulled the door open, standing as if pulled up by a set of strings, and slammed the door hard enough to rattle my teeth. I sighed, steeling myself for this encounter, and opened my door to get out. I had never met Erick, I had no idea what kind of person he was, but a vampire didn't gain his level of power without being very savvy.

I checked the back of my jeans, making sure the 45 was in place with the extra magazine of special bullets in my left front pocket, and felt in my other pocket for my silver stiletto. If the shit hit the fan, neither would do much, not with two Masters in the room, but they were better than a sharp stick. I also had my handheld 410 shotgun in my purse in place of my 38 special, loaded with silver plated self defense rounds, a concoction of birdshot and buckshot. Anyone who got too close would have a really bad day. I hoped things wouldn't come to that, but I had a premonition they might.

Svetlana had wandered off quite some distance, not bothering to look back and see if I was following, confident she held the winning hand. I shrugged and followed, apprehensive but committed.

We entered an elevator to the main lobby of the building, a lavish display of expensive wood work with a thick red carpet and real art on the walls. Svetlana walked past the door man, gliding purposefully toward another set of stainless steel elevator doors at the end of the hallway. She punched the button to the penthouse, turning a key she produced from seemingly nowhere, and activating the elevator. She settled back into the corner of the elevator car and waited, staring at the floor. With a start, I realized she was scared, too, dreading the upcoming meeting with her Master. As ridiculous as it was, the knowledge of her fear calmed my misgivings, allowing me to hope this whole plan might work out.

When the stainless steel doors of the elevator parted, they revealed a beautiful two story foyer with white marble steps leading up in front of us and a door to either side. Two hallways spread out right and left from the top of the stairway, circling back over our heads as railed balconies lined with doors. At the top of the stairs was a set of French doors, set with frosted glass in dark wood. Svetlana started up the stairs without a word, gliding up the steps like she was floating and I hurried to follow. She flung open the double doors, revealing a broad windowed vista overlooking downtown Denver, the window panes arching overhead to reveal the crystal clear winter sky, stars like diamonds set in velvet.

The floors were hardwood, a burnished blood-red wood I had never seen before, with an ebony wood wainscoted up to waist level and cream colored sponge painted walls to the tall ceiling. To the right was a white leather sectional couch, plush and comfortable looking, with a simple coffee table made of the same red wood. A massive television screen hung on the wall opposite the couch, but there was little else in the room. Two doors to the left led deeper into the penthouse I assumed, but there was no one I could see. Maybe Erick wasn't home.

Svetlana stopped, turning to me and gliding up to look me in the face, standing easily as tall as me in her heeled boots. "I want Erick to think we are lovers," she said, tracing my jaw line with a manicured fingernail. "It will be safer for you if he thinks lust motivates your conversion. Besides, it will be true, soon enough," she finished with a cruel, lustful smile.

She slid an arm around my waist, pulling me close, and breathing in my ear. "This way," she said softly, leading me toward the nearest door, pulling it open and walking through with me in tow. "Lean your head on my shoulder, Jamishka, try to look convincing," she whispered. I desperately wanted to pull my 45 but I knew that would be a death sentence. I hoped, prayed, Kris had been able to find a good vantage point for the apartment, but I needed to see if I could lure everyone into the living room with the big windows to help him out.

Chapter 30: Erick

We walked into a large dining room with a massive white linen and lace covered table set for eight people. Erick was sitting at the head of the table furthest from us, or I assumed it was Erick, along with six other people. He was huge, easily three to four inches taller than me and two hundred pounds heavier with a shock of wiry black hair and eyes the color of finest sapphires. His face was square, with a lantern jaw, thin, cruel lips, and a Roman nose. His suit was of the finest quality, charcoal gray wool with a pale blue silk shirt and a black and gray striped tie.

I recognized Jordan with a start, her face smooth and healthy again as she shot me a look of fear from the chair closest to us on the left. She was dressed in a revealing little black silk spaghetti strap dress with a ruby the size of an almond set in platinum around her throat. Someone had done her makeup just right to accentuate her startling round blue-green eyes and her hair cascaded around her in chestnut waves.

Next to her was another male, this one average height with styled copper hair and eyes the color of summer grass. His face was handsome in a rugged sort of way, heart shaped with a masculine nose and a thick lipped mouth made for smiling. His suit was well tailored, gray with a green silk shirt to compliment his eyes, no tie. I'd seen the ring on his right ring finger before in the vision Jackson had conjured from the ransom letter, but I didn't have time to dwell on that right now.

Between him and the one who I assumed was Erick was another woman, this one raven haired with blue eyes, a long face, and a sour expression. Her lips were thin, with a smattering of freckles across her hooked nose, and her blue silk dress hung awkwardly on her skinny frame.

To my immediate right was a little girl, maybe eight to nine years old with straight dirty blonde hair and buck teeth protruding from her little mouth. She wore jean shorts and a yellow tank top over scuffed white sneakers with no socks, completely out of place with the rest of the table. Her eyes were ancient and I knew she wasn't a little girl at all. She was a vampire, but Master or servant I didn't know.

I caught my breath, staring at the woman across from the copper haired man. She was tall and slender with a carefully styled straight white blonde hair and huge dark eyes. Her face was long and slender, with full red lips, a pert nose, and an arrogant expression. Her dress was silk as well, a pale ivory in color with one sleeve and the other shoulder laid bare, her small breasts pressing against the fabric as she shifted her attention to Svetlana and me. Adora Johanson.

Suspended over the table was a naked woman, bound hand and foot, spread eagle for easy access to her vital points. Her face was slack, unseeing, but her chest rose and fell in a gentle rhythm so I knew she was alive. She looked rough, her face much older than her thin body, hair stringy and unkempt with several missing teeth. *Meth addict*, I thought, gorge rising in my throat as I realized we had walked in on dinner.

"Ahh, Svetlana, right in time for dinner," said the red haired man jovially. "Sit, sit, join us," he gestured toward two empty seats between him and Erick, and stared at us expectantly. Svetlana made no move to sit, instead taking my arm in hers and leading me to the red haired man, standing between him and me protectively.

"Master," she said, touching her forehead with her fingertips, and going to one knee before the red-haired vampire, pulling me to the floor with her. "Thank you, I have already fed tonight, I wished to present Jamie for your approval. One of my servants bit her, but she fought her off. I sought her out and I offered her the Choice which she accepted. If she's acceptable, I

will convert her and add her to our family."
Master? I thought, looking at the red-haired vampire and finally understanding. *The big one must be a bodyguard or something*, I mused.

I looked at Erick in a new light, seeing his easy style and commanding presence, and wondered how I could have missed it. The head of the table wasn't a place of honor here, it was a place of shame, as far from the biggest veins of the suspended woman as one could get. Erick and Adora were sitting directly in front of the limp arms with direct access to the large veins in the wrist.

Erick frowned, flicking his gaze to me and back to Svetlana, considering.

"Svetlana, you have a pet, Jordan has been your favorite for twenty years, are you going to just throw her away?" he asked, his voice like melted chocolate, warm and oh so fattening, turning toward Jordan and arching an eyebrow. She looked away, flushing, but I thought I detected a hint of a smile hovering around her lips.

"I tire of her," said Svetlana dismissively, flicking a hand like she was shooing a fly. "Jamishka is strong, she would have killed me in Oregon but she chose not to. Now, I could kill her, leave her to die of the Wasting, but I too choose not to. Instead she will be one of us."

"Until you tire of her too," said the raven haired woman snidely, her voice high and nasal. Svetlana stared daggers at her, power like heat waves rolling off her to engulf Raven. A similar wave of power, this one cold as the grave, rose off Raven, shimmering like a wall between her and Svetlana's power and preventing whatever Svetlana had intended. I stared, dumbfounded. I'd never seen psychic power before, not in any tangible way, and I wondered if it was a side-effect of my treatment. Both women scowled, strain showing clearly on their faces, until Erick put a stop to it.

"Do grow up, you two," he said lazily, but his words were as effective as a slap to the face for the two Masters. Both shimmering walls disappeared as quickly as they had arisen, fading into nothing. "You've been at it for three hundred years," Erick continued, "it grows wearisome. One day one of you will best the other, but not tonight."

He turned his gaze to me, I could feel it on the top of my head like a searing wave of heat. His mind touched mine, softly, brushing the surface, and then withdrew.

"Svetlana, you are a fool," he said, sighing as he stood. "Come, the rest of you may feed, I will deal with this little matter and return shortly." Adora rose along with him, following us to the living room, as did Jordan who brought up the rear. I eyed Adora, noticing she didn't act like a prisoner, more like an honored guest, and tried to keep my distance from the two Master vampires ahead of me. I wasn't worried about Jordan, but Erick and Svetlana were way out of my league if I was alone.

Chapter 31: Confrontation

Erick and Adora sat on the couch, hip to hip, as Svetlana led me by the hand to the center of the room. Adora flung her legs across Erick's lap like a lover, his hand slowly caressing her thigh, and my theory gelled into fact. Jordan stalked to the corner of the room, sulking with her arms crossed over her chest.

"Svetlana," Erick's voice cracked like a whip, making me cower and Svetlana jerk. "Take her mind; make her tell you the truth of why she's here."

Svetlana turned to me, eyes wide, and then abruptly narrowing to slits in her alabaster face. Her power rose from her, shimmering in the track lighting like fog in a set of headlights and then rushing toward me with a psychic howl. I flinched, throwing my arms up and bracing for impact. I'd never seen her power before, every other time it had simply hit me like an invisible truck.

It never came. I snuck a peek between my fingers, and saw her power a hands breadth from my face, snapping and snarling at some unseen barrier just inches away. I straightened, pushing Svetlana's power even further away, a look of shock on both of our faces. I realized the barrier was my power, my sensitive abilities manifesting. I'd never heard of anything like it happening, especially with an untrained sensitive. Reaching out, I pushed her power away, forcing it further from my body with a supreme act of will.

"You were staring at my chin earlier, Jamishka," she said softly, an appraising look on her lovely face. "You see the scar from when I was a child, don't you?"

"You are a fool, Svetlana," Erick said, not giving me time to answer, his voice thick with contempt. "You've allowed your lust and fear to blind you. I should let you pay the price for your folly, but you're too powerful to lose over something this silly." He pushed Adora's legs from his lap, standing and raising him arms out to his sides. Power rose from him, a searing, freezing hurricane that made Svetlana look like a kitten. He turned to face me, flinging the power at me with a careless gesture.

My own power rose just as it had with Svetlana, but this time it shattered like a pane of glass. He grabbed my mind and bent it to his will, jerking my spine erect and forcing me to look him in the eye.

"Did you not notice her smell, Svetlana? She doesn't even smell like prey, she smells... different, almost like vampire but not quite. Tell me, Jamie, how is it that you aren't infected any longer?"

I struggled, trying not to reveal anything, but his power forced the words from my mouth like he was a ventriloquist and I his dummy. "I was treated with an experimental process developed by my friend, a vampire researcher. Her research has led to a modified version of Stoker-Dracul syndrome which prevents infection by SDS. I'm the first person she has tried it on, we don't know what kinds of side effects it will have because I'm a sensitive. She hopes to be able to create a vaccine against SDS and prevent monsters like you forever." I gasped, fighting every word and failing.

"That would be the illustrious Dr. Schmitz, I would wager, we call her our Bogeyman..." he replied, lowering his arms and slackening his control of me, a thoughtful expression on his face. "It appears we have found at least one side effect of this treatment. Svetlana should have been able to jerk your marionette strings with ease, instead you stopped her. Fascinating." He sat back down, pulling Adora back onto his lap and caressing her arm.

"Now tell me why you are really here, if you can't be converted," he said, idly, pulling my strings again and forcing more from my lips.

"Adora," I said, turning toward them, each word feeling like a knife being pushed down my throat. "I was hired to find Adora.

I mentioned to Svetlana about her being kidnapped and she let your little secret slip. Adora wasn't kidnapped; she's here of her own free will, isn't she? You wrote the kidnapping note. I'm just not sure why."

Erick smirked, leaning over to kiss Adora while she leaned in to meet him halfway. "Simple," Adora said, breaking the kiss and turning toward me with a sultry smile, her voice surprisingly deep. "If Harold had found out about Erick and me, he'd have divorced me and invoked the prenup. I'd be out on the street with nothing. I've grown so accustomed to the good life, I came up with the idea of writing the kidnapping note to get his money that way. I added the part about dissolving CFIC because I am so tired of hearing about Illegals this and Illegals that. He's a foolish old man, he doesn't even realize if he accomplishes his goal it will mean the end of his civilization. I knew he was shopping for people to try and find me, but I never thought he would find someone dumb enough to take the case but bright enough to actually find me."

"Why did you leave Harold then? Why not just have Erick as a lover on the side?" I asked, confused. Erick had loosened his hold, maybe it was enough for me to reach my pistol.

"He's getting old, something Erick will never do." She replied, gazing at Erick with adoration. "His charity is a joke, the whole reason your civilization has survived is because we aren't part of it. You can't compete with us, if you give us the same rights you have it will cease to be your civilization and become ours. We don't want the same things you do, we live to kill and we'll kill all of you if you give us the power."

"We? Us?" I asked, horror dawning on me.

"We," she replied, spreading her legs and showing me the inside of her thigh. Red and swollen with two dark, round holes, the bite on her thigh looked fresh. "I will be a vampire soon, it will require a different ritual but we think it can be done."

A vampire angel? I could scarcely believe what I was hearing. I'd never heard of a fallen angel wanting to be converted. Until tonight, I would have said it was impossible. If they succeeded, she'd become horrifyingly powerful, the equal of any Master, maybe even a King or Queen. I couldn't allow it, not if I could stop it. I reached for my pistol, trying not to think about it before I could get the pistol out, but Erick seemed to sense my intent. He wrenched my mind around again, freezing me in place.

"Tsk, tsk, Jamie, what awful manners. Go ahead, take it out," he said, smiling mockingly. My arm moved on its own, pulling my pistol from the holster and throwing it to the ground to my left. Next came the stiletto, landing with a resounding thud. He forced my hand into my purse, closing my fingers around the butt of my 410 pistol and forcing the barrel to my head.

"I can't let you leave now. If you tell Adora's husband the truth, she won't get the money she needs, and we can't have that. I'd give her all the money she could ever want, but she wants to be independent, and I don't begrudge her that," he said conversationally, a congenial smile on his face.

Svetlana had stood, mouth agape, during this whole exchange. Now she moved, drawing herself up to her full height and stalking toward me, rage radiating from every pore of her being as she approached. I whimpered, unable to move, hoping she'd kill me quickly and praying Kris would be able to do something. She drew up face to face with me, her face a mask of rage, snarling like an animal, and winding up her arm to slap me and probably take my head from my shoulders. Then, all Hell broke loose.

A shot rang out, stopping all movement in the room. Gore sprayed me in the face and chest, hot and sudden, as Svetlana's eyes grew as big as saucers, her arm falling back to her side. I thought for a moment Kris had come through, but all the windows remained intact. Erick's grip on my mind abruptly vanished, staggering me and I almost fell. Svetlana lurched forward, grabbing my shoulders with both hands and slumping to the floor, pulling me with her. I caught her as she fell, pulling her head into my lap.

Jordan was standing behind her, my 45 in her hand, still smoking. She had blown a hole straight through Svetlana's chest with a look of purest hatred on her face. She turned, taking aim at Erick and cracking off a shot that went wide into the wall just as Adora threw herself in front of him to act as a shield. Jordan fired once more, but the silver plated round did nothing but tear a hole on Adora's dress, ricocheting off her white skin like it was steel. Jordan hesitated a moment too long, giving the rest of the vampires in the other room a chance to come running.

Mr. Big was first, bursting through the door and skidding to a halt when he saw Svetlana lying in my lap, her life's blood spilling out onto the red wood floor. His eyes snapped to Erick, then to Jordan holding my gun. He roared, a great inhuman sound, as he charged Jordan, but he took a shot to the head for his trouble, blowing half his skull away. Falling with a wet sucking noise, Mr. Big became a speed bump for the next vampire through the door, Raven hair slipping in his blood and falling to her knees. It probably saved her life for a moment, because Jordan's next shot went high, striking the wall at the back of the dining room. Her next shot took Raven hair in the upper right chest, spouting a splash of gore on the wall behind her and knocking her to the ground. Jordan's final shot tore into her heart, killing her. The child vampire never came through the door, I didn't know if she had run or was hiding, but I didn't really care.

Jordan's eyes went blank, the arm holding the gun jerking like clockwork until she was pointing the gun at her own head. She whimpered, obviously no longer in control of her own body, as Erick shoved Adora aside to confront Jordan. I had never seen such a cold fury before so I waited to see if he would make her pull the trigger. Stalking toward her, his face purple, Erick crossed the room slowly and deliberately, passing in front of one of the windows.

The window next to him shattered and he staggered, gore blossoming from his left ribcage as his side exploded in a gout of blood and bone. Adora screamed, running to him and catching his body in her arms as he fell, his heart's blood pumping out with staggering speed, staining the red wood floor a noxious black. Jordan lurched back to herself, training the gun on me but hesitating.

"Is she dead?" she asked hoarsely, shaking and crying, tears running down her face.

I looked down, uncertain, only to see Svetlana staring up at me with wide, tear filled eyes. Her mouth worked but nothing emerged, just a horrible liquid filled gurgling. She reached up and touched my face with a blood drenched hand, whispering in my ear as I leaned down to listen.

"I could have loved you, Jamishka. We would have made a beautiful pair, you and I."

Her hand fell and her eyes went blank as she died, the light fleeing from her eyes like a firefly winking out. I stared at her, uncertain how to feel, when I heard my 45 hit the floor with a thud. My head snapped up as Jordan fell to her knees, shaking and crying, whether in fear, elation, or sorrow I had no idea. I stood, pushing Svetlana's lovely mortal coil from my lap and approaching Jordan carefully, gun ready in my hand. She didn't notice me, staring at Svetlana and half laughing, half crying.

Movement flashed out of the corner of my eye, my gun hand snapping up to aim and fire on the child vampire as she made a flying leap aiming for Jordan's back. The four buckshot pellets and twelve birdshot pellets took the little monster full in the upper chest where her neck met her body, severing her spinal cord and killing her instantly. Her momentum carried her into Jordan, but she was too small to do more than rock Jordan forward. Without looking, Jordan reached behind her and shoved the little corpse away.

Chapter 32: Adora Unleashed

"Traitor!" came a shriek near the windows. Adora stood over Erick, her power snapping around her like a flame dancing in a breeze. She raised her eyes as I looked at her, fire burning in them with an unholy radiance. Belatedly, I realized a pissed off angel was every bit as dangerous as a Master vampire. I pulled my arm around, training the 410 revolver on her and pulling the trigger as fast as I could. The cylinder clicked empty after five shots and I dropped it, desperately looking around for anything else I could use.

My shots had done nothing more than shred Adora's dress, exposing a pale breast and flat, white abs. She raised her hands, slamming them together and summoning a sheet of fire to cascade through the penthouse as air swirled in a mini tornado around her head. Jordan and I hit the floor, eyes wide, as Adora went nuts, beginning to glow and rise off the ground, supported by a pillow of her own power, her white blonde hair floating around her face like a cloud.

My eyes locked on my 45, just inches from my fingers, and I inched forward reaching for it. Closing my fingers around the butt, I pulled it closer, thumbing the magazine release. The magazine had one more bullet in it, but it was silver plated and would be useless against Adora. Fishing in my pocket for my special magazine, feeling my back start to blister from the raging angel power in the room, I slammed my extra magazine home and rolled over onto my back, taking aim at Adora.

My first shot took her in the stomach, the second her chest, and the third went through her heart, the gold bullets tearing through her body to punch through the window behind her, leaving shards of bloody glass to fall to the streets below. She fell out of the air, falling to her knees and then forward onto her face, eyes confused and then fading to unseeing in death. I shot her one final time in the head, gore splattering the walls, but I had to be sure she was truly dead. My heart hammered like a trapped bird in the sudden silence, only broken by the sobbing still coming from Jordan.

I turned to her, gun ready in my hand knowing gold bullets would kill a servant just as easily as silver bullets would, and stared at her.

"Why?" I asked finally. She didn't hear me, still staring at Svetlana's body and laughing and crying. I approached her cautiously, but she wasn't paying attention to me at all. I shook her, talking to her and trying to get her attention, resorting to slapping her after a few unfruitful attempts at rousing her. Her eyes cleared and her breathing slowed, staring up at me in undisguised elation.

"She's dead," she hiccupped. "She's dead, no more being her slave, no more having to sleep with her. She's dead, do you hear?!" she shrieked, hugging herself and rocking back and forth. I slapped her again, a full arm strike with all my strength behind it, bringing her back to herself.

"Why?" I asked again. "Why now?"

"Because of you," she replied wiping her eyes and taking my face in her hands. I almost flinched away, but I sensed she wasn't going to hurt me and let her do what she needed to do. "You were infected, she infected you intentionally, I know because she bragged about it, saying she knew you would decide to live even if it was a half life like mine. But now you're not! They cured you, your friend and her research, they saved you! Maybe they can cure me, maybe I can go back to my life, live as we are supposed to. Please," she looked in my eyes, begging, "please help me. I don't want to be a vampire anymore, I want to live and die, have children and live out my life as a human being!" She was laughing and crying again, hysterical, but I couldn't really blame her.

"But why did you shoot the rest of them?" I asked, still confused.

She turned to me, a manic expression on her face, and pulled me close to kiss me on both cheeks.

"They would never have let me go," she said, hugging me to herself, hard. "I had to, had to get rid of them, I knew when you talked about your cure that I had to be rid of them for good. Especially her," she spat, staggering to her feet and giving Svetlana's body a savage kick and then another. Over and over again, screaming and crying she kicked Svetlana until she collapsed, sobbing, pulling Svetlana into her lap and weeping, apologizing and cursing her in turns.

I was majorly creeped out by now, but she wasn't hurting me so I stood to try and see who'd made it through the carnage. I thought Svetlana was dead; she had died in my arms. Mr. Big was gone, his remaining eye staring up at me, accusing in death. Raven was also dead, her heart shredded, her blues eyes staring sightless, looking surprised. The child vampire was dead, too, this one my work and I knew with a quick look she had died instantly.

Adora and Erick were slumped together, her pale corpse covering most of him as I approached. She was dead, I was sure of that, not even a fallen angel could survive a head shot, but I needed to know for sure Erick was taken care of. I pushed her off, not worried about blood, I was already covered in Svetlana's. I pushed Erick onto his back with my feet, bracing myself against the now red splattered couch. He rolled over bonelessly, arms flopping as I shoved him over, rugged face slack and green eyes wide and unseeing.

Jordan had calmed down, rocking and singing softly to Svetlana, sitting cross legged in a pool of blood. Adrenaline crash was setting in, causing my hands to shake as I took gulping breaths to try to calm down. Bad mistake, I realized, as the stench of death flooded my nostrils, somewhere between the smell of an outhouse and a slaughter house. I gagged, trying not to throw up as I breathed shallowly through my mouth.

Chapter 33: Escape

A distant ringing caught my attention, helping me focus, but I couldn't tell where it was coming from. Confused, I peered around, looking for a phone, the doorbell, anything that might be making the noise as I realized it was coming from my pocket.

I laughed, mostly to keep from crying, and dug into my pocket until I found my phone. I'd missed a call from Kris, but I knew he'd call back so I sat back on my haunches and waited. Moments later, he did.

"Hello?" I asked, still coming down from the adrenaline high.

"Oh God, darlin', are you all right? What happened in dere? When you got into de elevator, de call dropped, I's worried sick! I saw de gunshots from de street, are you all right, cherie?" It was Kris, and he sounded frantic.

"I'm fine, unbelievably. Things, uh, didn't turn out exactly the way I thought they would, I need some help up here and your opinion."

"You're *okay?*" He asked, incredulous.

"Yeah, as I said, things went weird really quick. I'm just glad you were able to get that shot off, where are you?"

"Me, cherie? I didn't shoot at all, I couldn't get into de building across from your position. Nevermind, I be dere soon,

I'm in de lobby, on my way up. By de way, your SER friends are here, too, the big one, he comin' with me, we see you in a bit." He hung up, the phone going dead. I really needed to teach him better phone manners.

I walked over to Jordan, putting my hand on her shoulder and shaking gently. She looked up at me, her blue eyes clear, rimmed with red from her crying. She was covered in Svetlana's blood and looked a horror.

"Thank you," I said simply, helping her to her feet. "I'd be dead if you hadn't done what you did. I'll talk to Allison for you, see what she says. I know very little about her treatment, only that it hurts like nothing you've ever experienced."

She eyed me warily, maybe wondering if I was going to shoot her, so I stashed the 45 away in my holster. She sighed, looking very young all the sudden, as she turned to me with a questioning look on her face.

"What happens now?" she asked softly, worry making her eyes huge in her olive skinned face. "I've destroyed my life, everything I have known for the last fifty years lies dead around me. Maybe you should put a bullet in my head right now," she finished, miserably.

"Stop that," I tsked. "You don't know that you have ruined your life, maybe you've rescued it. We'll talk to Allison, maybe she'll know what she can do to help. Right now, I need you to stay behind me, SER and another hunter are on their way up and I'll need to do some fast talking to keep you from ending up like them," I pointed at Mr. Big for emphasis.

I retrieved my stiletto and my other pistol, stowing both away, as a sharp knock sounded on the front door. Jordan came with me as we went to the foyer, remaining at the top of the stairs while I went and opened the door.

Kris' eyes were as wide as I had ever seen them, and Coleman almost shot me before he recognized who I was. I realized I must look frightful, covered in blood in the lair of a Master vampire. Svetlana's blood was beginning to get sticky and I realized I'd ruined another pair of jeans and a t-shirt.

"I thought you say you okay, cherie. What happened here?" Kris asked, walking in and surveying the entry way. There was nothing to see here, but he looked at me expectantly anyway, eyebrow arched under his Saints cap.

"It's not mine, it's Svetlana's," I replied, trying to stay between them and Jordan. Coleman saw her anyway, snapping his rifle up and bellowing at her to put her arms up. Fortunately, she did, putting her hands up and lacing her fingers together atop her head.

"Stop, stop, stop!" I yelled, reaching over to push his rifle to the right, away from Jordan. He lowered it, giving me a quizzical look but no longer pointed at anyone.

"Okay, talk," he said, giving me an evil eye, one hand on his hip to indicate his displeasure, his rifle not as low as I'd like. Suddenly I was at a loss. Last time Coleman had seen me, I'd been injured with a death sentence hanging over my head and no light at the end of the tunnel.

"Er, well, let me show you instead," I said, turning to walk back up the stairs, gesturing for Jordan to lead the way. She turned and walked stiffly back to the horror show, hands still on her head.

We walked back into the living room, Jordan leading but trying to stop at the door. Coleman prodded her from behind, forcing her into the room. Kris came next, while I brought up the rear.

Coleman whistled softly as he entered the death zone while Kris grinned a horrible, creepy grin. I stopped dead, ice forming on my spine as I realized not everything was as he had left it. Svetlana wasn't where we had left her, only a blood stain remained where she'd been lying. Mr. Big and Raven hair were where we had left them, as was the child vampire, laying sprawled bonelessly where Jordan had shoved her. Adora hadn't been moved either, laying half on her side, dark eyes staring at nothing. Erick was gone, a single blood trail leading deeper into the house.

Jordan screamed, cowering in the corner, her eyes darting wildly around the room. Coleman snapped his rifle up, scanning the interior walls, and I pulled my 45 from my holster to cover the door we had walked through. Kris had my 10mm out, his eyes following the blood trail, but he didn't follow it just yet.

Coleman took point, crouched and tense, his rifle flicking back in forth as he motioned for us to follow him. Kris and I followed, shoulder to shoulder, while Jordan stayed in the room and whimpered. The blood trail wound through the dining room, into the kitchen, down a hallway and to a wood door that opened inward. Blood glistened darkly on the knob, enough that Coleman hesitated, so I pushed past him and pulled it open, knowing Kris and Coleman would cover me.

Apparently we had found the back door, because stairs led down, multiple flights switching back and forth out of sight.

"Shit," Coleman grunted, pulling his phone from his belt and thumbing the walkie-talkie function on. "Reynolds, we've lost one, there's a..." he looked at me inquiringly.

"Master, male, red hair, likely injured and covered in blood and another Master, blonde, female, also severely injured and covered in blood. He may be carrying her, there's only one set of footprints," I supplied.

"Master, male, red hair, likely injured and covered in blood and another Master, blonde, female, also severely injured and covered in blood. He may be carrying her," he echoed into the phone. "Set up a perimeter, I don't want nothing through, these two're powerful." He motioned us forward, again taking point and gliding down the stairs, stopped on each flight to whip his rifle back and forth. We could see the blood trail leading down to a landing at the bottom of the shaft and through a steel door.

I was worried about Jordan, we had left her alone up in the penthouse, so I motioned for the boys to continue while I went back up the stairs and back through the apartment.

Jordan still stood in the corner of the living room, staring out the expansive windows at the night time streets of

Denver. It really was an amazing view, too bad we had ruined so much of the apartment. We'd completely ruined the living room, five vampire deaths and bleed outs would probably mean the place needed to be gutted and completely redone.

She didn't react as I walked back in, my gun pointing at the ground but at the ready.

"Jordan?" I said softly, approaching her with caution. She might not want to be, but she was still a vampire, if just a servant. I didn't know if Erick or Svetlana might be able to take control of her mind and force her to try and kill us all. She turned pain-filled eyes on me, the haunted look on her face hard to look at.

"Erick or Svetlana didn't come back here, did they?" I asked, the hair on the back of my neck standing up.

"I've ruined my life, haven't I Jamie?" she asked softly, ignoring my question.

"Have you, Jordan?" I asked, equally softly. "What was it like before?" I asked, curious.

"Hellish," she replied, looking out the window again, staying quiet for a long moment. "I met Erick in 1961 at the University of Oregon. I was a student, studying engineering, and I met him at a frat party. We hit it off, seeing each other whenever I had time. I thought I was in love, worshipped the ground he walked on, and then one night, we were getting intimate, and he bit me, infected me. He gave me a choice, die, or become his servant. I loved him, I didn't know what he meant, so I allowed him to convert me.

"After he converted me, he treated me like dirt, ignoring me or beating me, making me run errands like kidnapping homeless people for our feedings. When Svetlana joined us, she liked me, so he gave me to her. I don't like girls, I don't swing that way, but she made me... made me pleasure her or let her pleasure me. She enjoyed my pain, sometimes causing real damage but always healing it. I didn't have a choice; you don't know how vicious their society is.

"I thought about suicide, but I was raised Catholic, I didn't want to go to Hell. When you came in tonight and told your story of how you were cured, I knew it was my only chance to get out of here. I saw your gun, picked it up and knew what I had to do." Her face had grown harder and harder as she told her story, anger making her lips tight and her eyes flash. "It doesn't matter if I ruined that shadow of a life; I couldn't live like that any more. Maybe your friend will be able to help me, maybe she won't, but either way, I'm free of her," she spat, glaring with loathing at some unseen presence outside the window.

"To answer your question, no, they didn't come back up here. I hope they find them, your friends, and shoot them until there's nothing but bloody meat left. He ruined my life, he's ruined so many lives, I hope he burns in Hell, and she's no better." She stood, approaching me with a strange look on her face. "You're covered in blood, you should clean up before you contaminate your friends. You can borrow some of my clothes, they'll be a little short but with those boots it'll be fine. Follow me," she said, walking through the door in the far wall.

Chapter 34: Cleanup

I followed, not trusting her sudden change of attitude, and I didn't put my gun up just yet. She'd shown herself to be mercurial more than once in the short time I had known her. I walked into a lush bedroom, thick, dark carpet spongy under my feet. All the furniture in the room was real wood; the same iridescent red wood of the floor in the living room. The four post bed was big enough for three people and the dresser would hold enough clothes for two Hollywood starlets.

On the far wall, a massive silver backed mirror reflected our images, our auras flashing around our heads. Jordan's aura was gray laced through with white, black, and red streaks, a standard vampire aura, but mine had changed. The same normal gray background with white and black streaks showed along with the usual green and blue pinpoint flashes, but there was now an overlaying pink phosphorescence shot through it. Not like a vampire aura, but nothing like anything I'd ever seen before. I stopped and stared for a moment, shrugging it off as a side effect of the treatment that had saved my life.

Jordan had disappeared through a door on the right hand wall; I could hear the faint sound of a shower running on the other side. A few minutes later she emerged, clad only in a dark red towel, her wet hair dripping down her back, as she went to rummage through the dresser. She pulled out two pairs of black leggings and two short sleeve t-shirts, one pink and the other a pale blue. She tossed one set onto the bed along with the blue shirt, brushing past me to get dressed in the bathroom. Emerging moments later fully dressed, she gestured for me to follow her lead. I shook my head, not willing to take make myself vulnerable with a Master vampire still on the loose and one of his servants standing next to me. She shrugged, sitting on the bed to pull on a pair of wrinkled gray knee high boots

"They're gone, you know," she said softly. "SER didn't find them; they were gone before they set up their perimeter. They're hurt, your friend wounded him very badly, I don't know if he'll survive. If he does, it will be a long time before he recovers if he ever does. I can't feel her, she may be dead."

"How do you know that?" I asked, suspicious.

"I can feel him, I know he still lives, barely."

"So you knew he wasn't dead when we left the living room to let Coleman in?" I demanded angrily.

"Yes."

"Why didn't you say something?" I advanced a step closer to her, contemplating bringing my pistol up.

"I guess in some small way, I still love him," she replied, turning to leave the room. I followed, keeping my weapon ready, but she never so much as looked back at me. Coleman was back in the living room, looking around at the carnage and shaking his head. Kris was nowhere to be seen, he must have stayed down on the street to continue looking for Erick.

"Ya sure know how ta make a mess there, McKinsey," Coleman commented, eying the vampire bodies and trying not to step in anything. He stopped suddenly, staring at Adora, turning to me with a surprised expression on his face.

"Is that... who I think it is?" he asked, pointing toward Adora remains.

"Yeah," I said, mildly embarrassed.

"I thought you was hired to find her, not blow her away," he said, a smirk on his dark face.

"I was, but you know, I wasn't going to let her kill me, it was self-defense."

"You sure about that? Them gold bullets ain't cheap, nor somethin' most people carry around regularly. You sure you didn' come up here to whack her?" His eyes narrowed as he said it, the implications working their way through his mind.

"She didn't even know she was here," piped up Jordan from behind him, making us both jump. Not good to forget the vampire in the room, not good at all. "She couldn't have come up here to kill her if she didn't know she was here, right?"

Coleman pursed his lips, thinking. "Yeah, that's true. McKinsey, you keep this little girl close to you, she may be your ticket outta jail. I'm goin' downstairs, check on the rest of the team, see if they got your buddy," he said, picking his way to the front door. He met Kris as the elevator door opened along with someone else I wasn't expecting to see. He was a brunette, below average height but very slender, with a long face and a square jaw. Morgan van der Slavv.

"Hey darlin', you still up 'ere?" Kris called, starting up the stairs with Morgan in tow.

"Yeah!" I shouted down to him "We'll be there in a second!" We met them at the top of the stairs, both men walking into the living room and peering around. Morgan stared at Jordan, looking like a predator sizing up his prey. He shifted his gaze to me, never changing his expression.

"Morgan! So great to see you, I didn't realize you were in town!" I said, the false words ringing flat in my ears.

"Jamie," he replied, nodding his head. I noticed the rifle slung across his back, it looked very familiar.

"Hey, you have the same rifle I have, what caliber is yours?" I asked, walking around to peer more closely at the caliber stamp.

"It's your rifle, Jamie, Kris was kind enough to allow me to use it. I was sent to the top of that building," he said pointing out one of the windows behind me, "to assist you should you need it."

"You shot Erick," I said, the pieces falling into place. He nodded, no expression on his face. I didn't like Morgan too terribly much, but I had to admit he made great backup.

"I called 'em last night before I made my reservations," Kris said, an unapologetic smile on his face. "You and me, we good, but no' good enough to take on two Masters, so I called him even dough you tol' me not to, cherie. I pay him outta my cut of de bounty, no worries. Although I don' know how ya got up dat building dere, dey wouldn' let me in," he continued, turning to Morgan with an arched eyebrow. Morgan shrugged, his expression never changing.

I squirmed, feeling guilty for not calling Morgan because I wouldn't be here if he hadn't been on the case. "No, I'd be happy to give him a cut, his timing couldn't have been better if he'd tried. Jordan actually killed Svetlana, so a piece of that bounty is hers, but she's not legal so we'll decide what we want to do later. For now, we need to get the cops up here and get this stuff sorted out."

The rest of the SER team arrived a few minutes later along with some regular police. They took all of our stories, including Jordan's, but we glossed over who she was, none of us wanting to explain. The fact that all of the dead were Illegals meant none of us would be facing any legal trouble, but we were still asked to go downtown to give our stories.

I asked if I could take a shower first, clearing it with Jordan, and Coleman agreed. I retrieved my extra set of clothes from my car, another pair of jeans and a navy blue tunic top, and took a quick shower, pulling my hair into a pony tail and dressing quickly. When I reentered the living room, the police had cut the meth addict down and EMS was tending to her wounds. She had a blank expression on her face, not seeing anything, and I wondered how long the mind control would last now that Erick wasn't physically here.

Jordan rode with me, seeing as she had no license, while Kris, and Morgan rode together in Morgan's rental car. We rode in silence most of the way. I didn't feel like talking and she probably had nothing to say. Gray buildings rushed by in the darkness as a sharp winter wind gusted my car around the road, the red and blue strobe lights of our SER escorts lending a lurid air to the night.

Chapter 35: New Roommate

We arrived at the downtown station, a windowed gray monstrosity with a brick courtyard, and proceeded to give our statements to the dispatcher on duty. She was a no-nonsense woman with her dark hair pulled tightly into bun on the back of her head, her face plain and without any makeup. Her pointed questions were direct and to the point, occasionally making me squirm, but I had nothing to hide besides Jordan's identity.

Surprisingly, Jordan proved quite capable of taking care of herself, producing an ID from her wallet that apparently passed muster and answering with responses that sounded impressive but provided little real information.

Morgan produced a permit for the rifle he had used, I had no idea how, and things wrapped up within an hour or so. We said our goodnights, promising to work things out in the morning, and headed our separate ways.

"Where to, Jordan?" I asked, hoping she had a place to go. She looked at me with her round blue eyes and said nothing, a look of distress on her olive skinned face. I sighed, afraid of that, and made the offer I never thought I would ever make.

"Do you want to crash at my place until you can get a place of your own?" I said, each word forced from my lips. I so didn't want a vampire staying at my apartment, but I owed her my life and I had promised to introduce her to Allie. She turned her away from me, not answering, perhaps understanding my reticence.

"I have nowhere else to go," she said softly, not turning to me, but I could hear the tears in her soft voice. "May I please stay with you? I won't hurt you, I swear to God, and I'll make myself useful. Please. I can pay you, I swiped some of Svetlana's jewelry before we left. Please." With that last please, she turned to me, her eyes huge and pleading.

"Okay, but don't take it personally when I lock my door at night. You don't need to pay me," I said, peevishly. It was a good thing I had a two bedroom, there was no way I was letting a vampire stay in my room. She smiled, a cheerful grin, and I wondered if the shifts of mood were a vampire thing, a result of her last fifty years of experiences, or just Jordan.

The rest of the trip was made in silence, me thinking about what the Hell I was thinking, Jordan thinking mysterious vampire thoughts. My apartment was dark but the door was locked, so we walked in without much hesitation. I set her up in the spare room, blowing up my inflatable mattress and throwing some sheets on it.

We had to block off the windows with cardboard because any light leaking in could be fatal for her. She seemed awake and active, helping me however she could. I was ready for bed, the last few days having really drained me.

"Jamie?" Jordan said as I wished her good night.

"Yeah?"

"Thanks, for everything. I won't be a burden, I promise."

"I believe you," I said, soothingly, wondering if I did. Just to be safe, I slept with my 9mm under my pillow, just in case. She wouldn't infect me, if Allie was right, but I still didn't want to wake up with a painful vampire bite.

Morgan and Kris showed up bright and early the next morning, both far too cheery for what time it was, and I answered the door bleary eyed. They begged off coming inside, claiming an early flight, so they handed over my firearms and I promised to mail them a check when the bounties came in. I secretly thought they just didn't want to come into my apartment with a vampire there.

I trudged into the kitchen after checking on Jordan, who was snoring softly in the extra bedroom, so I made myself some eggs and microwave sausage along with my morning mint tea. After showering and dressing (skin tight skinny jeans which showed off my figure and a fitted green button up shirt unbuttoned a ways to show some cleavage, along with black leather riding boots) I headed into the office. Hoping Jordan would sleep through the day, I didn't worry about her getting a hold of any of my guns. They were either on me or locked up safely.

Traffic was bad, but I was in to the office by about 10:00. I had to steel myself to call Harold Johanson to tell him his wife had been in league with Erick McBean and I had to shoot her, but the decision was taken off my hands. My phone rang, a single buzz indicating a call from Kristen.

"Yeah, what's up?"

"Hey Jamie, got a call from Johanson on the line, you want me to transfer it into you?"

My heart sank. I'd been dreading this conversation all night and all the way into work this morning, but I knew it had to happen. The line clicked over and I answered it in my best professional voice.

"Hello, Jamie McKinsey, how may I help you?"

"Hi Jamie, this is Harold Johanson, how are you this morning?" his smooth voice flowed over the phone, not giving any hint to his state of mind.

"Mr. Johanson, nice to hear from you, I was just about to call you."

"Good, I needed to talk to you about Adora. I was called down to the precinct earlier today to identify her body; I needed to talk to you about exactly what happened." His voice was flat, emotionless, and I didn't know if that meant he was angry, grieving, or thrilled.

My heart sank through the floor, horrified that he had to find out from the police, but it really wasn't my place to tell him. I couldn't tell how he was going to react, so I threw myself into the story, starting with my suspicions about her and Erick McBean and ending with the shootout in Erick's penthouse. He stayed silent for a long moment after I had finished, his breath a soft static over the phone line. I was about to ask if he was all right when he finally spoke.

"I see. You've been completely honest with me so I will be completely honest with you, at least as far as this case goes. I had my suspicions, and some circumstantial evidence, but nothing concrete. I hired you hoping you would be able to get close to her without tipping her off that I was onto her and to prove she was cheating on me, trying to bilk me of my money. It was a lot cheaper to pay you half a million dollars than pay her twenty million dollars for her ridiculous kidnapping scheme or half a billion dollars if she had chosen the honorable way and asked for a divorce. I knew the ransom note was a fraud, Adora was very powerful in the Forbidden Arts and wouldn't have been taken against her will." Things fell into place at that moment, why the comments by those around me pertaining to Adora being taken against her will had bothered me. He was still talking while I was lost in my reverie.

"Two of Erick's family contacted me around the time the ransom note appeared, Jennifer and her husband, Timothy. I believe you made their acquaintance last night. Timothy was the large, dark haired vampire while Jennifer was the slender dark haired Master. I must admit, I never once conceived Jordan wanted out of Erick's family so badly she would kill the rest of them to get out. If I had known, I likely would have provided her the tools myself, but that is neither here nor there.

"I'm off on a tangent, my point was simply that Jennifer and Timothy contacted me, wanting me to rein in my wife. They considered her a threat to Erick and their family and they wished her gone. They didn't have the power to go against Erick's wishes, so they reached out to me.

"I hired you along with some other hunters, feeding you a couple clues to lead you to Adora and Erick, and letting your hunter nature take care of the rest. The ghoul you encountered? One of Jennifer's minions I had her send to clue you into the vampire presence in town. I was sure you'd succeed, but if I was wrong and they killed you, I had other hunters lined up to take care of the whole affair in a more direct manner. By the way, don't bother paying Mr. van der Slavv, I hired him well before Mr. Delaroux called him. If you succeeded, Adora would have gone to jail or been killed, neatly removing her from both my life and Erick's family.

"I regret she attacked you and you were forced to defend yourself, but it solves my problems in a neat little package. Thank you, Jamie, I will send your fee to you in the form of a cashier's check by the end of the day. I'm glad you survived and I know if I need a hunter, you are the best. Until then, good day." *Click.*

I sat there dumbfounded, realizing I had been played like a fine violin, and then swore. He'd used me to keep from having to pay alimony and to assassinate his wife, of all the underhanded things to do. I didn't appreciate being the pawn in his game, and certainly didn't like being an unwitting assassin, but I had to admire the cold-blooded manipulation of everyone involved. His earlier erratic shifts in mood when I first met him suddenly flashed through my head as I realized they were the result of a bad acting job. Still, I'd fallen for it hook, line, and sinker.

Abruptly I realized it didn't really matter, because I still got paid even if I had to pay out some to Kris. I didn't Hunt for charity, I didn't take the case out of the kindness of my heart, I was a business woman and this was my business, brutal as it was. I would have appreciated a more direct dealing with Johanson, but I understood he had an image to maintain and having his wife killed wouldn't have gone over well in the community. I'd be very wary dealing with him in the future.

Chapter 36: Werewolf

The calendar behind the door caught my eye, as I noticed tonight was the full moon. With all the excitement, I had almost forgotten about my appointment out at the Bateman ranch. I needed to be out there by dark, no telling when the lycanthrope would show up.

I waited until around 2:00 when the check from Johanson showed up, then I headed home to spend the afternoon asleep with a stopover at the bank. I'd never seen so much in my account, Hell, I'd never made that much in a year, much less off one case. The government would take a huge chunk and I owed Morgan and Kris for their help, but I'd be able to catch up on my bills and live pretty well off that money for a while. Maybe I'd buy a new car, or even a house. No apartment neighbors sounded wonderful.

I checked on Jordan, surreptitiously peaking into the room, but she was out cold. She looked dead, but I knew she wasn't. I took a quick nap, getting up an hour before dusk to change into insulated camo pants along with a camo jacket and knee high thinsulate-lined tan boots, pulling my hair back and spraying myself with a scent neutralizer. My .45-70 rifle was the best option for closer range lycanthropes because it caused more hydrostatic shock and had better knockdown power.

Leaving a note for Jordan to stay out of trouble, I headed out to Bateman's farm, calling him on my way out there. He picked up immediately and said he'd be ready to take me out there as soon as I arrived.

Mike met me in front of his house; MUV already prepped and ready to go, so we headed out to the field where the carnage had taken place. He wished me luck, agreeing to have his phone handy when my nasty business was done, and heading off back down the road. Setup for my rifle was easy, I had a tripod and a scope already mounted on it, so all I needed to do was wait.

It was cold, below freezing, so I brought a camo blanket to wrap myself in while I waited. As the night wore on, it grew colder and colder, but the snow combined with my heavy clothing kept me from freezing too badly. By about 11:00 PM I was severely questioning my choice to wait out in the middle of the field, when one of the cottonwood trees swayed in the still night. A dark figure crouched on the branch over the field, snout raised to the night, sniffing the air. I couldn't tell what kind of lycanthrope it was from this distance, even through the scope, but it definitely wasn't human. It crept out onto the branch, its weight sagging the heavy limb almost to the ground, making a swishing noise as the lycanthrope jumped off.

It prowled toward the cow almost in the center of the field, loping forward on all fours like a hunchback parody of a natural wolf. As it grew closer, I realized it wasn't running on all fours, but rather on all threes. It only used three legs to move, the right hind leg looked twisted and was pulled in close to its body. Not having time to consider this new development and not really caring, I sighted my rifle in, squeezing the trigger and exhaling as the shot rang out like a crack of thunder in the still night, the butt of the gun slamming into my shoulder. The lycanthrope shifted at the last second, my round catching it in the shoulder instead of the chest. I swore, clambering up and pulling my pistol to move in for the kill. It wasn't dead so I needed to be extra careful.

I slid through the grass as best as I was able, holding my 45 in a two handed grip pointed at the ground, keeping an eye out for any movement from the lycanthrope. As I approached, I saw a dark figure splayed out on the ground. Its chest was rising and falling in a rapid sequence, but it wasn't making any move to rise. When I was within ten feet, I lined up my shot for the kill, aiming for the great shaggy head, when it spoke.

"Please... Jamie... Don't kill me," it gasped out. I reeled back, shocked, thumbing the safety on and backing off. I flicked my flashlight on, aiming the powerful beam at the struggling figure on the ground. It was a werewolf, coppery red fur streaked with blood.

"Pleassse... You don't underssstand..." it gasped, rolling onto its side, blood leaking from the shoulder wound with every beat of its heart. The words came out with a growling hiss, difficult to form with its canine muzzle, but the eyes looking at me from its distorted face were completely human, green as summer grass. I reeled back, thinking of the only human I had met recently with copper hair, grass green eyes, and a twisted right leg.

"Dr. Winston?" I asked, shocked.

"Yesss," he hissed through his muzzle. "Pleassse, don't kill me."

###

About the Author

Victoria Pritchard lives in Charlotte, NC, with her significant other and stepson. She grew up in Louisville, CO, until going off to graduate school at the age of 22. She is a chemist by education, but a long time reader and she enjoys creating her own worlds in her writing and hopes to someday make a living as an author. In her spare time, she likes to read, play video games, and visit the firing range. Her house is a menagerie of two dogs and four cats but she loves them all the same.

www.ingramcontent.com/pod-product-compliance
Lightning Source LLC
Chambersburg PA
CBHW050320030726
47505CB00003B/785